A Chance in Hell . . .

"Please," Ben whispered. Let there be a chance. He turned back to find his way.

And *it* was there. He slammed into it and rebounded.

With an awful realization he knew that it had circled him. Not hunting . . . *taunting* him. Playing with him.

The thing moved with hideous speed and Ben felt lines of fire ignite along his cheek. Hot blood poured from the gashes and ran into his mouth and down the side of his throat.

Ben whirled and ran straight through the dense brush.

His legs were as heavy as iron weights but he willed his feet to move. Out of the tangles of withered grass a set of pale stone steps rose to the foot of a massive door.

Ben realized where he was. It was a mausoleum carved into the living rock of the cliff. The ponderous bronze door was bound with thick iron bands that ran from top to bottom and side to side. The panels between the intersecting bands were inscribed with complex prayers and spells.

Hope flared like a spark in the darkness of his mind and he raced toward it. In the woods behind him he could hear the thing as it smashed through the brush in pursuit. He lifted the ten-thousand-pound weight of one foot onto the first step, but when he tried to lift the other he simply could not. With a cry of pain and defeat he collapsed.

Even so, Ben Talbot did not give up. The door stood ajar. If he could only reach it, then he could haul himself inside and slam it. That great door would hold back Hell itself.

Then he heard the click and scratch of clawed feet on the stone steps, and he knew that he would never reach that door. Ben's numb fingers scrabbled for his knife but the thing loomed up huge and terrible over him and the knife clattered to the cold stone.

OTHER BOOKS BY JONATHAN MABERRY

THE
WOLFMAN™

A Novelization by
Jonathan Maberry

♦

Based on the motion picture screenplay by
Andrew Kevin Walker and David Self
and the motion picture screenplay by
Curt Siodmak

TOR®

A Tom Doherty Associates Book
NEW YORK

THE WOLFMAN

Copyright © 2010 by Universal Studios Licensing LLLP

The Wolfman is a trademark and copyright of Universal Studios. Licensed by Universal Studios Licensing LLLP. All Rights Reserved.

Edited by James Frenkel

A Tor Book
Published by Tom Doherty Associates, LLC
175 Fifth Avenue
New York, NY 10010

www.tor-forge.com

Tor® is a registered trademark of Tom Doherty Associates, LLC.

ISBN 978-0-7653-6516-3

First Edition: February 2010

Printed in the United States of America

0 9 8 7 6 5 4 3 2 1

For Sara Jo

THE
WOLFMAN™

PROLOGUE

[1]

The hunt is eternal.

Her hunger is eternal.

For four billion years she has hunted the night while the world below rolled and changed. The Goddess of the Hunt is pale and hungry, her wicked eye alert, her teeth ready to bite; her mouth aches for the taste of life flowing down her throat. The stars flee like sheep from her, and at the full flush of her power she rules the whole of the night sky.

At the new moon, when the Goddess of the Hunt sleeps, the flocks of stars return to their endless fields, each time thinking that the beast has gone. Each time unprepared for when she comes again, bright, shining and newly hungry, to hunt among them.

Eternally hungry.

Eternally hunting.

[2]

Blackmoor, England, 1891

HE STOPPED ON a ridge that ran to the top of the cliff and looked up through the twisted fingers of the leafless trees at the sky. The clouds were thin and the night winds peeled them away in layers to reveal the moon—impossibly huge and bright, a cold white

1

face that ruled the sky. She was the only light in the sky; every star and planet had fled before the moon's stern face.

Ben Talbot lingered on the ridge for a full minute, his lantern hanging from his fingers, his mouth open in a silent "oh." He had seen the moon in a hundred forests, in distant fields far from cities, aboard ships lost in the vastness of the oceans—but every time he beheld her again in her fullness he was stunned to stillness. By her power . . . by her beauty.

Ben closed his eyes to force his wits to focus on the matter at hand. He wasn't out here to gape at the sky, and as he came back to his purpose he felt a pang in his heart. With great trepidation he turned away, moving carefully past the spillway of a waterfall that roared down into a hidden pool, down the cracked rock of the ridge until he was at the foot of the cliff wall near the pool. He paused, looking first the way he'd come and then turned to pick out his path among the thick yews. The evergreens had long since won back the path, cracking paving stones with their indefatigable roots and spreading backward until they washed hard against the cliff wall. These trees were ancient, Ben knew, some of them planted by the Romans and still reaching up from the black soil to scratch at the roof of heaven. He held out his lantern, first in one direction and then another until he saw the path: a shadowy tunnel formed by the outstretched arms of the trees.

Ben nodded to himself. That had to be the right way, though it had been so long since he'd walked these woods that it seemed entirely new and alien. The way a boy sees the forest and the way a grown man remembers it are so different.

He moved forward, bending his tall body nearly in

half in order to enter the tunnel of branches; though within a few steps the roof of the tunnel rose in a gentle slope and Ben could straighten to his full height of six feet. He was not yet forty, fit, and every nerve and sense he possessed was attuned to the night around him. As a boy he and his brother had been out here a thousand times, but never in the dead of night. Perhaps it was the distortion of nighttime as much as the questionable integrity of memory that made this all feel unreal and unknown. With unsure steps and a fluttering heart he moved forward.

The corridor of yews paid out into a clearing and Ben stopped again to make sure he was going the right way. He began to raise his lantern for a better view—

Crash!

Something smashed through the dried bracken behind him. Ben spun and leaped to one side, his heart racing now, pounding on the walls of his chest. Something moved through the brush . . . invisible in the darkness.

What the hell was this? Ben tensed to fight or run. One hand held the lantern out—as much a talisman as a light—and the other scrabbled at his belt for his knife. It was a sailor's blade, six inches and sharpened to a wicked edge. As his fingers closed around it he felt a fragment of confidence fall back into place, but still the thing moved through the shadows.

Ben drew the blade slowly, keeping it behind him, not wanting the polished steel to catch light from the lantern.

It was closer.

The blade cleared the sheath and Ben eased slowly down into a crouch. If he had to fight, then he would make a real fight of it.

Closer still.

"Come on, you bugger," he murmured, his fingers

flexing on the handle to find the best grip. If it rushed him he'd slash. Stabbing is a fool's move, the blade gets caught. Ben knew that quick slashes could fend off even a big hound or a boar.

Suddenly the thing burst from the bushes and drove right toward him. Ben growled in fear and fury and raised his knife. The creature flew into the spill of lantern light and Ben fell back a step, a laugh escaping his chest.

It was a pheasant. Plump and beautiful and indifferent to the big man with the wicked knife. It flapped past him down the corridor of yews.

"Bloody hell!" Ben gasped and slammed the knife back into its sheath. "Bloody bird," he called after it, and then to himself, "Bloody fool."

With a rueful smile and a shake of his head, he turned and found his path. But ten steps deeper into the forest his lantern guttered, the light dimming for a dangerous moment before waxing again as he shook it. Ben peered at it. The oil was almost gone. He had snatched up the first lantern he found and had not stopped to check the oil first. "You bloody fool," he said again. It was not the first time a hasty act had come around to bite him.

Ben lingered for a moment, looking back the way he had come. As silence reclaimed the shadowy landscape the night seemed bigger, darker, less familiar. Silence was like a presence, he could feel it watching him.

"Are you out there?" he called, but without wanting to he pitched his voice as a whisper.

Silence answered him, but Ben still felt as if he was being watched, as if familiar eyes were on him.

He cleared his throat and pitched his voice louder. "Come," he yelled, "we have to talk!"

Nothing.

The flame of his lantern flickered and he realized that if he didn't find his quarry soon the oil might not last and he'd be lost out here in the darkness.

He looked up, and even through the dense ceiling of evergreen branches he could see a paleness like frost. The touch of moonlight on the trees. Ben nodded to himself. If he lost his lantern he could find his way home by going to higher ground. That moon was bright enough to read by and it had just begun its long hunt across the sky. He would have hours of light left if it came to it, and the Hall only *felt* far away.

Even so . . . the thought of being without light, even for a few minutes, was daunting. Ben squared his shoulders and took a steadying breath.

On his first step the lantern sputtered again.

"Stay with me," he murmured and the light seemed to steady at his words. Encouraged, Ben moved forward. And as if to mock him the light guttered low and nearly went out.

He chewed his lip. Moonlight would get him back, but it would not help him find what he was looking for. Maybe it would be better to give it up as a bad job and come back tomorrow. Ben shook the lantern again and then, as the light flared once more, he caught movement off to his left. Just a flash of moonlight on something that moved behind the trees.

"What the hell?"

He tried to track it through the woods but it was already gone.

A sound made him turn and he caught another flash of it. There and gone.

Suddenly there was a blur of dark movement that slammed into him with impossible speed. As it whipped past Ben it made a strange ripping sound.

His lantern struck the hard-packed dirt behind him and rolled away, the fickle flame flaring brighter for a moment. The impact knocked Ben halfway around and he stared numbly in the wrong direction, his eyes bulging and blinking. The world dwindled down to an envelope of darkness that seemed to wrap itself around him. He heard the delicate sound of a raindrop on the scattered leaves beneath his feet. Another drop, and another. He looked up, wondering why he felt no rain on his face. The sky beyond the roof of trees was clear.

Ben smiled crookedly at the moon, wondering how rain could fall on such a night. And then looked down at the splattering of drops on the leaves. Dark rain. Black in the moonlight. Glistening like oil, smelling of freshly sheared copper. Ben opened his mouth to comment on the strange rain that seemed to be falling from his own body but no sound came out.

He heard a soft sound, the crunch as someone stepped on the wet leaves, but when he looked at the foot it was wrong. So wrong. Shoeless, misshapen. Not a human foot at all. Not an animal either. Ben raised his head and saw the eyes of the thing that stood near him. They were not the eyes of the person he came looking for out here. They were large and as yellow as a harvest moon. The eyes glared at him and Ben felt his hammering heart suddenly go still in his chest.

Understanding struck him harder than the blow that had stalled him.

He screamed, and then he *ran*.

His stomach was a furnace that sloshed loosely and Ben clamped his hands over his abdomen as he blundered through the brush. His fingers closed over wet ropes that threatened to spill out of him. His mind refused to accept the reality of what had been done to him—to accept it was to allow it and he could not.

He ran. Staggering, stumbling, leaving a widening trail of red behind him. Even through the sound of his own desperate breaths and the slap of his feet on the leaves he could hear the *thing* following. Not running. Stalking.

"God . . . ," he breathed, but his voice was ragged and wet.

He risked a single backward glance. Just one.

And it was not there. Moonlight painted the corridor of trees with a ghostly light and nothing behind him moved except the tree branches he himself had disturbed.

"Please," Ben whispered. Let there be a chance. He turned back to find his way.

And *it* was there. He slammed into it and rebounded.

With an awful realization he knew that it had circled him. Not hunting . . . *taunting* him. Playing with him.

The thing moved with hideous speed and Ben felt lines of fire ignite along his cheek. Hot blood poured from the gashes and ran into his mouth and down the side of his throat.

Ben whirled and ran straight through the dense brush.

His legs were as heavy as iron weights but he willed his feet to move and move. The brush abruptly thinned and then gave way to a small clearing that skirted the base of the cliff wall. Out of the tangles of withered grass a set of pale stone steps rose to the foot of a massive door.

Ben realized where he was. It was a mausoleum carved into the living rock of the cliff. It was ancient, with a massive lintel carved with the faces of forgotten gods and nameless kings. The ponderous bronze door was bound with thick iron bands that ran from top to bottom and side to side. The panels between the intersecting bands were inscribed with complex prayers and spells of such antiquity that much of their meaning was lost to time.

Hope flared like a spark in the darkness of his mind and he raced toward it. In the woods behind him he could hear the thing as it smashed through the brush in pursuit. He lifted the ten-thousand-pound weight of one foot onto the first step, but when he tried to lift the other he simply could not. With a cry of pain and defeat he collapsed onto the steps.

Even so Ben Talbot did not give up. He crawled, leaving behind him a red-black trail like a bloody slug. The door was near, and it stood ajar. If he could only reach it, then he could haul himself inside and slam it. That great door would hold back Hell itself.

Then he heard the click and scratch of clawed feet on the stone steps, and he knew that he would never reach that door. Ben's numb fingers scrabbled for his knife but the thing loomed up huge and terrible over him and the knife clattered to the cold stone.

Ben heard the sound of his own death. He saw the flash of claws as they tore at him. He heard his clothing rip, heard the separate sounds of parting flesh and tendon, heard the scrape of claw on bone. He heard all of this from a great distance, detached from the pain that must be coursing through his nerves. He heard, but did not feel. The tethers that held him to the broken flesh were stretching, stretching.

The thing leaned over him and he saw those dreadful yellow eyes. He saw himself reflected there.

When it suddenly stopped tearing at him and ran away into the night, Ben watched as if he were only a spectator watching a gruesome play. It was not real, this was not him.

A gust of the night breeze blew the branches aside and there above the cliff was the screaming face of the Goddess of the Night. The moon, in all her mad glory.

Framed against it, standing powerful on the crest of the ridge, Ben saw the thing that had hunted him. The thing that had killed him. Huge, misshapen, an impossible figure against an impossible sky.

"No . . ." Ben said as the thing on the cliff turned and vanished, fleeing this place, running free into the world. "No."

But his protest was heard by no ears other than his own. The darkness that crept toward him from all sides was black and infinite. The last thing he heard was the long and terrible howl of the beast, a sound that rose from the forest into the night sky.

Above the world the full white moon watched it all in glorious triumph.

CHAPTER ONE

London, England, 1891

He reached down and lifted the skull from the grave. It was old and battered, its jaw missing, the eye sockets fixed in an eternal stare. The man who held it brushed dirt from the cheeks and brow and held it in one hand, considering the lines and planes of the old bones. The eyes of the skull and the eyes of the man met and for a long minute they shared the secrets of eternity, the subtle truths of the grave.

"Alas," murmured the man in a voice that could hide no trace of the real hurt that wrenched his heart. "Poor Yorick." He half turned to his companion. "I knew him, Horatio."

In the shadows beyond a row of candles, thousands of invisible hands began applauding. Lawrence Talbot did not flick so much as a covert glance at the audience. His eyes remained locked with those of the skull, though his features shifted with a half dozen emotions as he turned the skull this way and that. When he regarded the brow his own brow knotted as if remembering old conversations; when turning it away from him his mouth betrayed the sadness of a boy suffering the disappointment of a beloved tutor; when he tilted the head back he smiled in remembrance of countless old jests. He shared the moment with the skull while the applause ran its course, and when it abated he spoke softly.

". . . a fellow of infinite jest, of most excellent fancy. He hath borne me on his back a thousand times. And now how abhorred in my imagination it is! My gorge rises at it. Here hung those lips that I have kissed I know not how oft. Where be your gibes now, your gambols, your songs, your flashes of merriment that were wont to set the table on a roar? No one now to mock your own grinning. Quite chap-fallen?"

Lawrence did not shout or bleat. He spoke with tenderness to the skull and everyone in the theater bent forward to be included in the private discourse, hanging on his words, their senses entirely given over to the soft voice of the Prince of Denmark, for—to the watching crowd—this was not Lawrence Talbot, the American actor, this was Hamlet himself. Alive, real, his mocking words clear evidence of the tortured pain within his troubled soul.

Except for one man, a well-dressed buffoon to whom Shakespeare was a bore and Shakespeare performed, a torment. Before Hamlet and Horatio had wandered into the cemetery the man had nodded and drifted off to sleep and now his buzzing snore sought to undercut the moment.

But Lawrence was too practiced a professional to allow a fool to upstage him. He tossed the skull into the man's lap and continued with his soliloquy as if the act had been staged to include this moment. The skull landed hard on sensitive softness and the man shot upright in his seat, flushing red as the crowd around him erupted into laughter.

"Now get you to my lady's chamber and tell her," continued Lawrence as he drew his energy and all eyes back to center stage, "let her paint an inch thick, to this favor she must come . . ."

Lawrence wore a suit of dark velvet and a ruffled shirt open to midchest. His wavy hair was as black as the pit and it framed a face that was rough and thoughtful and angry and handsome. "Brutally handsome" was the phrase used by *The Times* theater reviewer. He knew that everyone packed into the theater had read that review, and more than half of them were there because of it. When he stepped close to the footlights he was able to see past them to the rows of faces, each as pale as the moon, tilted up toward him, eyes fixed on him. The naked adoration in the faces of the women stoked fires within him, but the similarity of the faces—each as empty and vacuous and uncomprehending as the next—made him feel cold, empty. Gutted.

His full lips curled into a sneer. But they saw it as a smile and the applause rolled over him in waves.

CHAPTER TWO

The broadsheet tacked to the dressing room door read:

LAWRENCE TALBOT
The Eminent American Tragedian
Stars as the Melancholy Dane

■ in ■

William Shakespeare's

*The Tragical History of Hamlet
Prince of Denmark*

The stagehand pushed through the door with a grunt, stepped over the velvet jacket and nameless frilly detritus that belonged to who knew whom, ducked under the wild swing of an actress demonstrating a wobbly pirouette that she performed while drinking from a champagne glass, sidestepped a couple—a man and woman? Two women? He couldn't tell—passed a dozen other performers in various stages of undress and inebriation, and set the heavy tray down on the dressing counter. He off-loaded the six chilled bottles and clean glasses, accepted a couple of coins from

Lawrence, tried not to goggle at an actress wearing a very sheer slip who was sucking on an opium pipe, and crept out of the madhouse before his sanity fled entirely.

In the hall he passed another stagehand who was tottering under the weight of a tray laden with steaming loaves of fresh bread and a dozen different wheels of cheese.

"Whotcher, Tom?" said the second hand. "You look like you've had a fright."

The first hand jerked a thumb over his shoulder. "Just come up from the underworld, Barney. Bleedin' Sodom and Gomorrah in there." Tom leaned close. "Some of those ladies aren't exactly dressed, mate."

Barney, older and more seasoned, grinned. "Tut-tut, lad. Those aren't *ladies*, if you catch my meaning. Besides . . . it's all good fun."

"Not if you're just passing through," complained Tom.

"There you have me, lad. But wait 'til the spring when they do *Midsummer Night's Dream*. You can't keep those scalawags in their britches, male or female."

Tom shook his head. "I tell you, Barney, it's these Americans. They're uncouth."

"And what's 'uncouth'?"

"They ain't got class and breeding."

Barney snorted. "And here we are, the two of us grown men carrying trays of food for the animals in the zoo, and you're going on about class and breeding. Are we a bit above ourselves, lad?"

A girl opened the door and leaned out. She wore a red silk ribbon around her throat and nothing else. Wafts of opium smoke curled around her thighs like lecherous fingers. "Is that the food? Get your gnarly ass in here you bloody old sod!"

She slammed the door. Barney and Tom exchanged a long look.

"Aye," conceded Barney, "I take your point."

He took a breath and headed into Lawrence Talbot's dressing room.

LAWRENCE WAS ALMOST indifferent to the debauchery around him. It had become old hat to him and with familiarity had come a contempt of the excess. He required it as a matter of course because it fed the newspapers and it drew his audience. He had also long ago lost amusement of the irony that the theater seats were filled by idiots who came to share in the reflected glory of his own legendary excesses, but who came *back* because of the quality of the actual performance. A cosmic joke. Very droll.

He sighed and sipped wine from a goblet encrusted with glitter and jewels. It was the prop used for the poisoned cup in the final act. The goblet Gertrude drank from before her death scene. Lawrence searched the mirror for the actress who played his "mother." She had her skirts up around her waist and sat astride the young buck who played Rosencrantz. She certainly looked alive at the moment. Next to the wrangling couple, the impresario nibbled the wrist of one of the makeup girls. He gave Lawrence an amused nod, Pan to Bacchus. Lawrence returned his nod and turned back to the mirror. He was shirtless—that confection of fluff and frills had been clawed off of him by . . . by . . . God, he couldn't remember the name of the girl he had spent twenty minutes kissing after the performance. Just as well. She was over there kissing Polonius.

Lawrence slumped in his chair, sipping his wine,

brooding as profoundly as the character he played. That irony was not lost on him as well. The energetic rush of the performance was gone and now the black tide of depression lapped at him. It was always like this. He was only ever alive onstage; he was only ever himself when he was *not* himself. Here, when things were supposed to be real, Lawrence felt cheap and artificial and alien.

A mass of blond curls obscured his vision of the mirror as Ophelia leaned in to kiss him. She was very drunk and barely dressed, but when she kissed she put her whole soul into it, God bless her. He resisted for half a second, but then gave in to the moment. This, too, was a performance of sorts, and Lawrence could never let his audience down. Ophelia's hot mouth moved from his lips to his cheeks and chin and ears and throat. Lawrence felt little fires ignite under his skin. Her burning line of kisses trailed lower to his chest . . .

"Naughty little minx . . ."

The room went out of focus as she nipped his skin with the skill of an artist.

God! What was she doing to him . . .

"Lawrence . . ."

He jerked erect and looked around to see who had spoken but there was no one behind him.

The girl looked up. "What's wrong, love? Did I hurt you?"

"What? No . . . no," he said, distracted. "I thought I heard . . ."

But he left it unsaid. What he thought he'd heard was impossible. For just a moment he could have sworn he heard his brother Benjamin speak his name. Not Ben as he would be now—a grown man, full in his prime— but Ben as he had been all those years ago, a boy.

Suddenly the noise and smoke and laughter was oppressively loud and coarse. The room swam in and out of focus, and he blinked his vision clear. In a moment of clarity the scene around him shifted from a Roman debauch that was perfect in every sinful sense of the word . . . to a debauch that was fractured and wrong. He felt suddenly sickened, unclean. He pushed the woman aside.

"What is it?"

Lawrence fought the urge to bark at her like a dog. He bit down on the words that rose like bile to his lips.

"Nothing," he said. "It's nothing . . . a headache."

She smiled and sidled closer. "I'll bet I can make you forget you even have a head, let alone an ache—"

"No," he said quickly. He stood up and snatched a dressing gown from the back of chair. "No, I'm fine. I just need some air."

He pulled a robe from a rack, thrust his arms into it and yanked the flaps tight around him as if that could separate him from the squalor. A few of the revelers cast vaguely questioning looks at him, but he shook his head and picked his way to the door, opened it, stumbled up a flight of steps and shoved open a door to the alley. The cold air cut through the thin cloth of his robe, pebbling his flesh with goose bumps, but at least he could breathe.

Lawrence opened his eyes and he was alone. He was always alone, no matter how large the crowds, no matter how thronged the parties.

"Ben . . ." he said aloud, but the name echoed emptily off the brick walls of the alley and vanished into the limitless black of the sky.

CHAPTER THREE

L awrence walked naked to the window. The breeze was cool and thick, and the sheers moved as if in slow motion. Ever since he'd left the party earlier that evening everything had a surreal air, as if he had stepped into one of those obscure French plays that made no sense even to the playwrights.

Lawrence saw the white face of the moon through the curtains, huge and full, but as he parted them with his hand he saw that it was only the face of Big Ben. Equally cold, but far less threatening. He stepped through the curtains and leaned against the frame, watching as the mist from the Thames curled like a nest of snakes through the gaslit streets. It was a typically thick London fog that rose like drapes to cover most of the clock tower and virtually all of the city.

There was a soft moan behind him and Lawrence half turned to look at the woman on the bed. She was beautiful and lush, her naked skin painted to porcelain whiteness by the misty light. Her dark hair lay scattered around her lovely face like a dreamy chestnut storm. Her nipples were dusky in the filtered light, her lips dark and parted, black lashes downswept against perfect cheeks. Lawrence saw her and didn't see her. As he stood there in his melancholy and weariness, his waking mind was subsumed by his unconscious and he slipped into a dream of memory that swirled like fog around him and took him back to another place and time. . . .

AT NINE YEARS old Lawrence Talbot was a thin boy. Not yet strong, not yet the muscular predator he would become as he strode the stage and stalked the avenues of the world's great cities. At nine he was pale and brooding, as dreamy as a poet, lost in frequent reveries whose particular nature he shared with no one.

Except his mother. Solana Talbot knew all of her son's secrets.

Lawrence lay with his head on her lap, his dark curls lost against the intricate embroidery of her gown as if he were still, years after his birth, enmeshed with her. Solana sang an old Spanish song to him, a fanciful rural ballad so old that its meaning has changed a hundred times in as many years. Lawrence lay with his eyes closed, listening, flowing in and out of dreams, guided by the melody and the promises hidden in the words. . . .

LAWRENCE LAY IN the big hotel bed, awake in the depths of the long and roiling night. The woman had welcomed him back to bed with a sleepy moan and snuggled up against him, and Lawrence had allowed it while detesting it. It wasn't where he wanted to be. This wasn't who he wanted to be with.

It wasn't who he wanted to be.

The night ground on. Boats on the river bellowed warning calls with muffled horns that sounded like the moans of the dead. Through the open window, past the black spike of Big Ben, Lawrence saw the night pull back its garment to reveal the swollen white breast of the moon.

He wished that he could tear free of his skin and become anyone else. Anyone who was not Lawrence goddamned Talbot. He hated living the pretense of who he had become. He closed his eyes and pretended to sleep. But that, too, was a lie.

IN THE MORNING, after the woman had left him, there was a discreet knock on the door and Lawrence opened it to see a liveried footman holding a crisp envelope.

"Sorry to disturb you, sir," said the footman, "but this was just delivered and it was marked urgent."

He handed the letter to Lawrence, who grumbled something and thrust a handful of coins into the man's hand and slammed the door on his grateful smile.

His name had been written on the envelope in a woman's hand, addressed to him here at the hotel. He held it up to the light and saw that the smudged cancel stamp was for Blackmoor in Northumbria.

Home, he thought. Or, the place that had been home to him a million years ago. Who there knew he was in London? Ben?

He tore it open and read the single page.

"God . . . ," he breathed.

Five minutes later found him running for a hansom cab to take him to the train station.

CHAPTER FOUR

Northumbria

The train was old, and though the first class carriage was newly refitted it still creaked and rattled as it rolled across the ancient trestle over a deep gorge cut down into the wild lushness of Northumbria. Some miles back Lawrence had finally managed to find a comfortable nook between wall and seat and sat cross-legged, his traveling cloak shed, his unadorned walking stick beside him on the bench seat to discourage anyone from sitting too close.

Lawrence held a daguerreotype in one hand and for the last quarter hour he had alternately studied it and stared thoughtfully at the rolling hills. In the photograph he and his brother Ben stood beside their mother. It was deeply unnerving in a thousand different ways for him to realize that everyone in that photo was gone in one way or another. His mother, dead all those years ago; and now Ben gone missing. As for himself . . . he had felt absent from reality all his life, more like a ghost haunting the life of some stranger named Lawrence Talbot.

He raised the photo and traced the crenellated folds of his mother's dress with one fingertip, and then touched Ben's image, placing his finger over his brother's heart.

Where are you, Benjamin?

Even if Ben was found hale and happy somewhere—as surely he must—the old photograph was a lie gouged like a thorn into his heart. In that picture they were all happy, all gathered together as a family. Anyone looking at the picture would see happiness and unity. They would see life and possibilities. All lies. All promises proved false by the unwavering cruelty of circumstance.

"Your mother?"

Lawrence looked up from the picture to the old man seated across from him, the only other passenger in this compartment. He was wizened but looked healthy, dressed in French fashions of the more subtle and severe cut. A moneyed look that Lawrence recognized but did not share. Though he was wealthy himself, his clothing was more flamboyant, befitting a star of the stage; though perhaps a bit too flamboyant for a tragedian. This man had the simple elegance of someone who had possessed money for so long that it had become commonplace to him.

"Yes," he said.

The man nodded. "My oldest memory is of my mother," he said, his accent a cultured provincial French. He sat comfortably with his hands propped on the handle of a cane with an ornate silver animal head. A hunting dog or a wolf, Lawrence was not quite sure.

"We have something in common then, Monsieur."

"In my memory, we are gathering grapes in her father's vineyard." The French gentleman smiled wistfully. "It is my Garden of Eden."

Lawrence felt his defenses falling into place like shutters. He had too much on his mind right now to wander down memory's pathways with an old French fool. He fitted a polite smile onto his face but offered no comment, not wishing to encourage further conversation.

The Frenchman, however, was warming to his recollection. "Fathers give us the strength to survive this harsh world, but mothers make it worth the effort." He nodded, pleased at his aphorism, then raised an eyebrow. "You are paying yours a visit?"

It occurred to Lawrence that truth was often rude, but he could not change the script that the moment had written in his head. "My mother passed not long after this was made."

"Ah," said the old man, unabashed by his own faux pas.

"My ancestral home is near Blackmoor," Lawrence said, surprising himself by continuing to engage this old man. "My father and brother live there."

"You're English? Forgive me," said the Frenchman, "but your accent . . ."

"I've been in America for a very long time," said Lawrence. "A very long time."

The Frenchman smiled. "Ah . . . a wandering spirit."

It was casually said, but Lawrence didn't think it was as casual a remark as it appeared. "Well," he said diffidently, "not exactly."

"Ah, a fellow exile then."

For some obscure reason the comment amused Lawrence and he smiled. "Yes . . . I guess you could say that."

The Frenchman settled back against the cushions as the wheels clicked along the rails. His long, clever fingers turned the shaft of his cane in a slow circle so that the silver head seemed to search the whole of the room. Lawrence saw clearly now that it was a wolf: fierce and snarling. A beautifully made stick, but somehow repugnant.

The cane made a final turn and as the wolf's head swung around toward him, Lawrence felt—as absurd as the thought was to his civilized mind—that the eyes of a real wolf glared out at him through the lifeless metal. It required effort to wrench his own eyes away from the cane and he caught the Frenchman in a split second of unguarded interest, the old eyes keen and sharp, and an enigmatic smile curling the corners of his mouth. Then the moment passed and the old man was just old and wizened and the cane was nothing more than metal and wood.

"A man needs a good stick on the moors," mused the Frenchman. "I purchased this in Gévaudan . . . oh, it seems like *lifetimes* ago. Isn't it lovely? The work of a master silversmith, an apprentice of Pierre Germain. Do you know Germain's work? One of the Rococo artists. Very beautiful art . . . so alive." He bent forward and offered a warm and inclusive smile. "You would do me a great honor, sir."

The Frenchman gripped the wolf's snarling head and with a deft turn of the wrist he released some hidden lock and pulled the head away from the wooden shaft. Not entirely, but enough to reveal a hand's breadth of a wickedly sharp rapier that was hidden within the heart of the stick.

Lawrence gasped, but the Frenchman's smile turned genial as he slid the rapier back into place with a quiet click. He took the sword cane in both liver-spotted hands and offered it to Lawrence.

"I . . . can't," stammered Lawrence, and in truth he was as unnerved by the look that had been in the Frenchman's eyes when he said that he'd obtained the cane *lifetimes* ago as he was by the deadly potential of this unexpected gift. "We've only just met." He picked up his own stick—stylish but no match in either form or purpose with the Frenchman's cane. "This one will do me just—"

The old Frenchman interrupted with a chuckle and a shake of the head. "Nonsense! It would give me great pleasure to know that my old stick was in the keeping of a civilized man. Besides . . . its heft is somewhat too much for me these days."

Lawrence opened his mouth to rephrase his refusal, but the old man beat him to it.

"It is one of the few privileges of the old," the Frenchman said, "to pass on our burdens to the young."

He held the cane out again.

"*Merci*," Lawrence said after a long pause. He accepted the cane with a gracious nod.

"From one exile to another," the old man said softly.

The sword cane was light but solid, the heavy silver head balanced by a thick brass ferrule that showed signs of hard use in rough terrain. The wood was unmarked and lovely, with a tight grain that swirled throughout the polished hardwood. "You are overly kind," murmured Lawrence.

"Not at all."

Lawrence picked up his own cane and held it out, intensely aware of how shabby it looked by comparison. "I insist you take mine in trade, then."

The smile the old Frenchman gave was mostly gracious, but sewn through the wreath of wrinkles on his smiling face were traces of some other emotion; and as he accepted the stick his finger brushed one of Lawrence's fingers. It was a casual accident, but Lawrence nearly recoiled. The Frenchman's skin was as cold as the tomb and strangely rough. The Frenchman's eyes were hooded as he sat back and examined his new stick, a smile of some rare kind trying to blossom on his lips.

The train whistled like a shrieking ghost as it sped along through the tangled vines and twisted trees of Northumbria.

Chapter Five

Near Blackmoor

The country lane twisted and turned through forests more ancient than any of the races of men—both savage and civilized—who had lived there. Vast oaks with trunks as stout as stone towers; gullies that dropped away into spider-infested darkness; paths that led into the hearts of bottomless bogs.

Lawrence sat in a corner so that he could watch the countryside and have enough light to read and reread the letter that he held between thumb and forefinger. The paper was expensive, the handwriting precise, flowing and emphatically feminine. He read the letter again, perhaps the twentieth time since it was delivered to his London hotel, and his heart hammered as forcefully and as painfully as it had the first time he'd read it.

Dear Mr. Talbot,

I beg you to pardon this overly familiar and desperate appeal.

I believe your brother Benjamin has mentioned me to you in his correspondence: I'm Gwen Conliffe, his fiancée. I'm writing to inform you of your brother's disappearance. He has not been seen for three weeks now and we fear the worst. I have recently learned that you are currently here in England with your theatre company.

I understand that your schedule takes you back to America soon, but I would implore you to help us find him. Please come to Talbot Hall.

We need your help.

With each line the handwriting had become more passionate, the pen digging more desperately into the paper. The signature was a scrawl and the letter had been hastily blotted before it had been folded. Speed and urgency, he determined. And fear.

Lawrence folded the letter and placed it in an inner pocket of his coat. He rearranged his clothes but his hand lingered over the place where the letter rested. Over his heart.

"Ben . . . ," he murmured.

For most of the way the hooves of the horses thudded dully on hard-packed dirt, but when they began clattering on stone, Lawrence glanced out the window. He looked out just as the carriage passed under a great stone arch that he thought he would never see again. The massive portal was topped with a hunting scene of snarling hounds on either side of a trapped stag. The words TALBOT HALL were engraved with cool severity into the keystone, but the letters were mostly obscured by tangles of vine. A flock of threadbare ravens were roused from their slumber by the passage and they leaped into the air, salting the afternoon with their rusty protest. A fox with one milky eye watched the wheels roll, its body hidden by shadows thrown by stones long ago fallen from the arch.

Lawrence turned and looked back, trying to remember the arch as it had been and catching only embers of memory that had long since burned away.

The carriage rolled on, moving quickly down a lane once guarded by double rows of beech trees, but scavenger maples and tall weeds had invaded their ranks and the trees now looked like a line of beggars. The fields beyond, once immaculate and trimmed, had become tangles where crabgrass and wild onion ran rampant. Crass shrubberies of a hundred unnamed varieties now clogged the flower beds and unswept piles of leaves lay in rotting dunes in the cobbled turnaround. Even the stone hounds and wolves that stood like gargoyles on marble pedestals along the drive were gray with dust and strangled by vines.

The carriage stopped and Lawrence hesitated before turning the door handle. Even though he knew that much would have changed since his boyhood, he had never expected this total descent into squalor and dissolution. The house itself had an abandoned air about it. Most of the windows were dark, a few had cracked panes, and from one empty frame on a top floor Lawrence could see finches flutter in, one after another, carrying twigs and worms.

" 'Ere you go, sir," said the driver, hopping nimbly down. He cast an appraising eye at the hall but kept his own counsel as he pulled Lawrence's expensive steamer trunk out of the boot. He carried it to the top of a flight of heavy stone stairs and left it standing on one end beside the door, then retreated hastily to the carriage. His charge had not yet emerged, so the driver folded down the wrought-iron step and opened the door. "Talbot 'all, sir."

Lawrence debated telling the driver to fetch back the trunk and get the hell out of this place. He tasted the words and how clean they would feel on his tongue, but then an old memory stole like a thief into his mind. Lawrence and Ben, a pair of boys playing at being pirates, running from the portico to the shelter of the trees. Ben with a wooden cutlass, Lawrence with a tree root shaped like a boarding pistol.

Where are you, Benjamin, he wondered for the thousandth time since he had first read Gwen Conliffe's desperate letter. *Come out, come out wherever you are.* He sighed and unfolded himself from the carriage and stepped down on the same flagstones across which those boys had run a thousand times. But that was before Hell came to Talbot Hall and all things merry and light had been torn away. Now he and his brother were grown men who had never once met face to face. Lawrence wondered if there would ever be a chance to walk these grounds with Ben, just a couple of young men sharing brandy and cigars and chatting about the separate worlds in which they lived. Lawrence feared that it would never happen, even if Ben was found hale and healthy. This place seemed drained of all of its potential for comfort.

The driver, no lout, caught something of Lawrence's air. "Shall I wait, sir?"

Lawrence looked at him for a moment, lips pursed, but then he shook his head. "No, thank you. This'll do."

He handed over a fistful of uncounted coins and the driver beamed a great smile and climbed back onto his carriage. The horses moved off sprightly as if happy to be quit of such a dreary place and soon even their echo had vanished away down the lane, through the arch, and out through the iron gates. Lawrence stood as still as the ancient trees until only silence rolled back toward him.

"Ben? . . ." Lawrence called lightly, but not even the birds in the trees answered him. Lawrence sighed again and began the long climb up to the front door.

The door was closed and Lawrence had never

possessed a key. As a boy he hadn't needed one, and he had never been here as a man. He knocked on the heavy wood.

A chill wind sent dry leaves skittering across the steps as if even the moistureless debris of autumn wanted to flee this place. He turned and looked around, saw nothing, and knocked again.

No one and nothing answered his knock.

On a whim Lawrence tried the doorknob and was surprised when it turned under his hand, the heavy lock clicking, the oak panel yielding to a little pressure. Lawrence grunted and pushed it open and stepped in, leaving his trunk behind. Even though the carriage had gone, just knowing that the trunk was still outside made him feel that he still had the option of flight.

He stepped inside, his eyes adjusting from the dappled sunlight to the gloom of the enormous entry parlor. Rich wood paneling covered the walls, paintings of old relatives scowled from their dusty canvases, a once luxurious and now moth-eaten Turkish carpet stretched forward into the brown shadows of the inner house.

Lawrence looked around, listened. Nothing.

Silence.

"Hello!" he called. "Father?"

Nothing.

On a whim he called, "Ben?"

The only sound he heard was the steady ticking of the old family grandfather clock. That at least was a sign of life; somebody had to wind it. Lawrence moved to the foot of the sweeping double staircase that led to the upper landing. Between the stairways hung a tapestry depicting strange monsters and heroes from Hindu legend. Lawrence studied it for a moment, as fascinated now as he had been as a boy, always discovering a new creature, a new brave warrior. He absently twirled his new cane through his fingers, the wolf's head chasing itself through the air. Lawrence sighed, slid the cane into a Ming urn full of umbrellas that stood beneath the tapestry, and turned to call out again . . .

. . . but a fierce growl froze him in place as something huge and furry rushed at him from behind.

Lawrence cried out in shock and recoiled as the massive form of a great Irish wolfhound—two hundred pounds of muscle and sinew—galloped toward him across the big foyer, its savage teeth bared in a terrible snarl of pure rage.

Lawrence instantly backed away, backpedaling until his heels found the stairs and then he began to climb backward as the hound stalked him. He raised an arm across his throat, but even the thick wool of his greatcoat would be like tissue paper to those fangs. The hound began barking with a deep-chested bay that shook the whole foyer. Lawrence flinched at the noise and then cried out again as he collided with something behind him on the stairs. He whirled.

And there was his father.

Sir John Talbot stood tall and imposing, a huge rifle in his hands.

"I—" began Lawrence. He awkwardly retreated a step or two, caught now between the barking hound and the sudden and powerful presence of his father.

Sir John's eyes were cool and calculating and he looked down at his son, but spoke to the dog. "Samson!"

The hound instantly went quiet.

The hall fell into an electric silence. Lawrence stood on the bottom step, one hand gripping the banister, the other frozen halfway into a gesture of contact—hand open as if to touch his father, but his reach withheld. He swallowed and took one last retreating step, standing on the landing. Close to the hound, but closer to his walking stick, totally uncertain how this drama would play out. There were so many ways it could turn bad.

Sir John descended the stairs until he stood in front of his son.

"Lawrence . . ." he murmured, and there was surprise in his eyes. Confusion, too, as if Sir John was waking from a dream and found that fantastic images had followed him into the real world. "Lawrence?"

Lawrence cleared his throat.

"Hello, Father."

Sir John's eyes roved over Lawrence, taking his measure. "Lo and behold," he said softly. "The prodigal son returns. . . ."

Despite everything, Lawrence smiled.

Sir John blinked and looked down at the big Holland & Holland "Royal" double rifle he held, smiling bemusedly as if surprised to see such a thing in his hands.

"Not too many visitors these days," he said as he broke the rifle open and draped it comfortably over the crook of his arm. With that done the tension in the room eased by slow degrees as father and son stood there, each lost in the process of calculating all of the possible meanings behind this encounter, and feeling the tides of memory surge in on them.

"Shall I slaughter the fatted calf?" said Sir John with a rueful grin.

Lawrence stiffened. "Don't go to any trouble on my account."

Sir John stepped closer and once again took his son's measure. As an actor, Lawrence was skilled at reading faces, but as bits of emotion flitted onto and away from his father's face he found it impossible to get a read.

When his father nodded to himself, Lawrence said, "What? . . ."

"I've often wondered what you'd look like."

"I doubt that."

"It's quite true." Sir John wore a heavy robe trimmed with leopard fur. His hair and beard were snow white but his blue eyes were youthful and charged with vitality. His personal energy was completely at odds with the rundown state of the grounds; however, his cool smile was in perfect harmony with the chilly and cheerless house. "Yes," he said more to himself than to his son, "I've often wondered . . ."

Lawrence didn't know how to respond to that, and didn't want to try. Instead he said, "You seem well."

Shutters dropped behind Sir John's eyes. "Do I?" He paused. "You come here for your brother, then?"

"Of course."

"Of course," echoed Sir John.

"Has there been any word?"

Sir John turned away without answering. He crossed the hall and entered his study. After a moment's hesitation Lawrence followed.

The study was a man's place, with many sofas and chairs and bookshelves crammed with volumes in a dozen languages. Tables were scattered about, some bearing bottles of wine and brandy, others covered with maps, and one with an open book on astronomy. Tall windows of thick leaded glass let in filtered light, which was warmed and colored by the glow from a thick knot of logs in the fireplace. Pistols, swords and weapons of ancient design were mounted on the walls or set in cases of museum quality. But as much as it was a man's room it was also a predator's room, with the heads of a score of animals—rhinoceroses, lions, bears—gazing fatalistically into the chamber, tiger and leopard skins on the walls, and a plaque on which were mounted claws and teeth from ten species of great hunting cats.

Lawrence lingered in the doorway, his attention not drawn by the violent majesty of the décor but by his father's odd behavior. It was true that Lawrence had not seen his father in many years, but a chance meeting of this kind should have provoked some flicker of humanity. Instead, Sir John seemed distracted, his attention drawn inward instead of outward to his son's presence.

Lawrence said, "Miss Conliffe learned that my company was in London. I was going to invite you and Ben. . . ."

"I see," said Sir John, stopping by a globe and idly tracing a line of latitude.

"I was going to send word to you," said Lawrence. "To invite you to a performance. You and Ben. . . ."

But his voice trailed away as Sir John turned to face him. The look on his father's features was oddly twisted as if he was in physical pain.

"Well," said Sir John quietly. "A fine idea. Some years too late, but a fine idea." He was trying to sound offhand, but Lawrence could tell that something was wrong and his father's next words drove home that suspicion with terrible force. "Unfortunately your brother's body was found in a ditch by the priory road yesterday morning."

The words hit Lawrence like fists. He staggered back against the door frame.

"Good God! Father . . . *what happened?!*"

Sir John's eyes went cold, his conflict resolved into an icy control that Lawrence remembered from all those years ago. Sir John clasped his hands behind his back and stood ramrod stiff. If he had any compassion for what his words had just done to his son, not one flicker of it showed on his stern face.

"I assume you have something to wear to the funeral."

Lawrence had no words. There was a soft sound behind him, a discreet clearing of the throat, and he turned to see a tall Sikh in a deep blue turban, loose jacket and trousers.

"Sir John, I heard Samson, is . . ." The Sikh stopped talking as he realized that the man in the doorway was not the master of the house. His eyes snapped wide and he smiled in delight. "Master Lawrence!"

"Singh!" cried Lawrence as he clapped the other man on the shoulders. "My God!"

Singh regarded him in a more fatherly way than had Sir John, looking him up and down and appearing to be greatly pleased at the tall, handsome man he saw before him. But then his face clouded.

"I'm so very sorry, Lawrence. We're all shocked. This has been a terrible, terrible event."

"Thank you, I—" as Lawrence fished for words Sir John gave the globe an irritable spin and stalked past him. His footsteps echoed with force and anger throughout the hall. Lawrence and Singh watched his stiff retreating back.

Singh met his eyes and then busied himself with taking Lawrence's traveling cloak and hat. "It's good that you're here."

"Is it?"

Singh hung the cloak and paused for a breath before turning to face him. "Yes," he said, "it is."

"Ben's fiancée . . . Miss Conliffe?"

"She's here," said Singh. "Sleeping upstairs. Poor lass is in a very bad way."

"She must be devastated," Lawrence said, his eyes drifting toward the staircase.

"Her father arrives tomorrow. For the funeral."

"That's tomorrow as well?"

"Yes."

"This has all happened so fast." Lawrence shook his head. "Where . . . where's Ben?"

"Being cared for," said Singh.

"I want to see him."

Singh shook his head. "It would be better if you did not—"

"Tell me," said Lawrence.

Chapter Six

Blackmoor Village

None of the horses Lawrence had ridden as a boy were still at the estate but there were several healthy animals stabled behind the house. Lawrence saddled a sturdy black gelding and as he rode away from the Hall he wished the horse could sprout wings like Pegasus and fly far and away, not back to London— no, he wanted to go home to America. Home was there, not here. This place had not been home for a long time, and he suspected it never would be again.

There were too many ghosts.

Ben. *God almighty, Ben!*

He had lived so long without Ben in his life that he should have been better prepared for such a catastrophe, but with every second the knife of grief drove deeper into his heart. Benjamin. He could *not* be dead.

Not now. Not when Lawrence was here, at home. It was so unfair, Lawrence wanted to scream at God.

He walked his horse as far as the stone arch and finally stopped and sagged against the wall, all of the power gone from his muscles. He clutched the reins with one hand and balled the other into a fist.

"Ben . . . ," he whispered and beat the side of his fist on the ancient stones. "God damn it, Ben. . . . God damn you!"

Tears boiled in his eyes and ran down his cheeks.

Lawrence pounded on the stones over and over again as sobs wracked his big frame. The horse nickered nervously and the ravens chattered in the trees like noisy mourners.

"Ben," Lawrence said again, and this time his voice was choked and raw, "I'm sorry. . . ."

THE VILLAGE OF Blackmoor was small and rustic. Nothing seemed to have changed in the last thirty years, and probably not in the hundred before that. The thatched houses still sat at odd angles to the road as if the inhabitants didn't want to be reminded that their neighbors were a short stone's throw away. Gardens were well tended and embowered by low stone walls overgrown with creeping vine, and smoke drifted prosaically from each chimney. As the gelding followed the road into town Lawrence caught the eye of several villagers, some of whom tapped their companions to notice the stranger passing among them.

Lawrence tried hoisting a genial smile onto his face, but the scaffolding of grief wouldn't support it and each grin collapsed into a brooding scowl. It was all the same to the villagers, who gave him only calculating stares and suspicion.

He rode into the town square, which was anchored on one side by the gray pile of the Presbyterian church whose stained glass windows depicted scenes of righteous fury and harsh celestial judgment. Never a cheery place, and Lawrence could not imagine his brother— his lighthearted and smiling brother Ben—getting married in such a temple to gloom and damnation. But was it any more fitting a place for a burial? Lawrence wavered on the edge of not caring and feeling that the murkiness of the church matched his own mood.

The other anchor to the square was the tavern, and Lawrence knew that it saw a more religious attention from its devoted followers than did the church.

But he passed both and headed down a side street to a massive wooden structure with the ill-chosen name of Black Ice. The icehouse was a major employer in the town and many of the men of Blackmoor started their working lives there as boys and ended them there, as Ben did now, as bodies laid out on slabs of ice awaiting burial.

Lawrence nearly gagged at the thought, but he steeled himself. He dismounted and tied his horse to a post. He walked to the big barn doors, which stood slightly ajar. A waft of chilled air brushed his face as he stood there, and he knew that going inside was going to cost him.

If Ben can endure it, then so can I.

With that he pushed the doors wider and stepped inside.

THE ICEHOUSE FELT colder than any place he had ever been. The air was thick and damp and the lanterns did nothing to dispel the oppressive murk. He moved down the main aisle, past empty wooden bins for shaping the ice, past the great saws that cut it into slabs or cubes, past long blocks of ice covered with straw to slow their melting, past side rooms where butchers stored and cut their meats.

Ben Talbot lay on the last block of ice at the end of the row, deep inside the building by a back wall. Someone had draped him with a sheet and though the color had faded to a muddy brown, Lawrence could tell that the stains on the sheet had once been bright red. It hurt him to see his brother laid out in such a place, displayed on ice like a choice cut of beef. Defenseless and vulnerable, without dignity.

And alone.

Alone in this cold and terrible place.

Lawrence reached out an unsteady hand and pulled the sheet down. At first he just uncovered his brother's face, and for a long moment Lawrence stood there and tried to impose the memory of his brother's boyhood features over the landscape of this dead man's face. Ben's eyes were closed, and though that was a mercy it also removed the element of personality. This was a man he did not know who had been the boy—the *brother*—he had loved.

Ben's face was turned away, the exposed cheek smooth, but when Lawrence bent over to examine the landscape of his brother's features he saw with horror that the opposite cheek had been slashed from temple to jawline. Four long, deep wounds.

With trembling hands, Lawrence pulled the sheet down to Ben's waist.

"Dear God!" The cry was torn from him and he staggered back, hand to his mouth. There did not seem to be enough air as the whole room spun crazily around him. He staggered forward until his thighs bumped against the unyielding ice of the slab. "What . . . what . . . *did this?*" he demanded, but his only answer was his own echo.

Ben Talbot had been eviscerated by some terrible and savage claw. The flesh of his muscular abdomen had been slashed as if by swords, but the tears were too jagged to have been made by edged steel. These were definitely claw marks, but nothing short of a tiger or a bear could do such horrible damage. Ben's skin was bloodless and white and hung like strips of stage canvas, and in the gaps of the wound Lawrence could see striated muscle, yellow globules of subcutaneous fat, coils of purple intestine, and the jagged ends of shattered ribs.

He sensed movement behind him and turned to see a grim-faced butcher in a stained leather apron standing near. The man knuckled his forehead.

"You'd be Mr. Lawrence I expect?" he said, his breath steaming in the frigid air. "Mr. Benjamin's brother?"

Lawrence nodded, unable to speak.

The butcher reached past him and pulled the sheet up until it covered everything except Ben's face. It was a merciful act and Lawrence nodded his mute thanks. He turned away to blink tears from his eyes. Lawrence leaned on the wooden wall and breathed with great care until he was sure that he would not disintegrate into tears.

After a few moments, the butcher cleared his throat. "We were all sorry about your brother. He were a good man."

"Was he?" Lawrence said distantly. He turned and looked down at Ben. For just a moment it seemed as if his brother were merely sleeping. "I missed his whole life . . ."

The butcher shifted uncomfortably. "Sir . . . I might be overstepping meself . . ."

Lawrence turned to him. "Speak your mind."

"Well, sir . . . your father instructed me to bury your brother's effects with him." He dug into a large pocket and removed a small leather bag. "But it seems a shame, though. Especially you being his brother an' all."

He offered the bag, and Lawrence hesitated only a moment then took it from the butcher's bloodstained fingers. Lawrence mumbled a disjointed thanks, and the butcher nodded and vanished back into the gloom of the icehouse. Lawrence lingered for ten minutes longer, staring at Ben's face and holding the bag of his possessions to his chest. He could feel his heart beating against the clenched fist that held the last things Ben had touched before he died.

Then Lawrence stumbled out of the icehouse and into the light.

CHAPTER SEVEN

Lawrence brooded into his whiskey, thinking some of the darkest thoughts he owned. The tavern was nearly as dark as his temper. A haze of pipe smoke and burning peat hung like a cloudbank beneath the creosote-soaked wooden rafters. The voices of fifty men and a handful of women filled the air with a constant din that nearly drowned out the off-key tinkle of the piano and the tone-deaf voice of the drunk singing the wrong lyrics to the song the pianist was playing. An eight-year-old boy walked backward through the room, scattering sawdust on the floor that he scooped from an old leather ship's bucket. Portraits on the walls showed the haughty faces of landed gentry who had sponsored the tavern at different times in its long history. A two hundred-year-old blunderbuss was hung on pegs over the bar, and the barman—an evil-faced exsailor with a knife scar that made him look like a pirate—tugged on animal-headed beer taps to fill pewter tankards with dark local beer.

Lawrence saw all of this when he'd come in but little of it registered. He found a table in a corner and had settled down to examine Ben's belongings and lose himself in the strong whiskey of the region. It was rough and raw and nasty and suited his mood to a tee.

He sipped his whiskey and used one finger to push the items into an uneven line on the table. Ben's reading glasses were bent and scratched, showing much wear, and Lawrence wondered if Ben had become a scholar. He'd always loved stories as a boy. What would he have read as a man? Lawrence did not think that Ben would tend toward the scientific—natural philosophy was their father's passion; Ben had always seemed more of a dreamer. Novels, perhaps? Or poetry. Lawrence decided that he would find out. Gwen Conliffe would know, and might perhaps enjoy talking about the things that fascinated Ben. Singh would know, too.

Lawrence would not ask his father.

There had been a pocket watch among Ben's things, and Lawrence recognized it as the one that had belonged to their maternal grandfather—someone they'd never met but whose belongings had been shared out among the boys by their mother. Lawrence had owned a silver cigar case as a boy and he'd used it to keep crickets and other bugs that he could catch. Thinking of it nearly carved a smile into the harsh frown that was etched onto his mouth, but then he thought about its loss, along with everything else he'd owned, after his mother's death, and his frown deepened.

Two items were of particular interest to Lawrence and he picked each of them up several times. One was a daguerreotype of Gwen Conliffe. Lawrence had never met her and he studied the picture with great interest. She was quite a beautiful woman. Quite extraordinarily beautiful, he decided, with intelligent eyes that—in this picture at least—showed a great depth of kindness, perhaps of insight. And despite the tradition of austerity when posing, there was a hint of a smile to quicken the pulse. Though her manner of dress was the height of propriety, there was no hiding the lushness of her womanly curves. Even moody and in his cups Lawrence was self-aware enough to be wryly amused that his animal instincts were drawn more powerfully by this woman in her proper dress than from the oceans of naked flesh that had been available to him for the asking over the last few years. And for that insight a tiny smile did touch his mouth, just for a moment.

He held her photograph and wondered what kind of woman she was. His mother had been brilliant and sad and funny and complex. Few of the women he had met in the theater—whether as fellow actors or among the legions of theatergoers who flung convention to the wind to dally with a "star"—had half of her wit and charm, and none of her grace. He studied Gwen Conliffe's smile and the lift of her chin and the expression in her eyes and thought that he saw in those features a woman of more complexity than he would have credited for the fiancée of a country gentleman. If, indeed, that was what Ben had aspired to be. And somehow this insight into Gwen jabbed him because it suggested so many things about Ben. If Ben had wooed and won such a woman then he must have been a remarkable person, and Lawrence felt guilty for not having worked to cultivate Ben's acquaintanceship beyond letters. And he felt anger for having the opportunity stolen from him forever.

He set down the photograph and picked up the oddest item among Ben's meager possessions. It was a medallion on a silver chain. Lawrence held it up to the lamplight to study the image stamped onto the metal disk: a monk in medieval robes surrounded on all sides by snarling wolves. How odd, he thought, and he could not determine if the monk was in peril of being devoured or if some celestial power was holding the wolves at bay. The carving was too crude to clearly present the meaning of the scene. In either case the medallion unnerved

Lawrence in ways he could not clearly define. Doom or salvation? Why would Ben carry it? What did it signify to his brother? The butcher had said that it was among his possessions, not on his person. Something carried rather than worn.

A shadow fell across the medallion and Lawrence looked up to see the middle-aged publican who owned the tavern. The barman nodded at the empty glass at Lawrence's elbow and gestured with the whiskey bottle he carried.

"Another, sir?"

Lawrence nodded and watched distractedly as the man poured a hefty slug and moved off. Lawrence glanced at him as he passed and saw a look of faint recognition on the man's face. Putting two and two together, perhaps.

A noisy group of men called for fresh drinks and the publican and his assistant hurried over to pour whiskey and beer. They sat in a loose circle around a large table on which sat their hats—bowlers, cloth caps and top hats—and an assortment of tankards and wineglasses. Lawrence idly took the measure of this group as they were the centerpiece of the whole room, the kind of group who felt themselves to be of sufficient importance to speak louder and with less circumspection than anyone else. One of them was dressed in severe black with a Roman collar and Lawrence marked him as the village vicar. There was a very well-dressed man wearing expensive clothes. Local squire, Lawrence determined, and next to him was a ramrod-straight man with thick salt-and-pepper hair that Lawrence would have wagered was exmilitary, and from his patrician features probably an officer. Next to him was a fellow with a fierce Lord Kitchener mustache and suspicious eyes who was almost certainly the local constable—he was in shirtsleeves but there was an official-looking tunic draped over the back of his chair. The bald man with spectacles had an educated look, and Lawrence figured him for a scholar or a doctor, and the broad-shouldered man with the weathered face and piercing hunter's eyes looked like a farmer or gamekeeper—but definitely an earthier man than the others.

This was a game Lawrence often played when he was out and about, and now he did it to distract himself from the heartbreak that threatened to unman him. Like most trained actors, Lawrence was well practiced at guessing professions from dress, mannerisms and patterns of speech. Observation of real people in such situations was part of what made him so good at his craft. If he listened for ten minutes he could play each of these men convincingly on stage.

The men jabbered, each of them trying to dominate the conversation so that their remarks overlapped and commingled.

"It's going to be hard to replace young Toland," said the squire. "One of my best men. Widow and five little ones now on my rolls. Not to mention I'm down two hundred pound on that flock. I'd put another two hundred on the head of the beast that did this if I had it in hand." He shook his head. "A widow and five little ones . . ."

"I feel for Sir John," rumbled the constable. "Poor sod. Losing his son like that. 'Course he always was a bit on the edge of mad in my opinion. If anything puts him over, this will."

The squire sniffed. "What becomes of Talbot Hall when the old man passes, I wonder."

Lawrence's hand tightened around his whiskey glass. *Were they talking about my family?*

"Cor blimey," said the constable to the squire, "but you're a vulture, Timothy."

"In all seriousness," protested the squire.

"I should think some long-lost relative gets a happy letter from his solicitor."

The pastor cut in, shifting the topic away from material concerns. "I saw the bodies with my own eyes." He bent close and his voice took on a mysterious timbre. "Unnatural wounds. Most unnatural. Made by a fell creature I say. Not merely an animal," he said, cutting a disapproving look at the constable, "as some would wish it."

Lawrence almost opened his mouth to say something but restrained himself. His hand was closed tightly around his whiskey glass.

The military man pursed his lips. He spoke in a voice better suited for a parade ground than a quiet tavern. "What if it wasn't a beast at all, but a cunning murderer? Someone who bore a grudge against one of these men?"

"What do you mean?" asked the squire.

"It's a simple tactic. To misdirect the authorities he kills the men, then he tears the bodies up to make it *look* like a wild beast was responsible. I've seen it before—"

The others all jumped in to offer counterarguments, their volume rising to become a shouting match.

The constable slapped his hand on the table. "Ridiculous, Colonel! Who would go to such lengths? And why risk killing anyone other than the intended victim?"

The colonel spread his hands. "To conceal his true intentions. Like I've been saying."

Throughout the debate the vicar was shaking his head and now he held up a hand as if he was about to give a blessing. "Satan's minions are manifold," he said gravely. "He has forms and bodies far more terrible to draw upon than those of mere men and beast."

The tavern keeper shook his head. "What about them Gypsies' dancing bear? It could've done it."

The colonel snorted. "That mangy thing? Kill three grown men? Doubtful, Kirk, very doubtful."

The publican, Kirk, shrugged. "Then what, sir?" When the colonel didn't answer Kirk turned to the vicar. "You agree, Pastor Fisk, don't you?"

Fisk pursed his lips. "It might *not* be the bear," he said dubiously, "but those Gypsies are behind it. Mark me. A curse on us—and we're to blame. We allowed their paganism in our community."

The man with the hunter's eyes snorted. "Got nothing to do with the damned Gypsies, and ye all know it."

All conversation at the table died away, as did much of the chatter elsewhere in the room.

"We've seen all this a'fore."

"What are you saying, MacQueen?" asked the colonel.

MacQueen popped a lucifer with his thumbnail and held it over his pipe as he took a long pull. Despite his roughhewn clothes the other men waited him out, clearly invested in his opinion. MacQueen exhaled blue smoke up to the rafters and settled back in his chair, his keen eyes roving over the men as he spoke. His voice was quiet and even Lawrence found himself leaning forward to catch his words.

"It were twenty-five years ago now. My pa found him, way up on the dun. Quinn Noddy. Pastor, you knew him and his people. You, too, Constable Nye. Noddys have lived in these parts since times back. My pa was out early, following a blood trail and thinking there was a hound gone wild. He found Quinn Noddy and his whole flock. Torn to pieces. Half eaten they were. Just like these poor souls. Brains and guts and God-knows-what lying across the moor for a quarter mile. And Quinn . . . the look on his face like he'd been eaten *alive*."

"Good lord," murmured the bespectacled man.

"Aye, Dr. Lloyd. The Good Lord weren't looking after Quinn and his that night. Whatever it was that done it was big, too. Had claws. And didn't mind a load of buckshot, on account of we found two empty shells inside Quinn's shotgun. Quinn were a good shot, too. He and my pa took many a wily pheasant, and he weren't one to miss what he shot at."

"Anyone can miss," said the colonel, but his voice lacked conviction.

MacQueen turned a knowing eye on him. "If something was killing your whole flock o' sheep, Colonel Montford would you miss? *Could* you miss if something were close enough to tear you apart? Maybe one of your green recruits, but Quinn was nobody's fool and he could hit what he wanted to hit. But there was nothing . . . no body, no wounded animal spoor. Whatever it was killed Quinn and tore him and flock to guts and gore was something that could not *be* killed by buckshot. Think on that for a spell."

Dr. Lloyd opened his mouth to speak but shut it again. Constable Nye cleared his throat. "Did your father know what killed Noddy?"

MacQueen gave him an enigmatic smile; not a comfortable smile at all. He sucked on his pipe. "Well, sir, after what my pa saw, he went home and melted down my ma's wedding spoons and cast silver slugs of 'em. Always had one barrel loaded that way and the other slugs in his pocket anytime he walked out onto the moors, even in the bright midday." He paused and the tavern was as silent as the grave. "And at night? Well . . . my pa wouldn't leave the house on a full moon from then on."

Colonel Montford laughed, trying to break the spell of MacQueen's words. His laugh sounded hollow. "Come now, MacQueen."

Dr. Lloyd shared a knowing look with Pastor Fisk.

Montford said, "Your father thought it was a were-wolf?"

MacQueen smoked his pipe and said nothing.

The squire patted MacQueen on the arm. "Your father was an excellent gamekeeper, God rest him . . . but a gullible soul."

"Strickland's right," agreed the colonel. "Your father would throw salt over his left shoulder and knock wood at any mischance. I've seen him do it."

Squire Strickland nodded, but MacQueen continued to sit in silence, the blue fog of his pipe surrounding him like an aura.

Into the silence Pastor Fisk spoke, his voice low and tentative. "Maybe, Squire . . . and again maybe not. MacQueen lives closer to the land than we do. His people see what we in town miss. Besides . . . my uncle complained for years that his livestock disappeared at the hands of the Devil's beast."

The publican grunted. "I still say that bear's to blame. Damn Gypsies. You don't need to look past them for the Devil's work, Pastor. Them dark-eyed buggers always wandering the countryside, bringing their woe and deviltry with 'em. They show up, and two weeks later this happens. . . ." He shook his head. "My guess is that Ben Talbot went to their camp to twiddle a Pikey whore. Bear gets him and they dump what's left of him in a ditch."

"No, no," said Dr. Lloyd, "that's all well and good, Kirk, but how does that explain—?"

Squire Strickland cut him off. "You'd think the Talbots would have learned their lesson consorting with the Roms!"

"Right," agreed Colonel Montford. "Remember that black-eyed Salome the old man married? Gone crazy up there in the hall, killed herself? Wasn't she a gypo whore queen or somesuch?"

Lawrence stood up with such violence that his chair legs scraped back with a furious squeal. He stalked straight to the edge of their table and as one the gathered men stopped speaking and looked up to face the tall, broad-shouldered stranger. The scowl on Lawrence's face was so charged with dangerous fury that most of the men at the table recoiled.

"Yes, she *was* crazy," Lawrence snarled. "To have come to this shit-hole you call a town."

His words struck them to dumb silence except for the half-deaf pastor who turned to the squire. "What did he say?"

Colonel Montford was the first to recover. "You're in your drink, boy," he said with quiet control.

"Am I?" Lawrence sneered. "Then you must be awash in gin if you allow your mouth to jabber on about things you know nothing about!"

Montford jumped to his feet so suddenly that his chair fell over with a crash. His face flushed with red fury as he stepped face-to-face with Lawrence. Kirk moved behind the colonel and his glare showed that he was ready to back a regular against a stranger if this came to blows.

That was fine with Lawrence. He loathed these men as deeply as if he'd known them as enemies for years.

Hearing them speak of Ben was bad enough, but then they had dared—*dared*—say such vile things about his mother. He balled his fists, ready to tear into them; ready to defend his brother's honor and see their blood. He stepped toward Montford, his lips still curled in a sneer that gave his features a lupine cast.

"I—" he stared to say but then Constable Nye was on his feet, thrusting his bulk between Lawrence and the colonel.

"We'll have none of this!" he bellowed.

"Get him out of my tavern, Nye!" growled Kirk.

Lawrence started to go around the constable, but Nye put a restraining hand on his chest. "No!"

Lawrence looked down at the hand and then brushed it aside. Gently. He looked at the colonel with such a cold contempt that Montford looked taken aback.

"My mother was a Marquesa, you idiot. Solana Montrosa de Verdad." He spat on the floor. "And she was no Gypsy."

With that he turned and stalked out of the room leaving behind him a stunned silence so profound that the gathered men could hear the soft hiss of the log burning in the fireplace on the far side of the room.

It was Dr. Lloyd who broke the silence. "That man . . . that was Lawrence Talbot."

Nye looked at Colonel Montford for a long and ugly moment, and the echo of Lawrence's words seemed to haunt the air around them. The colonel turned away, snatched up his wineglass and threw it back. He sank into his chair without comment.

CHAPTER EIGHT

The sun was down, its last feeble light staining the sky as it tumbled into the distant west. Lawrence stalked down the street, fists still balled in rage, his jaw aching from the clench of his teeth. God how he wanted to pound those men, especially that pompous military buffoon.

He made it as far as the church and then wheeled around and headed back to the tavern. Maybe beating some sense into them was the right thing to do. Maybe that's what it would take to—

But Constable Nye stepped from the shadows into his path. Lawrence squared his shoulders, ready for a fight, but the constable gave him a sad smile and held out the small pouch of Ben's belongings. "I'm sorry for your loss, Talbot . . . but it's time for you to go home."

Muscles bunched and flexed at the corners of Lawrence's jaws. He looked past Nye to the tavern door and the moment stretched.

"Truer words were never spoken."

Then he drew in a breath through his nose and exhaled slowly and took the pouch from Nye. As Lawrence turned and began walking to where his gelding was tethered, Nye fell into step beside him.

After a dozen silent paces, Lawrence said, "What happened to my brother and those other men?"

Nye shook his head. "It had to be some kind of animal."

"And what are you doing about it?" Nye hesitated and Lawrence wheeled in front of him. Lawrence stepped closer. He was bigger and taller than Nye and the constable was forced to look up in order to maintain eye contact. "You're not doing *anything*."

For all the raw menace that Lawrence exuded, Constable Nye held his ground. "There's been no sign of it for weeks, Talbot. It's likely moved on . . . whatever it was."

"And what if it hasn't?" Lawrence asked. "What then?"

Nye did not even try to answer it. It was clear that he had thought about that and did not have a clue as to what to do.

"I thought as much," said Lawrence with venom and pushed Nye out of his way. He stalked to the hitching post and whipped the tethers away from the wrought-iron rail and swung into the saddle. He threw one black look at Nye and a longer, far darker one at the tavern door, then nodded to himself as if he'd made a hard decision, and kicked his horse into a canter.

CHAPTER NINE

Lawrence's foul mood was with him all the way home and only slightly diminished when Singh informed him that he was expected at the table with Sir John and Gwen Conliffe. The image of the young woman was captured in his mind as if the photograph had sunk beneath his flesh, and as he bathed and dressed he felt conflicted. Gwen had been engaged to Ben. She was a stranger to him. Nevertheless his baser self had been powerfully drawn to her image.

The lust, guilt and anger at the townsmen were all bandages to hide the real wound: grief. Lawrence knew it and that just pumped more bile into his demeanor.

By the time they sat down to dinner his troubled feelings had not much diminished. In person Gwen Conliffe was even more beautiful than the photograph had suggested. She was young and lovely in a way that made all of the beautiful actresses Lawrence cavorted with suddenly seem *plain*. She was uncorrupted, unsullied. Her fair skin was not the product of powder and paint, and her eyes were bottomless.

She was dressed in a mourning gown of black, but it was beautifully cut and did nothing to divert his attention from her beauty. By contrast, Sir John wore a suit with an old-fashioned cut. Elegant but out of place and showing wear. The old man's white hair was sketchily combed, his face unevenly shaved. Lawrence himself had no mourning clothes, though he wore his most somber colors and a cravat that was as modest as he could manage with no notice.

The dining hall itself was a strange setting for the meal. The big ballroom was in disrepair and this smaller room had been intended for informal meals, which this should have been. The table was too large, the draperies too heavy, the paneling too dark, the chandelier burning with too many candles so that the overall effect was ostentation shoved to the edge of claustrophobia. The walls were crowded with tables and sideboards, and the dining table itself groaned under the weight of an absurdly large feast. Lawrence suspected that Singh had used every piece of silver plate in the house. Platters were laden with eels baked with lemon and black pepper, whole pheasants sitting in nests of roasted chestnuts, grilled brook trout whose eyes glared in apparent shock at the room, a rack of rare lamb's ribs in mint sauce and a massive boar's head with an apple larger than Lawrence's fist shoved between its jaws. Bowls of roast potatoes stood alongside the last of the autumn greens.

Under other circumstances Lawrence would have dug in with the rapacity of a Roman at a bacchanal, but under the circumstances it all seemed too much, and it was far too soon. A feast like this would have been better suited to entertain a crowd of mourners after the funeral.

He briefly caught Gwen's eye as she picked delicately at a sliver of fish. Her manners were those of a cultured London lady, though he could not yet tell if she had the snobbery to go along with them, or if her reserve was like his own. Grief and awkwardness.

In truth they'd barely said ten words between them since Sir John had made introductions prior to ushering Miss Conliffe to the table. Sir John, on the other hand, had set to the feast with a will and had managed to keep a flow of conversation going between hefty portions of every meat on the board. Lawrence watched Gwen as she in turn watched Sir John reach across the table to tear another rib from the rack. The fragile bones cracked and he smiled at the sound, then laid into it with his strong white teeth. Gwen colored slightly and turned away, apparently interested in the arrangement of the silverware beside her plate. Sir John must have caught the movement of her head and flicked a glance first to her and then to Lawrence.

"You should have sent word you were coming," he said while chewing. "The telegraph line does reach us here at Blackmoor."

Lawrence said nothing. He was trying not to stare at Gwen as he played and replayed the moment when he first saw her. He and his father had already sat down, and Sir John had started eating without preamble. When the door to the cramped dining room opened, Lawrence turned but Sir John had leapt nimbly to his feet. Lawrence stood slowly, entranced and, for once in his life, unaware of the emotions on his face.

Sir John was a clumsier host than Lawrence expected. He was gruff, possessive and even rude—but all of this was directed at Lawrence. To Gwen he was overly deferential and courteous. Too much so.

Now, half an hour into the meal, Sir John was still eating and both Gwen and Lawrence seemed to be looking for an open window through which they could separately escape. Lawrence was hoping to make direct eye contact with Gwen so they could share that fragment of awareness. Would it make her smile? Even a rueful smile would be a wonderful thing to see on so beautiful a face.

"You find it surprising?"

Lawrence blinked, realizing that his father was talking to him. He read back the script of the last few moments and understood that his father was making a challenging follow-up to his remark about the telegraph. Lawrence had no intention of rising to the bait. He offered a meaningless smile and token incline of his head and sipped the wine. That, at least, was excellent.

Sir John reached for a platter and held it out to Gwen. "May I suggest some baked eel? Singh has outdone himself."

Gwen smiled—as meaningless a gesture as Lawrence's had been—and selected a piece of eel that looked less alive than did the others.

"Lawrence seems surprised that the telegraph wire reaches us here, even at lonely old Blackmoor." He chewed for a moment. "Also—I hear that the Americans are running lines for their new telephone system in the Boston area. How about that?"

"Is that so?" Gwen said with feigned interest. Had an actress read the line that way Lawrence would have scolded her for a poor performance, but Sir John was a devoted audience and took it as a cue to continue his ramble.

"I don't think I could stand the intrusion," the old man said, forking more eel onto his plate, "being at the beck and call of every Tom, Dick and Harry with such a device."

"I'm not surprised," murmured Lawrence, and immediately regretted it as Sir John turned a hostile eye toward him. For a moment the air crackled with tension but then Sir John cut another covert look at Gwen and jammed another forkful of eel into his mouth.

Gwen used the moment to shift the topic, and she turned her smoky blue eyes toward Lawrence.

"Do you find your home much changed, Mr. Talbot?"

Without looking at his father, Lawrence said, "Blackmoor does seem rather the same as I left it."

"How?" Sir John's question was almost a grunt.

Lawrence affected a casual expression as he said, "The villagers have some wild ideas."

"Yes," said Sir John, "we're a provincial lot, I must confess. Ignorant. Superstitious. To a worldly man such as yourself we're savages at the end of the Earth—"

Gwen cut him off. "I didn't intend to start a squabble—"

"No, no," persisted Sir John, overriding her protest. "I've *seen* savages at the ends of the Earth. All I am saying is that you dismiss the natural man at your peril."

The defensiveness in his father's voice amused Lawrence. He took a sip of wine and settled back against his chair. "I find your insecurity strange."

Sir John raised an eyebrow, equally amused. "Oh? And how comfortable are you in your skin, may I ask?"

"You can get used to anything," said Lawrence.

There was a sharp *clack* as Gwen set her silverware down with too much force and started to rise. Lawrence half rose, the gesture almost a bow.

"Please," he said. "Stay a moment."

She sat very tall, eyes cool and challenging. Sir John's eyes held equal challenge, but his eyes were almost palpably hot.

Lawrence knew that the moment was his to lose or repair. He nodded to Gwen and to his father, placing a hand over his heart in a gesture he contrived to look honest rather than affected.

"I want to apologize to both of you," he said, his voice quiet and guileless. "For not attending you in a more timely and . . . appropriate fashion." Both sets of eyes continued to watch. Neither said a word, so Lawrence continued. "It's a regret I'll carry with me the rest of my life."

The line was dramatic, and Lawrence had constructed it with the intent to manipulate the moment, but as he stared into the smoky depths of Gwen Conliffe's blue eyes, he realized that he meant it.

Sir John sat back and refilled his wineglass, his gaze probing, calculating. Gwen studied Lawrence as well, and he could feel the strength of her insight and intellect, and he saw the moment when she made her decision. She gave him a single, brief nod, but as she did so her eyes softened. Just a bit.

CHAPTER TEN

The rest of the dinner was extremely polite and no one wandered within biting distance of controversy or challenge. After Singh had cleared the plates, Gwen excused herself and retired.

That left the two Talbot men alone. Lawrence expected his father to return to their argument, but instead Sir John suggested they retire to the Great Hall for drinks. Lawrence was happy to agree.

In the Hall, Sir John poured scotch into a pair of cut-glass tumblers. The animal heads on the walls watched him with glassy indifference. He carried the glasses over to a pair of overstuffed chairs positioned before a roaring fire. Lawrence stood by one of the chairs, firelight flickering on his face, his dark eyes reflecting the blaze. He accepted the glass with a nod and sipped the rich single malt. They did not toast one another or even touch glasses. That would have been an absurd gesture on both their parts.

Sir John settled into one of the chairs and looked over the rim of his glass at a display of Masai spears that he had acquired before Lawrence had been born. His eyes were distant, as if he wandered through fields of memory.

Sipping his scotch, Lawrence wandered the room,

pausing now and then to examine the hunting weapons—and the stuffed and mounted proof of their effectiveness—that made up the room's motif. Then he spotted a newspaper that lay folded on the settee. He picked it up and opened it. The theater review page of *The London Times*. The headline read:

VICTORIA PLAYERS' *HAMLET*
A TRIUMPH FOR AMERICAN TRAGEDIAN TALBOT

"I've never understood it," said his father, and Lawrence turned to see that his father was standing by his elbow. He hadn't heard him come up behind him. "Acting. Playing at being other men . . . but, I understand that you're celebrated for it. *Famous* for it. Perhaps someday I'll see for myself what all the fuss is about."

Lawrence tossed the newspaper onto the desk.

Sir John threw back the rest of his scotch and as he poured a fresh drink he glanced up to see Lawrence looking at the beautiful portrait of Solana Talbot that hung above the fireplace. Sir John took a strong pull on his new drink.

"She was so beautiful," Lawrence murmured.

"She cared very much for the two of you."

Lawrence turned to his father, the sneer threatening to curl his lip again. "Why did she take her own life?"

Sir John was a long time in answering. "I don't know," he said softly.

But Lawrence was on the attack now, his earlier rage stoking the fires in his heart. "Was it something you did to her?"

His father turned from the portrait and looked at Lawrence with such honest hurt in his eyes that Lawrence faltered. "What do you think of me, Lawrence? What bizarre and wonderful stories have you concocted for yourself?"

"You're not answering the question," Lawrence snapped.

"Your mother was a regal creature." Sir John set the drink aside and came over to stand before his son. His eyes searched Lawrence's face for several painful seconds before he spoke. "I loved her dearly, and she never once gave me cause to raise my voice to her, let alone raise my hand. I miss her terribly, every single moment of every single day."

Lawrence opened his mouth to speak, but Sir John shook his head. His eyes were wet with unshed tears.

"I had never met a woman like her before. This world is seldom fortunate to be granted many of her kind. If we accept evolution as a truth, then she is of the kind we should be breeding so that we move farther and farther from the savagery of our ancestors . . . and the savagery of our own present kind. It may be that we're not ready for such a step forward, and it may be that we don't yet deserve it. So, perhaps women such as your mother are not meant for the troubled, corrupt and terrible world as it is. Your mother was not, and it kills me to say so. The world oppressed her, tore at her. Life presented too many horrors for her. She was brave, and she was strong, but in the end, after all of her struggles she . . . lost." Sir John's eyes burned with his loss and heartache. He swallowed and blinked slowly as if remembering where he was and to whom he spoke. In a softer voice he said, "Does that answer your question?"

"I . . . I don't know what to . . ." Lawrence felt his heart shift in his chest. No matter how many times he had rehearsed this conversation in his head he had never predicted these lines. Not their honesty, not their content. They sank through his flesh and into his heart. He looked deep into his father's eyes, looking for the lie, looking for the monster he had imagined him to be . . . but all he saw was a great and terrible pain that had never healed. Now he understood. The decay of the estate, the abandonment of care in the grounds, the distance from humanity. It was not a monster remaining aloof from the humanity to which it did not belong. It was hurt, it was retreat. It was an unconquerable grief.

He closed his mouth and eyes and took in a steadying breath through his nose. When he opened his eyes, he said, "Yes."

Sir John took a long moment before giving an accepting nod.

"I saw Ben today," Lawrence said, changing tack. "What could have done such a thing?"

"I have no idea," said Sir John, turning to face the fire. He rolled his glass back and forth between his palms. "I've seen the work of a Kodiak bear. A Bengal tiger. Nature at its most vicious. But . . . I've never seen the like of this."

"Could it have been a man?"

Sir John's eyes flicked toward Lawrence. "A man? You mean a raving lunatic at loose on the moor?" He shook his head. "Since this happened I've been over every inch of the region; I would have run him down with dogs. But you never know. On the other hand, the wounds are so terrible that . . . I think only a human being would seem capable of such wanton malevolence. Animals kill for food or to protect their own. They aren't cruel, and the damage that was done to Ben and to those other men . . . it was very cruel. As if the suffering of the victims was as much the intention as the need to feed."

"The locals blame the Gypsies," said Lawrence.

"They blame everything on the Gypsies. If a calf is born dead or a rooster crows at the wrong time of morning, they'll blame it on the Gypsies. They're guilty of half as much as they're blamed for and twice what you think them capable of."

Lawrence reached into his pocket and produced the medallion. He held it up by its silver chain so that the medal turned slowly, catching bits of hot firelight.

"This was among Ben's things."

Sir John looked at his son for a long moment before taking the medallion. He studied it closely as he sipped his drink.

"Hm. Saint Columbanus. An Irish saint. A favorite with Tinkers and Gypsies."

"So . . . Ben had dealings with them?"

"Yes. The local gentry pays a fee, and the Gypsies keep their criminal activities to a minimum. It's extortion, certainly, but it's often done. Here and elsewhere, probably everywhere. We pay a tithe and it guarantees that their stay is mutually tolerable. They move on once they've sold the local boys all the wine and dark-haired ladies they can stand."

Sir John handed the medallion back and turned away from his son's assessing eyes. He paused once to glance again at the portrait of the beautiful woman they had both loved—and still loved—and then walked out through the big glass doors that led to the patio.

Lawrence watched his father go. And he was aware that he was, in clear point of fact, seeing his father. Not the villain of all his fears. Not the culprit of his dark imaginings. But his father. A lonely man torn with grief, both old and new.

Grief that Lawrence shared, and knowing that the grief truly was shared opened doors in his soul that Lawrence had long since believed sealed shut forever.

He wiped tears from his own eyes and followed his father outside.

THE PATIO WAS broad and fashioned of decorative stonework from the last century. The trees beyond the patio were featureless with evening shadows, though their upper branches were painted with silver from the gibbous moon. Sir John was bent to the eyepiece of a magnificent old telescope that was a masterwork of the lensman's art. Sir John adjusted the delicate brass knobs with practiced skill.

"*'That orbed maiden with white fire laden; Whom mortals call the Moon . . .'*" he quoted softly.

Lawrence cleared his throat. "Still the natural philosopher, I see." He came close and followed the line of the telescope up into the darkness. "I always loved looking at the night sky with you."

Sir John's hand faltered for a moment then resumed adjusting a dial. "Yes. I recall that you did."

Somewhere away in the darkened woods an owl lifted an inquiring hoot.

"Father . . . ," Lawrence began softly, "do you ever think how it could have been different—"

"Never." Sir John cut him off as if he'd been dreading that question all night. He cleared his throat. "There's no point going down that road." After a moment, Sir John spoke again, his voice little more than a whisper.

"I only wish that I could have taken care of you properly," said Sir John. "That I had not sent you away to that asylum as I did."

Lawrence looked away. This was almost too much to bear. Behind him he heard his father fiddling with the telescope, clearly using it to hide his own discomfort.

The old man cleared his throat again, and when he spoke his voice was casual, offhand. "She exerts enormous power."

"The moon?" Lawrence asked, recovering.

Sir John raised his head and glanced at Lawrence, but from that angle his face was all in shadows. "That is who we're talking about."

"You always refer to it in the feminine."

"I do indeed," Sir John said as he bent back to the eyepiece. "Her power is subtle. Smoothly employed, like a woman's. And absolute. The Goddess of the Hunt, as the old legends say."

He straightened and gestured to the telescope. Lawrence nodded and bent to look, and the magic of the telescope brought the face of the moon to within arm's reach. Lawrence could see it with perfect clarity. Cold, powerful, luminous . . . and utterly desolate.

And hostile.

Lawrence raised his head from the telescope, feeling a wave of coldness pass through him as if he'd been standing knee deep in the airless, cheerless dust of that ancient rock.

His father bent to look again, and Lawrence thought he caught the flicker of a smile. They stood there, Lawrence and Sir John, both looking at the moon in their own way.

"Lawrence," Sir John said, his eye still pressed to the viewer. "I *am* glad you're home."

Lawrence did not know how to respond to that. Nothing in his life had prepared him for this moment, so he said nothing for fear of saying the wrong thing. He sipped his scotch and watched his father watching the great and icy Goddess of the Hunt.

For the first time in his adult life, however, Lawrence Talbot felt like he was home.

Above him, bright in the infinite darkness, the moon watched him and laughed. All Lawrence heard was the whisper of the night wind.

CHAPTER ELEVEN

Lawrence said good night to his father and retired. He climbed the stairs, hands buried in his pockets, his chin sunk thoughtfully onto his chest. Singh had seen to opening and airing his old room and Lawrence's feet took him there more through reawakened habit than conscious thought; however, as he reached for his doorknob he heard a woman's voice across the hall and turned to see that Ben's door was ajar and light spilled out from within.

He paused in the middle of the hallway and then took a tentative step toward his brother's old room. From the other side of the decorative door Lawrence could hear the muted sounds of women's voices.

Now, or not at all, he told himself, and gently rapped on the wood.

A moment later the door opened an inch and the stern eye of a dour maid peered out at him.

"Can I help you, sir?"

Lawrence was much taller than the maid and could easily see over her head into a sliver of the room, and that was enough to catch sight of the big stand-up dressing mirror that stood in the far corner. Gwen Conliffe was reflected in the mirror. She was turned away from the door and only half-turned toward the mirror so that she did not see him watching her. Lawrence's breath caught in his throat. Gwen wore a sheer petticoat and was absently drawing her arms through the sleeves of a gossamer dressing gown, and for a moment Lawrence could see her creamy skin, naked from the waist up. Her body was lean and finely made, with full breasts tipped with delicate pink nipples. She had no scar, no flaw, and Lawrence marveled at the purity of her beauty, especially seeing it this way—unintentional, without artifice, almost goddesslike in line and form. Lawrence saw this in a flash and immediately lowered his eyes to the maid's as if he had in no way intruded into the privacy of that chamber.

"I was hoping to have a word with Miss Conliffe. I'm Lawrence Talbot."

The maid gave him a frank, appraising stare and Lawrence almost blushed. Thank God the hallway was badly lighted.

"Just a moment, sir," she said with a tight mouth.

She closed the door a bit harder than was absolutely necessary.

Lawrence stared at the wood panel and sighed. "You sir," he said to his shadow, "are an incredible oaf."

DOWNSTAIRS, SIR JOHN Talbot was lost in thought as he played piano. His fingers caressed the keys, coaxing from them wistful music of an older time. Not specific pieces, but drifting overlaps of movements and airs from a dozen composers, interlaced with his own moody improvisations.

The house around him was huge, its bones made of timbers from trees that had been half as old as the empire. Many of the stones that anchored the corners of the hall had been taken from Roman fortifications and bridges. The décor reflected the ancient beliefs of a hundred cultures. Everything about Talbot Hall spoke of age, and the drafts that wandered the halls whispered secrets long forgotten.

Sir John liked the sense of age that the house represented; he valued its permanence, treasured its strength. In many ways it matched his own life: something that had become wiser and stronger from age rather than weaker. Though there were cobwebs in the high corners and finches in the attic, the essential house was strong. As strong as ever. Just as Sir John was strong. As strong as he had ever been, age notwithstanding.

He teased music from the keys. Samson sat beside him, his liquid brown eyes fixed on his master's pale hands, his great ears alert to every sound in the house. When Lawrence had stopped outside of Gwen's room, Samson had heard the shift of weight on the floorboards; when Lawrence had hastened to his own room and closed the door, Samson had noted each covert footfall. The dog was attuned to Talbot Hall. When he heard Gwen's softer footfalls cross the hallway, Samson chuffed quietly.

Sir John, never missing a note, flicked a glance at the dog and then looked at the ceiling with a knowing smile.

As he played his smile never once faltered.

LAWRENCE SLOUCHED DOWN the hall and threw himself into a chair that was one of a matched pair in a conversational nook. Years ago that nook had been the chart room of *The Captain* as Lord Nelson planned the destruction of the French fleet at Trafalgar. Lawrence was always Nelson, Ben was always one of his fighting captains. At other times the nook was a straw hut where Robinson Crusoe—Lawrence—and Friday—Ben— planned how best to deal with pirates. As he waited for Gwen, Lawrence bent and looked at the underside of the armrest and sure enough the initials were still there. BT and LT, carved with fingernails and long since varnished over. It made him smile.

"Mr. Talbot?"

He had been so lost in reverie that he hadn't heard her approach and he shot to his feet as nervously as a young heir at a debutante's ball. But the actor in him rebelled at the foolishness and immediately pulled his features into a smooth smile.

"Miss Conliffe."

"Thank you for coming," she said as he ushered her to the adjoining seat. She arranged her tightly cinched brocade robe primly. Lawrence was fully aware of the maid lingering down the hall, her face as stern as a beadle's, arms folded across her considerable bosom. Lawrence had no wish to challenge such ferocity.

"I'm sorry we're meeting like this." He reached beside the chair and lifted the small satchel of Ben's belongings.

"These were Ben's. He'd want you to have them."

But it was immediately clear that she recognized the bag. Her eyes glistened as she accepted it, and when she lay it upon her lap she caressed the worn leather. Then she opened it and removed the daguerreotype picture of herself. The memory of it, perhaps of the happy day on which it was taken, struck her hard and a sob hitched through her chest. Tears welled in her eyes.

"If . . . if there's anything you need," Lawrence said, feeling suddenly large and clumsy. "Anything at all, please let me know."

She looked up from the picture and Lawrence could see her eyes transform from the vulnerability of tears to something harder and colder.

"I want to know what happened to him," she said, and there was no tremble in her voice.

"So do I. And I'll do everything I can."

Those words, that promise, broke the fragile resolve and she disintegrated into tears. He moved quickly to sit beside her, drew her into the circle of his arms, and caressed her head as she buried her face into the hollow of his throat and wept.

The maid took a single defensive step toward them, but Lawrence caught her glance and gave a mild shake of his head. The maid paused, watching her mistress, then nodded and resumed her post.

Lawrence held Gwen as she cried. The sobs were so deep, the grief so huge and immediate that he wondered if she had been able to let it out before now. Certainly Sir John offered no haven of a shoulder to cry on. Lawrence felt awful for not being able to help, but he was glad he could do at least this much. Her tears burned against his throat like acid and he fought to keep his own sobs from tearing free of his chest.

CHAPTER TWELVE

L awrence knew that he would not be sleeping much tonight, if at all. Too much had happened. Too much was still happening. His brother's funeral was tomorrow, and his brother's fiancée was just down the hall. Lawrence's thoughts flowed like liquid mercury from one to the other, from grief at his loss and guilt over his desires. Sleep be damned.

He paced the length of his room over and over again, sipping too much whiskey, frowning at the shadows, imagining laughter and boyhood chatter from years ago. All of his and Ben's possessions were still in that room. When Lawrence had gone away after their mother's death Ben apparently moved across the hall and left every reminder of childhood behind. Shelves filled with clockwork toys and tin soldiers and tin weapons surrounded him. A clothes tree in a corner still held red cloaks from their adventures as Roman soldiers and oilskins in which they walked the decks of imaginary ships. A broken rocking horse leaned against a wall near a cricket bat and a pile of chipped building blocks. All the colors had paled like a faded photograph . . . like his own memories, which had lost so much clarity and texture as the years had burned away.

In the distance, miles beyond the estate, there was the sound of thunder, low and mean like an old dragon clearing its throat. Lawrence almost smiled, thinking of how Ben had convinced him that thunder was the voice of dragons, but then another thought raked its claws through that image. The thunder rumbled again and Lawrence stood there, staring at the big four-poster bed, remembering thoughts he had hoped never to revisit. Never, especially not here. . . .

THUNDER GROWLED IN the east and the shaking of the old house's timbers jolted young Lawrence Talbot out of a dream of dragons. His heart was in his throat and he crept out of his bed and crossed the cold floor to the edge of Ben's bed. He bent low over the sleeping form and hissed, "Ben! Wake up!"

"Ug . . . it's late . . . I'm asleep . . ."

Lawrence shook him by the shoulder. "I heard something."

Ben propped himself up on his elbows and listened, eyes still closed. "It's just the storm," he said and then collapsed back onto the bed and pulled the covers up over his head. A buzzing snore came faintly from beneath the blanket.

Lawrence made a frustrated face but he did not retreat back to his own bed. Instead he stood there, still bent over, his head cocked to listen.

There it was again. A strange sound. More of a growl than a rumble, but muffled. Was it outside the house . . . or *inside*? He crept to the door of their room and turned the handle as quietly as he could, trying to make sense of what he had heard.

Only silence greeted his straining ear.

Summing up all of his meager courage, Lawrence pulled the door open and stepped into the hall with all the care of someone putting a foot onto thin lake ice. He gradually shifted his weight, willing the floorboards not to creak. The hallway seemed a mile long and as lightning flashed outside the twist of shadows made it seem as if the rows of deer heads had turned toward him, their glass eyes searching for this pale intruder.

Lawrence shuffled sideways, his back to the wall, turning front and back to make sure that all of the shadows were just empty air, that nothing was hiding there waiting to reach out a taloned hand. On many wild nights he had dreamed of monsters in the dark—strange, shapeless creatures that skulked out of the black forest, sniffing for tender meat. Father and Singh always smiled at his stories, assuring him that the woods were safe and the house was a fortress, but Lawrence always feared that they were saying that just to fool him. To protect him from the truth. That maybe there were monsters out there in the dark.

Thunder rattled the windows and in the heart of their din Lawrence thought he heard the other sound, the one that had pulled him from his sleep. That indefinable noise that he knew was made by something that should not be here. At the top of the stairs he paused, his tongue nervously licking his dry lips. Should he wake up father?

No! Father was away on business.

The thought terrified Lawrence. Why would Father go away when a storm was coming? Father had his guns, he had shot bears and boars and all manner of creatures. Surely Father was unafraid of anything in the woods . . . but now the truth that his hero and protector was *not* here chilled Lawrence to his core.

What about Singh?

But the Sikh's room was on the other side of the Hall; with all these shadows it might as well be on the dark side of the moon.

Thunder slammed a fist against the walls and the whole house shook. Lawrence looked over his shoulders and he could swear that the deer heads had turned toward him, their antlers sharp as knives, their eyes glaring at him with unnatural ferocity. He backed quickly away, moving backward down the stairs. First a few steps, then more, and when the next thunderclap struck he whirled and ran down the rest of the winding stairwell, his bare feet slapping desperately on the icy wood. Outside, the storm had brought wind with it and it howled through every crack in the walls and under every door. The wind rose and rose until it was a piercing shriek and Lawrence wanted to stop up his ears, but at the same time he felt *drawn* to it. It called to him and screamed at him and tore at the night.

Lawrence ran down the last of the stairs and raced along the side passage, away from the great front door, heading toward the back door that led into his mother's glasshouse garden. She would not be there this late, of course, but it was a place where she always felt safe, and where she read to Lawrence and Ben. Even with all its glass walls it felt more like a fortress to him than this pile of wood and rock; so he tore along, chased by shadows, pounded by thunder. And the wind's wail continued to build to a banshee shriek.

Lightning flashed so brightly that the corridor was suddenly stark whites and blacks, and it outlined every curl and twist in the ornate wrought iron of the garden door. The reflection turned each pane of glass in the double doors to milky opacity, and then the lightning vanished and the doors were plunged into darkness. But not before Lawrence had found them and grasped the smooth, cold, familiar curves of the handles.

More thunder, and the wail of the wind was a white-hot needle in his brain.

As Lawrence thrust open the doors the wail spiked even higher and for a terrible moment he thought that the sound was a scream and not the wind at all. He stepped tentatively into the garden and winds buffeted him, and then he realized why he could hear the wind so well—the glasshouse doors were opened to the natural garden beyond. The exterior doors stood open, moving back and forth as waves of rain shoved at them. The glasshouse was soaked and frigid water washed around Lawrence's ankles, sending chills up his flesh in waves. And the wails continued. Hypnotized by the moment, lost in the dark sorcery of wind and thunder and rain and lightning, Lawrence moved forward as if in a dream, unable to stop his frozen feet, his eyes blinking as he stepped into the spray of rain by the doors to the outside garden.

Thunder struck again and again, and between the bursts he could hear the wail. Lawrence stopped.

The world stopped.

He looked down at the water flowing toward him from the edge of the patio. It was black with shadows, but even when the lightning flashed it remained black.

Lawrence frowned.

Black rain made no sense.

He followed it with his eyes back along the cracks in the flagstone to the base of the huge stone fountain that was carved with birds and squirrels and pinecones. The black rain came from there.

The lightning flashed once more, but dimmer now, as if the storm was moving away. In its glow Lawrence saw something that made no sense to him. A man knelt before the fountain, his head bowed as if in prayer. His shoulders shook as he knelt there.

Lawrence recognized those shoulders, the clothes.

Father?

How? How could Father be here when he was supposed to be away on business? Why was he here?

And . . . was he laughing? Weeping?

Then lightning flashed once more and the moment became stranger still, for Lawrence saw that his father was not alone as he knelt by the fountain. He had his arms wrapped around another person, cradling her to his chest.

A woman.

"Mother?" Lawrence whispered.

The wail tore through the night, rising upward from the kneeling figure as Sir John raised his head and screamed to the storm. As he did so the body in his arms shifted and Lawrence saw his mother's arm fall limply down, her hand striking the wet ground. The black rain flowed from her, from her arm, from her body, from her skin. A river of darkness that washed from her and across the flagstones toward Lawrence.

"Mother? . . ." Lawrence said again, and this time his father heard his plaintive little voice. Sir John turned, still cradling Solana to his chest. As lightning flashed Lawrence could see the lines of terrible, impossible grief carved into his father's face. His father's eyes were dark, a red that was filled with grief and fury and rage and an impossible loss.

Sir John opened his mouth and uttered a cry of despair that tore the night apart. Lawrence felt the blackness of the storm suddenly gather around him, closing like a fist on his throat, and then his own scream lifted into the air as the lightning and thunder exploded around him.

And then there was nothing but blackness.

Chapter Thirteen

Lawrence lay on his bed and stared up at the blackness of the ceiling. He felt old and used and damaged in a hundred ways. He had thought himself free of the memories of that awful night. His mother was thirty years in her grave, and Lawrence had not set foot in this house since.

But now, as if the wood and stone were a battery that had stored every minute detail of that night, it replayed over and over in his head. No matter how much whiskey he drank the images were relentless, undeterred. Every detail of that night . . . and of what followed. . . .

THE BLACK CARRIAGE was not a hearse but it looked like one. Large and heavy, with shaded windows and four black horses led by a grim-faced man in a dark suit.

Young Lawrence is only remotely aware that he is being carried. His mind does not process time or movement or action with any clarity or cogency. He feels like he is floating. When he hears voices he does not know who they belong to. His father's voice is that of a stranger. The other voice—people are calling him Dr. Hoenneger—is equally unknown to him. Lawrence is beyond the point of associating people with reality, because nothing is real.

This is all a dream. A nightmare. He knows that, because it must be a nightmare. What he saw last night in the garden. The black rain. His mother's body. The uncontrollable grief of his father. These are not possible in the real world . . . they belong in dark dreams. Lawrence understands this. Just as he knows that the black carriage and Dr. Hoenneger likewise do not belong to the waking world. And the dark horses and this strange building—they are all parts of a nightmare, too. The storm did this. It was too loud, too strong, and it broke the world. The wind and the rain washed all sense away.

Lawrence thinks these things without knowing that he is thinking. His mind is twisted into crooked shapes and self-awareness has been washed away with black rain down a gutter.

Lawrence's eyes see words painted on wood outside the building, but they're nonsense words. They don't belong to him, they don't apply to his world. In his world there is no Lambeth Asylum, and even if there was he would not be there, and his father would not be taking him there. Nightmares are like that. Strange things that make no sense are jumbled into shapes that don't fit in his head.

"Poor lad," a voice says. Lawrence does not know the voice, and doesn't care.

He stares upward with eyes that are drying from not blinking, but he doesn't feel discomfort. Discomfort belongs to a different world. Nor does he feel the jab of a needle. It's only pain and it doesn't belong to him either.

All that belongs to him is the darkness. He can feel it spreading through him and closing around him, and as he sinks into it Lawrence hears his mother's voice singing an old Spanish lullaby. He knows that he should remember the words. But he can't, and he can't find a way to care.

The blackness is so soft and smooth and it covers everything. . . .

THINKING BACK, REMEMBERING now with a cruel clarity those things that were fractured dreams to him as a boy, Lawrence threw his arm across his eyes in an attempt to deny, even to himself, that he wept.

Chapter Fourteen

They buried Benjamin Talbot the next day.

Funerals are supposed to be dreary days with gray skies that weep cold rain, but the sun stubbornly shone and the trees were filled with idiot birds who sang as if hurt and harm had not poisoned the air of Blackmoor.

The funeral procession began at the church, where a scowling Pastor Fisk gave a long and droning homily about the transience and fragility of life and the enduring suffering of the grave. During the church service Lawrence sat beside his father and glared hatred at the old vicar. To compound grief with religious guilt was, to his view, the greatest sin. Wasn't it enough to suffer irretrievable loss?

Lawrence cut covert looks to his left, where Sir John sat with wooden rigidity and allowed nothing at all to show on his face, and to his right, where Gwen Conliffe sat hunched over the knot of despair in her heart. She clung to her father and wept continuously, and Lawrence was sure that the pastor's words were doing her actual harm. Just when Lawrence's rage had built to the point where he was ready to jump to his feet and tell Pastor Fisk to go leap into his own dismal Hellfire, the sermon ended. The congregation stood and sang a hymn of grace that was, at least, not an actual condemnation of having lived, and then it was over. At least the church part of it was over.

From there the coffin was loaded into the back of a hearse pulled by four night black horses, and the procession to the cemetery began.

It was far, far worse than the sermon. At least in the church there was someone specific at whom Lawrence could direct his frustration and anger, but now it was a slow march to the place where Ben's body would rest forever. Rest, and rot, and probably be forgotten in little more than a generation. There were no more Talbots except for Lawrence and he had no intention of returning to the Hall to live. And Ben had never had the chance to marry Gwen. Ben had no sons to carry on his name, and Gwen was young . . . there would be an end to her grief. She would return to London with her father and in time her shattered heart would heal. She would marry some other man, and Ben would settle into being a foot-note in her life. His death would drift into local legend here in Blackmoor and he would be remembered more for how he died than how he lived.

That hurt Lawrence terribly, and as he walked behind the hearse tears ran down his face. If the sky would not weep for Benjamin, then the tears of Gwen Conliffe and Lawrence Talbot would stand as substitutes, even though those tears fell on cold ground and were absorbed by dust and trampled into obscurity by the rest of the towns-folk, who trudged along behind the procession more out of duty and obligation than sentiment.

BESIDE THE GRAVE the pastor spoke again, but this time his remarks were brief and he recited his lines straight from the scriptures; by then Lawrence was so set against the deaf old fool that he internally mocked the performance.

And then the words were done and the mourners had each dropped a ritual handful of dirt onto the coffin, and Gwen had scattered roses atop it, and all that was left was the reality that Ben was going into the ground. It was the end of all things for Lawrence's brother, and as he watched the coffin being lowered into the cold earth he could feel his heart descend to a lower place in his chest. He knew that it would remain there forever, just as Ben would remain here in the soil of Blackmoor until the sun itself burned to a cinder in the sky.

Lawrence wanted to scream. He did not.

Instead he stood there and wept. For his brother. For his mother. For opportunities lost forever. For himself.

The funeral party began to disperse. Gwen was one of the very last to leave, and she stood on the opposite side of the grave from Lawrence. They had not said a word all morning beyond a kiss on the cheek before setting off to the church. Her eyes were as red-rimmed as his own as she raised them from the grave and looked at Lawrence.

There were no words that could possibly define what he felt about all that had happened. Lawrence nodded to her and she nodded back, and though he was aware of some transfer of communication it was not on any level where his conscious mind could read it. But he felt it nonetheless.

Gwen's father took her arm and led her away from the grave, but once, for a fleeting moment, she turned and looked back. Not at the grave, but at Lawrence.

Lawrence stood there for a long, long time, watching her go.

He wiped his face with his hands as if to cleanse it of

more than tears, and as he turned he saw his father standing at the foot of the grave. Sir John was looking up the hill to where Gwen's father was helping her into a carriage, but then he turned and met Lawrence's gaze. Behind the lenses of his dark spectacles Sir John's eyes glittered with an understanding of the moment that was, perhaps, sharper and more accurate than Lawrence's own. Without a word or change of expression Sir John turned away and began walking among the headstones toward the road.

CHAPTER FIFTEEN

After a thoroughly depressing luncheon during which he had to be civil to townsfolk he disliked, pretend to remember relatives he had never met or couldn't recall, and was unable to have a private word with Gwen, Lawrence left the house. He walked down the lawn and into a path that meandered a crooked mile through the tall trees of the forest.

Last night, when he'd given Ben's things to Gwen, Lawrence had kept one item back. It wasn't intentional, it had been in his pocket and he hadn't found it until he'd dressed for the funeral. As he walked he fished it out and studied it. The St. Columbanus medal seemed to display different moods depending on how the light hit it. In bright sunlight the saint seemed to be holding the wolves back through some holy power, but when shadows caressed the design it seemed as if the carving showed the very last moment of the saint's life.

A frown etched itself onto Lawrence's face and remained there as the soft turf of the forest gave way to rocks. He glanced up, surprised at how far he'd come. His surprise deepened when he realized that he was not the only person who had walked this ancient path on this dreadful afternoon. Fifty yards ahead, Gwen Conliffe stood on the edge of the cliff that overlooked the deep gorge that marked one corner of the vast Talbot estate.

As Lawrence approached he was struck by the improbable beauty of the moment. Gwen, dressed in mourning colors, stood with her head high, looking out at the panorama of mountains and tree-covered slopes and the eternal blue of the sky. It was a moment of grandeur that took his breath away and he slowed his pace to delay the moment when she would become aware of him and turn, breaking the spell of eternal beauty.

But as he drew closer he saw how very near she stood to the edge of the cliff. Fearing to startle her, he called to her softly while he was still several yards away.

"Hello?"

She started but did not take an unwise step. Instead she turned toward him, alert now, unsmiling, a complex expression in her eyes. She waited until he joined her, then she nodded to the rocky shelves and paths that formed that part of the cliff.

"Ben said you played here as children."

Lawrence leaned out and stared down into the shadowy gorge. Its depths and the promise of catastrophe that it held had not frightened him as a boy, and it did not do so now.

"It was our refuge."

"From what?"

Lawrence straightened and turned toward her. "You mean from whom?"

Gwen digested that for a moment. "I've known your father for two years," she said. "In all that time, I've never been able to read him. One moment he would be happy, it would seem he never wanted us to leave, and the next it was as if he disapproved of our relationship entirely. Ben told me that it was because I reminded your father of your mother. And I can see that now. Having seen her portrait and seen you . . . I understand how it must have been a constant reminder for your father." She paused, then added, "He said you did as well."

The sneer came unbidden but unstoppable to Lawrence's mouth. "Which is why he put me in an asylum for two years and then shipped me off to my aunt in America. So when I killed myself he wouldn't have to find me, too."

"God . . . don't say such a thing . . ."

But Lawrence just shook his head. "Unfortunately, disappointing him has become something of a habit."

"He's suffered so much," she said. "Some people can't manage their grief. They never heal, it just consumes them, and in their anger they lash out at the ones they love. The ones who remind them . . ."

"I know, dammit," Lawrence snapped. "Don't you think I've known that my whole life? I lost my mother to suicide and my father to his own mad grief. I lost my brother back then, and lost him again now. I've lost everything. Don't tell me about the nature of grief. It's *defined* me my whole goddamned life!"

Gwen touched his sleeve. "You know . . . Ben wanted very badly to bring you and your father back together. If not in life, then maybe in death he can do it."

A cold wind blew up from the gorge and tousled his hair. He brushed it out of his eyes and stared down into her face. Several times he opened his mouth to reply, but each time he left his thoughts unsaid. They turned and stood side by side, watching small clouds sail like ships across the ocean of the sky.

Chapter Sixteen

They returned to Talbot Hall without saying much more to one another. There was so much *to* say, but Gwen's words had struck deeply. He retired to his room to think.

At sunset he heard noises from outside and came downstairs to find Gwen and her father standing with Sir John on the front steps. Beyond them the Conliffe carriage stood ready and waiting.

Sir John stood as straight and stiff as a ramrod, his face dark and unsmiling. Gwen reached up to give Sir John an embrace, but it was dutiful and careful and there was no joy in it for either of them.

"You're sure you won't stay with us one more night?" said Sir John with some frost.

"My father has secured lodgings for us at the inn," she said. "It will be convenient for the train in the morning."

Gwen's father was a thin man with the face and gait of a startled heron. He seemed flustered by everything that had happened and it was clear—at least to Lawrence— that Conliffe was intimidated by Sir John. He shook Sir John's hand tentatively and snatched his own back the moment it was polite to end the clasp. For his part, Sir John looked mildly amused and even almost pleased at the effect he had on Conliffe.

Gwen noticed Lawrence and looked discreetly relieved at his appearance. "Lawrence, when do you return to London?"

"After I find out what happened to Ben."

Everyone looked at him in surprise, except Gwen, who nodded. Those words straightened her back and stiffened her chin and, Lawrence thought, ignited a fire in her eyes. She rose to her toes and kissed Lawrence on the cheek.

"Godspeed," he said.

But her reply, whispered in his ear, was: "Good hunting."

She stepped back and the tears were gathering once more, so she fled across the courtyard to her carriage. After a sputtering moment, Conliffe bobbed his head at the Talbots, started to offer his hand to Singh, then stopped as if unsure whether it would be an insult to someone of his caste, and finally gave the Sikh a jerky nod and scurried after his daughter.

Lawrence and Sir John climbed the stairs to the landing and lingered there to watch the carriage wind its way down the weedy lane. Sir John stuffed his hands in his pockets and looked from the diminishing carriage to the gathering gloom of the afternoon sky.

"You're going to solve the mystery, eh?" murmured Sir John.

"Someone has to."

"You don't have much faith in that fool Constable Nye."

Lawrence shook his head. "Not much, no. He either doesn't know how to investigate something like this, or he's afraid to."

"And you feel you're better suited to the task?"

"I couldn't do any worse than he has," said Lawrence.

"Mm, true."

"And I have a stronger motivation. Nye has already given up. I won't."

Sir John turned to look at him for a moment, then turned back to his study of the growing twilight. "That's all well and good, but your inquiry can wait till tomorrow. The moon will be full tonight."

"So? Are you afraid I'll run afoul of a werewolf?"

Sir John chuckled. "I suggest you stay inside in case your lunatic notion is correct." When Lawrence did not reply, Sir John continued. "You do understand the etymology of the word? Lunatic. The root word is *luna*—the moon. *Lunaticus* is the Latin for 'moon-struck.' People have always known that the phases of the moon, her strength and her pull, affect the moods with the same regularity with which she affects the tides. Madness runs riot at the full moon."

"Yes," Lawrence said with great coldness, "I know full well the sound of an asylum filled with madmen on the full moon."

Sir John said nothing except to inhale deeply and sigh slowly.

The carriage was completely gone now and gloom began to cluster in the lane.

"Will you stay home tonight?" said Sir John.

"If you insist," Lawrence said with bad grace.

"I do."

The first of the evening birds raised its plaintive call from the darkening trees.

"I cannot lose you as well," said Sir John, and before Lawrence could respond the old man turned and entered the Hall. Lawrence stood and stared at the door, which Sir John had left ajar, and a thousand emotions became snarled on the thorns in his heart.

CHAPTER SEVENTEEN

As the sun dwindled behind the autumn trees, armies of shadows gathered in the forest and on the eastern slopes of the hills and then pounced on Talbot Hall. To Lawrence it seemed as if in the space of one breath and another the old house went from pale walls and reflecting glass panes to a featureless mass as dark as sackcloth. His father had gone to bed early and the house was silent and dark. Not a single light shone in the windows. Talbot Hall had closed its eyes for the night.

Lawrence was fine with that.

He led the black gelding out of the stable and walked him quietly up the lane. He had a pistol tucked into his belt and a folding clasp knife—a gift from a stagehand in Chicago—in his coat pocket and snugged into a saddle holster was a fully loaded heavy hunting rifle. If the moonrise drove the lunatic to murderous rage again, then let him come, thought Lawrence.

Let him come.

By the time they reached the iron gate beyond the arch the sky was beginning to grow ghostly pale. The moon was rising. *What was it father called it?* mused Lawrence. *The Goddess of the Hunt.*

That suited him quite nicely. His lip curled back in a

snarl of anticipation. Let Ben's killer come hunting for him. He'll find that the hunt is already on.

"Let him come," he said in a low, feral whisper. "God . . . let him come!"

He swung into the saddle and the horse gave a deep-chested nicker as Lawrence kicked his heels back. Together they raced away down country lanes that the moonlight opened before them.

DEEP WITHIN THE woods Lawrence paused at the crest of a hill and looked down on a ring of ancient standing stones, relics of a forgotten age. They stood like silent sentries at the edge of the ancient cemetry that formed one edge of the Talbot Estate. Lawrence remembered coming here with Ben as a boy, making up games of ancient adventure in the depths of the forest. But never before had Lawrence seen the great ring of stones by moonlight. He steered his mount down a switchback path and entered the ring.

The smallest of the stones was twice a man's height, and though they looked rough and crude, his father had insisted that the stones were made to calculate the movements of the stars.

"A more perfect lunar clock does not exist," Sir John had told them long ago.

Lawrence rode among the dark giants and then paused before the heel stone, which was painted with pale moonlight. He bent low in the saddle and looked across the heel stone's flat surface. Sure enough, the rim of the moon was rising in the precise center. Even now, with grief and anger and haste warring within him, Lawrence marveled at it, and for some reason this ancient proof of the dedication to the moon gave him a measure of insight into the obsession of lunatics.

He straightened in the saddle, wondering if this place itself would draw the killer, but after sitting there for five minutes he shook his head. Lingering here felt wrong.

He kicked the horse into a fresh canter and they moved through the woods, angling first toward the town and then skirting it. Finally Lawrence found what he was looking for. Not the madman, but something else that might offer both answers and clues. He heard it before he saw it: mandolins and violins, a concertina and a penny-whistle, and threaded through it was the tinny clash of finger cymbals.

Gypsy music.

He jerked the reins and picked his way through the woods to a distant point where fairy lights danced. The lights grew larger and resolved into torches and lanterns and cook-fires around which a dozen *vardos* were set. The sides and doors of the brightly colored wagons were carved with horses, birds, lions, griffins, flowers and vines interlaced with elaborate scrollwork. The vardos formed a loose circle around the camp and at its center was a dirt ring edged by a hand-packed rim of raised mud. Men and women sat on wooden folding chairs or sprawled on wildly patterned woven blankets. Children wrestled and played on the fringes or sat in the shadows of their parents to watch the entertainment. Lawrence sat on his mount and watched, too.

A handful of musicians played a rolling, hypnotic tune as a dark-haired, red-lipped, olive-skinned woman danced with erotic abandon in the center of the ring. As she whirled her many skirts floated high enough to show the sleek and muscular curves of her naked legs; sweat pasted her sheer half-blouse to her full breasts, and her eyes flashed dark fire as she moved. She moved like a snake. She had complete control over every muscle and her body rippled and twisted into impossibly erotic shapes as the firelight caressed her flesh.

Lawrence swallowed a throatful of dust and had to shake his head to clear it of her seductive magic. He dismounted and led the horse into a space between two wagons, watching the woman twist and turn and leap and undulate.

" *'Chavaia!*" cried a harsh voice and Lawrence turned to see a burly Gypsy emerged from the shadows, a rifle in his hands. The barrel was not pointed at Lawrence, but the man held it with professional competence and there was no smile of welcome on his dark face.

"I—" Lawrence began, but the man fired off a long string of incomprehensible words in Romany. Before Lawrence could protest his ignorance a boy slipped from behind the man and held up a warning hand. The boy wore baggy trousers that were gathered at his waist with a red sash, a white shirt and a black vest stitched with vines.

The boy listened to what the man said, and then looked up at Lawrence. "He says you must come into the camp and stay with us now."

"What?" Lawrence said, surprised.

"The woods are not safe."

It was then that Lawrence noticed that the man with the rifle was not looking at him, but was instead glaring into the shadows of the forest behind him.

"Take your horse, your honor?"

The boy could not have been more than eight or nine, but he already had a smile that was on the unctuous side of earnest. The double entrendre of his question was not lost on Lawrence. *Take your horse, indeed.*

Lawrence fished a coin from his pocket and made sure that he jingled the coins so that the child could hear the promise of others. He handed a coin to the boy along with the reins and watched as the boy expertly tied the gelding to a young tree. As the horse turned in place the boy caught sight of the rifle in its sturdy leather scabbard. It made the child pause and flick an uncertain look at Lawrence, who returned the look with a knowing smile.

Lawrence showed a second coin to the boy, producing it with a sleight of hand he'd learned long ago in his earliest days in the theater.

"Here's a second so you don't touch that," he said and then magically produced another. "And a third to take me to whomever sells these . . ."

With his other hand he drew Ben's medallion from his vest pocket and held it up so that it caught sparks from the campfires.

The boy paused halfway to taking the coins and the sight of the medal wiped the smile from the child's face. He looked at the image of St. Columbanus and the wolves as it turned slowly in the fire light, then back at the guard with the rifle, who gave a terse nod, and then up at Lawrence. He accepted the coins solemnly, all traces of Artful Dodger impishness gone from his face. Several seconds drifted past before he decided to accept that third coin.

"You want to talk to Maleva," he said softly and with grim reverence.

"I expect so," agreed Lawrence. "Lead on, MacDuff."

The boy did not ask who "MacDuff" was, figuring it for some foreign phrase. He pocketed the coins and gestured for Lawrence to follow him into the camp. As they passed by, the Gypsies watched him with calculated interest. There were fifty or more of them, many of them tinkering away on pots and sham jewelry, a few stringing beads and others engrossed in embroidering flowers on clothing. Cooking pots charmed him with rare spices and a roasted pig sizzled with juices as it was turned on a slow spit. A few of the more dangerous-looking men appraised him for whatever threat he might pose, or risk he might bring, while others calculated his value as a well-heeled customer. Everyone in the camp looked at Lawrence as he passed by, and he knew that each of them, from the youngest child to the oldest crone, could value his clothing and accoutrements to the last halfpenny.

Just beyond the dancing circle Lawrence saw a big cage on wheels in which a lumpy animal squatted dispiritedly behind the stout bars: the dancing bear the publican had mentioned. But Lawrence sneered inwardly, knowing that this mangy old beast could not have caught his brother, let alone killed him. The poor creature looked more than halfway into its own grave.

The boy led him to one vardo that sat apart from the others, tucked farther back under the boughs of a diseased maple whose leaves had been chewed to lace by moths. A pair of lanterns hung from posts beside the short stairs that led up to the colorful door of the wagon, and tapestries of almost regal beauty were hung on lines to create a palatial setting. Whoever this Maleva was, he thought, she must be of great importance.

The boy stopped just outside the spill of lantern light from the wagon. He pointed to a figure seated on a stool outside of the vardo and then, without a further word, he retreated back to the music and noise of the main camp. The boy wasted no time in leaving the vicinity of the figure seated in the shadows.

Lawrence had no such reservations and he strode

straight toward the figure. From twenty feet away he could tell that it was a woman, but as he drew close it was clear that the woman was ancient. Maleva sat hunched over, a colorful shawl pulled close around her bony shoulders. A thin cigarillo bobbed between her lips as she hummed along with the distant music. She heard Lawrence approach but without even turning her head she said, "You wish to have your fortune told?"

He stopped a few feet away and held out the medal of St. Columbanus. He stood silent, waiting for Maleva to turn. As she did the bored expression on the old woman's face darkened and when she raised her eyes from the medal to meet Lawrence's gaze she gave him a look of mingled dread and sadness. Maleva slowly reached out a thin and wrinkled hand to take the medal.

She held it for a moment, then closed her eyes and pressed the medallion to her chest. Maleva bowed her head, nodding to herself as if confirming a dreaded suspicion.

"You had better come inside," she murmured.

CHAPTER EIGHTEEN

The vardo looked like a junk shop to Lawrence. Strings of cheap beads hung from the rafters, dozens of bad imitations of holy relics overflowed from drawers and chests, and a pot of "good luck" coins had cracked and spilled its contents onto the floor. But past this debris there was another layer to the décor made up entirely of boxes of herbs and pots of compounds made from roots and exotic flowers. Strings of wrinkled plants and strange fruit hung drying in the corners, and streamers of animal hide were nailed to the wooden walls. Maleva waved Lawrence to a three-legged chair and he had to move aside several bolts of beautiful fabric to give himself leg room on the other side of a small divination table.

Maleva laid the medallion on the tabletop, and after studying it for a few moments leaned back in her chair and puffed her cigarillo. The flare of the coal showed her face: wizened, pinched, filled with age and pain, but Lawrence was long practiced in looking at actors and actresses made up to look old. He could easily imagine the face she had once worn many decades ago. She was probably beautiful once, perhaps arrestingly so. The bone structure was there, and there was still some fire in her old and rheumy eyes.

She handed Lawrence a deck of old tarot cards and

asked him shuffle, then she took the cards, cut them and began laying individual cards in a row. She rambled on for a few moments about pain, dark omens and the pain Lawrence felt for his dead mother. Lawrence wasn't impressed. Everyone in this county knew that Sir John was a widower.

". . . and you try to find solace in the women who pass you by, but this pain never goes away. It gnaws deeper—"

He placed his hand on hers, stopping the flow of meaningless words.

"That's not why I came here," he said. "And you know it."

The look in her eyes was sly and careful.

"Tell me about my brother."

Maleva lowered her eyes to study the back of Lawrence's hand. She took it in both of hers and turned it over to study the palm.

"There is a picture in your mind," she said, and this time her voice lacked artifice. "A terrible picture. It cannot be erased. It hides from you, but you know it's there. Which makes it more terrible . . ."

"The medallion I showed you. It was found on my brother's body."

"But he was not wearing it." She said it as a statement rather than a question.

Lawrence narrowed his eyes. "How do you know this?"

She said nothing.

"Your caravan showed up two weeks before three men were killed. I don't think it's a coincidence."

Maleva smiled thinly. "There are no coincidences. Only Fate. But she plays a hidden hand. What part we have in this we won't know till the game's up."

"What exactly is 'this'?" he said, irritated by the parlor mystic performance. He wasn't a believer and this felt like more Gypsy nonsense to him. But then he narrowed his eyes as another thought occurred to him and he leaned forward, placing his palm on the table. In a low and dangerous voice he demanded, "Did someone here kill my brother?"

If Maleva was intimidated by Lawrence's tone or words no flicker of it showed on her face.

"Darkness comes for you. You must leave Talbot Hall," she said in a voice as soft as a midnight whisper. "You must flee Blackmoor."

"I can't," he said. "I've only just arrived."

Outside there were shouts and screams.

"And you have come too late. . . ."

CHAPTER NINETEEN

Lawrence leaped to his feet and dashed outside, expecting the worst and hoping for it. He wanted the killer to be there . . . to be *here*. He wanted to catch the bastard in the middle of one of his murderous attacks; he wanted him red-handed so that no one could say that he was innocent. Lawrence was hungry for blood, he wanted—*needed*—to be face to face with Ben's killer.

He kicked open the door and stared at a scene of confused activity that was not at all what he expected, and it stopped him in his tracks.

Tableau.

A Gypsy lay on the ground, his face a mask of blood, hands pressed to a jaw that was clearly shattered. Broken bits of teeth were stuck against his lips and chin. A billy club on a thong dangled from his wrist. A woman knelt over him, using her body to shield him from four big men who stood in the center of the dancing circle. They were not Gypsies—these were clearly men from Blackmoor, and each of them carried a heavy shotgun and it was clear from the looks on their faces that they were willing to use either end of their weapons. One man wiped blood from the stock of his weapon, a cruel grin of satisfaction etched onto his heavy features. Lawrence recognized him. Kirk, the publican who owned the tavern.

Kirk pointed his shotgun across the clearing where the bear cage stood. A Gypsy man stood between him and the cage. He had a ball python curled around his neck and his rough hand rested on the hilt of a curved dagger in a sheath angled to allow a quick pull. Other Gypsies—men and women—appeared out of the shadows. They were angry, some snarling curses in Romany, their dark faces clouding with confusion and rage.

"Go away," he growled in a heavily accented voice. "You have no business here. Not tonight. Go away."

"Give us the bloody bear, you old snake handler, or you'll get what I gave your friend." Kirk kicked the fallen man in the leg. The other men kept turning to cover the gathering crowd with their guns.

The Gypsy with the python pulled the knife halfway from its sheath, but Kirk leveled the shotgun at him and thumbed back the hammer with an audible *click!*

"Pull that pig-sticker and I'll shorten you by a head." Kirk was enjoying himself and wore a vicious smile as he bullied his way through the crowd and threw open the drop-bolt on the bear cage. He and the other men stepped back as the bear moved forward; it shouldered open the barred door and stepped down onto the hard-packed ground.

"There's your killer, lads," declared Kirk.

"Nonsense!" cried the Gypsy. "He dances. That's all."

But the bear made the kind of noise an old man might make when sinking into a chair. It sat down heavily on the cold ground and began biting its own rump in an attempt to catch some fleas.

The momentum of the confrontation stalled. Kirk looked around as if he expected a second and much more terrifying bear to be on display. A few of the Gypsies laughed quietly.

One of the vigilantes lowered his shotgun. "Kirk, I think we might be off our mark here—"

Kirk was having none of it. His face was livid and the look he gave his companion was murderous. He swung around and leveled his shotgun at the bear. The snake handler stepped between Kirk and the bear but the moment was suddenly spinning out of control.

Lawrence had reached his limit with this nonsense. He jumped down from the vardo and shoved his way roughly into the clearing. He strode straight toward Kirk and slapped the barrel away, but Kirk took a half step back and brought the weapon up again. Several of the bigger Gypsies began closing in from all points of the circle.

"Stand back!" bellowed Kirk. "We have a right!"

"You have no rights, you idiot," Lawrence fired back. "You have no idea what you're doing."

"You should be with us, Talbot. That bear killed your own brother."

"Don't be a fool! I saw my brother's body. I saw the wounds. Only a fool would think that this pathetic creature—"

But he was immediately interrupted by a shrill whistle from the woods. Everyone turned and even the bear looked up with myopic interest as Constable Nye came wobbling into the clearing on a bicycle, his whistle caught between his teeth.

Lawrence almost burst out laughing. The moment had gone through drama nearly to tragedy and was now transforming mid-scene into farce.

"Get out of my way! Get out of my way!" Nye demanded as he skidded to a stop and dismounted. He took in the scene and blew out his cheeks like a gasping fish, then wheeled on Kirk. "Thomas . . . what the hell is going on here?"

The men with the shotguns lowered them, except for Kirk, who stood his ground.

"Thomas," Nye said to him, "what the hell are you about?"

"We come for the bear, Nye," said Kirk. "It done all the killing."

Constable Nye looked from him to the pathetic creature huddled in the firelight. The bear's hide was bare in spots and his muzzle was white as snow.

"For goodness sake, Thomas," Nye said with exasperation, "don't be daft. I mean . . . these poor beggars make their living off this sorry creature. It couldn't hurt a fly."

The bear handler nodded emphatically and reached over to stroke the bear's shaggy head.

"You see?" said Nye. "Harmless. It's not a—"

But his words were cut off as the threadbare old bear suddenly let out a terrible roar and rose up onto its hind legs, rising to full height above the startled crowd. There were shouts and screams—both male and female—and everyone staggered back from the bear. The vigilantes brought up their guns and the Gypsies stared in shock at the sudden ferocity of their old pet. The bear's stubby claws were out and it pawed the air—but it did not attack anyone. Instead it let out a howl that was almost human: high and piercing and thoroughly charged with naked terror.

"Oh my god!" someone yelled at the back of the crowd and Lawrence, along with everyone in the packed crowd, turned to see what had spooked the animal. There was a flash of movement and then a splash of red spattered everyone in the clearing. The rearmost of the vigilantes, the one who had shoved a Gypsy into Lawrence, staggered forward and dropped to his knees as a geyser of hot blood shot up from between his shoulders. His head spun through the air and struck the bear full in the chest and the moment froze into insanity and impossibility.

Then, from the outermost edge of the camp, something huge rose up out of the darkness. Not as bulky as the bear but taller and far, far more terrible. Lawrence stood transfixed, his mind juddering to a halt as he tried to make sense of what he was seeing. It was dressed like a man, but the shirt and waistcoat and trousers were split at the seams and hung in shreds. The thing was covered in brown fur that was tipped with silver and as it rose up muscles bunched and flexed under its skin. It stood on two legs, but the feet were gnarled and twisted parodies—part animal, part human, with claws that tore ragged lines in the hard-packed earth. It had a deep chest and shoulders that sloped upward to a bull neck and great muscular arms that were spread wide as if to gather and crush the entire crowd. The hands were dreadful, with long fingers tipped with claws that curved into wicked points. Fresh blood steamed from the tips of each wicked claw.

But the worst thing was its head, its face. Tufted ears rose above a knotted brow beneath which were yellow eyes rimmed with red. It had a short muzzle that wrinkled back as it opened its mouth in a snarl of primal animal hate. Teeth like daggers dripped with hot saliva.

Lawrence could not move, could not think; his heart slammed against the walls of his chest. He could not blink or swallow or scream. All he could do was stand there and behold this *thing*. This monstrous impossibility. This perversion of all sense and sanity.

This . . . *werewolf*.

Chapter Twenty

The creature threw back its head and the massive muscles of its chest and sides flexed as it let loose with a howl so loud that it threatened to break the fragile scaffolding of Lawrence's sanity. The sound was too loud. It exploded inside his head and though he was aware of other screams all around him, the howl of the werewolf muted them to meaningless noise. Then everything was in motion as panic swept through the crowd and pandemonium scattered vigilantes and Gypsies, young and old, like leaves in a windstorm.

The Gypsy snake handler shoved Lawrence out of the way and ran to gather up two small children; women screamed and ran, babies cried in uncomprehending fear. Horses reared and kicked the air.

The werewolf lunged forward and raked its claws across a man's chest and Lawrence saw lungs and heart slide through shattered bone and spill onto the ground before the man could even fall. Then the werewolf leaped forward and dove into one of the vardos, chasing a Gypsy woman who had fled inside. Lawrence saw the silhouette of the creature—a form painted in light and shadow and fashioned in Hell itself—as the monster rushed the length of the wagon and pounced on the woman. As the massive arm swept across her she seemed to fly apart like a doll and the inside of the vardo's canvas covering was splashed with dark droplets.

A Gypsy screamed a woman's name and rushed toward the wagon, a wicked knife held in his fist, but the werewolf exploded out through the back door. The man was impaled by splinters from his own wagon before he could even attempt to avenge his woman's death. The werewolf pounced on him, driving him into the dirt and then leaped at another man who was bent over trying to load an old cap-and-ball pistol. The werewolf clamped its jaws around his throat and tore away everything but the spine. The blood spray caught the creature in the face and for a moment Lawrence could swear that its eyes rolled high and white as if in ecstasy.

Lawrence saw Kirk—as shocked to stillness as he was himself, his shotgun pointed uselessly at the ground. Seeing that ignited something within Lawrence and he suddenly found himself moving forward, pulling the pistol from his belt, aiming wildly, firing, firing. He thought he saw one of his bullets hit home, saw cloth puff up on the thing's shoulder, but if it was a hit the bullet did no good. The monster didn't flinch or slow; instead it wheeled around and spotted Kirk standing nearby with one of the remaining vigilantes. The eyes narrowed and the mouth stretched in a parody of a smile as it slashed out with its paw.

Kirk tried to say something—perhaps a plea, perhaps a prayer—but then the claws struck him with such terrible force that his face was completely torn away. Eyes, nose, teeth and jaw . . . all of it gone in a red flash. The publican's body shuddered as shock and convulsions burst through his nerve endings and he fell to the ground, dying . . . but in a twist of perversity, not yet dead. He flopped on the ground as the monster stepped across his body toward the vigilante who had not managed to get off a single shot during the attack.

Lawrence grabbed the sleeve of a Gypsy man and bellowed at him. "Get the women and children to safety!" He hurled the man toward some of his fellows and, terrified as they were, they ran to obey.

Lawrence raised his gun and tried to fire, but as he shuffled forward for the best shot he stumbled over the dirt rim of the dancing circle and went down, his bullet firing into the campfire. He landed hard and the pistol fell from his grasp, landing in the hot coals.

The monster moved quickly past the vigilante, and for a moment Lawrence thought that the creature had chosen, for whatever reason, to ignore him, but in his mind there was an afterimage of a blurred movement and then Lawrence—and the vigilante—looked down and saw the truth. The man's guts slid out of a gaping wound and splashed heavily onto the dirt. The vigilante's finger flexed on the trigger and the shotgun exploded, peppering the still-twitching Kirk with buckshot. Then the vigilante fell across Kirk's body and they both settled into a terminal stillness.

The monster turned its head and its hellish eyes found Lawrence. It uttered a low, hungry growl.

Lawrence scrambled to his feet and ran. For his life and soul and sanity, he ran. He saw Nye ahead of him, running toward his bicycle, which stood against a tree near the tethered gelding. The constable was screaming like a girl as he fumbled for his pistol, but the lanyard had become hopelessly tangled. Lawrence ran past him. The knife in Lawrence's pocket was useless, his pistol was in the fire, but in the scabbard on his saddle was his father's Holland & Holland elephant gun. Monster or not, the huge bullets in that rifle would blow this beast's head off.

The last of the vigilantes rose up in his path and gruffly brushed Lawrence aside as he took up a shooting stance, seating the butt of the shotgun hard into his shoulder, aiming with professional skill along the barrel. Lawrence threw a backward glance to watch the shot, but the werewolf was not there.

Startled, Lawrence slowed to a half-run and looked around. People still screamed and ran, but the clearing was empty except for the dead and the bear, who had snuck back into its cage and cowered there, trembling like a whipped dog.

The vigilante shouted at Lawrence. "Where is the goddamned—"

It came out of the shadows to their left. Moving with inhuman speed it had circled them and come at them out of the forest, and it drove into the gap between Lawrence and the vigilante. One powerful shoulder clipped Lawrence and sent him spinning into a gorse bush. Lawrence wrestled himself onto his back and tried to find his footing, but as he raised his head he saw the werewolf use one paw to tear the shotgun from the vigilante's hand and toss the weapon a hundred feet into the darkness. With the other it slashed him back and forth, and the man seemed to come apart like layers of a paper doll.

Then it flung the man toward Lawrence and vanished behind the row of vardos. Nye stood at the edge of the campfire, his face white with shock and splattered with drops of blood. Lawrence slapped his shoulder to shake him out of his stupor.

"It's gone around back. I'll circle to the right, you go to the left. We can catch it in a crossfire."

The constable licked his lips and gagged as he realized that he was tasting blood. But his face hardened and he nodded and set off, pistol in hand. Lawrence lost sight of him almost at once.

Nye crept along the edge of a line of utility carts and saw the rearmost vardo. It trembled and shook, rocking sideways onto one set of wheels and then the other.

"Got you, you bastard!" Nye growled and hurried over. When he was ten feet from it he saw a figure slumped in the shadows. A man. He had no throat and his head lolled grotesquely from a single strand of tendon. The cart was no longer trembling. Had the monster done its bloody work and fled? Nye stepped over the dead man and parted the curtains with the barrel of his pistol. The interior of the vardo was black and he heard nothing. Then something bumped against his arm and he jerked it back.

He stared at it without comprehending what he was seeing. His coat sleeve was there, and the cuff of his shirt. But the hand that held the pistol was . . . *gone.*

A red geyser pumped from a jagged stump. The pain didn't hit him for a full second. But by then a massive, shaggy arm had reached out of the shadows of the vardo and grabbed his gaping lower jaw. With a jerk Nye was plucked off the ground and pulled into the vardo. He fell forward into the shadows and there was no end to his plummet into darkness.

LAWRENCE NEVER HEARD Nye's muffled scream. Instead his attention was drawn by the cries of a little girl who wandered through the carnage, crying aloud in Romany for her mother. Off to his left he heard—or hoped he heard—a woman's voice calling for her child.

He turned, spotted her, saw the moment when she located her child and began to run.

Then, up ahead, he saw the last vardo in the line begin shaking violently, then it abruptly stopped as the werewolf leaned its head and shoulders out to watch the woman race by. In an instant, driven by predatory mandates built into the core of its being, the creature leapt out of the vardo and gave chase.

Lawrence was on the wrong side of the line of vardos. He saw the creature in glimpses between the wagons as it raced down the line after the woman. Lawrence followed the line of flight and knew that the monster's prey was not the woman . . . but the *girl*.

He was moving before he realized it, running, racing, legs pumping as he tore past fire and blood toward the little child. The mother cried out, the creature spotted him and howled in hate and hunger. It threw itself into a long dive, but Lawrence was already in motion, already leaping, one hand holding his pistol, the other out and curled, scooping up the child, and as he fell with her he could feel the heat and mass of the werewolf pass directly over him.

The mother screamed, and the little girl screamed, and so did Lawrence. But the werewolf screamed loudest, a shriek of frustration and fury that tore pinecones from the trees and burst the worms in the earth beneath its clawed feet.

Lawrence rolled off of the little girl, who was dazed but unhurt, and as her mother raced up he thrust the child toward the Gypsy woman's desperate arms.

"Run!" he roared, and the mother gathered up her child and ran.

Lawrence bent and picked up someone's fallen gun. He'd landed badly and pain lanced through his joints, but he ate it and used it to fuel his own hate. He snapped off one shot, another, sure that he hit the thing, but it kept moving. Not toward him, but across the camp. He pulled the trigger again but it clicked on an empty chamber.

Lawrence clambered to his feet and staggered toward the horse, who was trying to tear free of its tether. Lawrence grabbed the bridle and wrenched the horse's head around so he could get at the rifle, and he yanked it from the scabbard. He spun and rushed back to the edge of the clearing, throwing the rifle to his shoulder, needing to kill this thing, to *hurt* it. For Ben. For everyone.

But the werewolf was not merely escaping. It was smarter than an animal. It had a cold and evil cunning, and there beyond the campfire, forgotten in all of the panic, sat another child. A boy, silent and shocked by everything that had happened, too terrified to move and confused by having been abandoned. The werewolf ran toward it and suddenly the boy screamed out in a shrill wail. The werewolf threw a brief look over its shoulder at Lawrence and for a moment it seemed as if the goddamned thing was grinning at him as if to say, *You can't save them all!*

"No!" Lawrence bellowed, racing to catch up but not daring to take his shot. The child was too close.

Then the monster bent low and snatched the child off the ground, tucked it under its muscular arm and leaped across the fire. By the time Lawrence had reached the fire and ran around it, the werewolf and the boy were gone.

Lawrence stumbled to a stop, his chest heaving. All around him there were people groaning in pain or crying in loss and terror. A man with a bloody stump sat with his back to a tree, staring in dumb amazement at the arm that lay between his outstretched heels. A woman held something in her arms that might have been an infant, but there wasn't enough left of it to tell. A muscular Gypsy with a broken nose and knife scars on his arms and face stood staring into the interior of a wrecked vardo, silent tears streaming down his face. The place smelled of death. Everything was splashed with bright blood.

The rifle sagged in his grip and hung from one nerveless hand as Lawrence looked around at all of the carnage that had been wrought by one creature in . . . how long? A minute? Less? Seconds?

The creature was gone. The leaves on the bushes and trees still trembled from where it had passed. The slaughter was over.

But it was chasing the boy.

Lawrence knew that it was death to pursue the thing. Only a madman would consider it. Only a fool would do it.

With a growl that began deep in his chest, Lawrence Talbot gripped the rifle in both hands and plunged into the woods.

Hunting something that could not exist.

Hunting a monster.

CHAPTER TWENTY-ONE

The moonlight showed him the way. He moved as fast as caution would allow, following a path of destruction that marked the creature's passage. Broken tree limbs, bushes smashed flat, the marks of clawed feet torn into the sod. Lawrence may not have been as practiced a hunter as his father, but he could follow this track. The monster was making no effort to hide its passage.

And then the underbrush thinned and the ground became rockier, and the trail petered out and vanished entirely. Lawrence slowed from a run to a trot to a cautious walk, bending low to search for any marks scratched onto the hardpan.

But there was nothing.

"No, goddammit," he growled. "Don't do this . . ."

He kept moving forward, hunting now by instinct rather than evidence. He climbed to the top of a hillock and saw that the rocky field led down to another part of the forest. A far older part, with huge trees that reached up from the earth like the fingers of buried giants. Their branches formed a heavy canopy that was so dense that it made the ground shrubbery very sparse. Though the ground cover was thinner there were bogs that belched up gray steam.

Taking a fresh grip on his rifle, Lawrence crossed the

rocks and entered the old-growth forest. Once inside, the moonlight was filtered to a murky gloom which made forward progress much more dangerous. Cold sweat burst from his pores and ran in rivulets down his skin and under his clothes.

"Help me," he murmured to a God who he had long ago ceased to worship. His faith had been torn away by the death of his mother, but here in this forest, in this terrible place, as he hunted a creature whose very existence was proof of a larger world, he sought for any help that might be offered. "Please . . ."

The forest was vast and empty and with every step it grew darker. The mist was cloying and smelled of sulfur and decay.

He pressed on, and after another quarter of an hour the pillars of the old trees began to yield to younger growth and thicker shrubs. But even here there was an innate hostility. The shrubs were mostly barbed holly or wild rose, and they nipped at his clothing like little teeth. Nettles clung to his trousers and the stiff leaves of wild rhododendron lashed his cheeks.

The ground beneath his feet began to yield but the mist had grown so thick that he had to bend and feel with his fingers to confirm that he now trod on thick moss. The ground sloped down and then began to rise again, and Lawrence stalked through the mist, thoroughly lost, his heart sinking as all hope of finding the child drained away drop by drop.

Then he heard a sound far off to his left.

Voices.

He stopped and strained to hear. Men were shouting, but the words were strange. Romany. The Gypsies were out hunting, too. Enough of them must have recovered from the attack to organize a hunt.

Good, he thought. Maybe their greater numbers would drive the creature toward him, like beaters flushing a tiger. But a moment later he knew that this guess was wrong. There was a single high scream of awful pain that rose above the mist and then stopped with a terminal abruptness. A second later Lawrence heard gunshots and more shouting.

And then the night was torn by the long, heart-rending howl of the werewolf.

For a moment it rooted Lawrence to the spot. Visions of claws and teeth and blood flashed through his brain, and in the next moment a murderous rage boiled up in his chest. He snarled aloud and began running through the mist, aching to reach the fight before it was over, needing to be the one to bring this monster down. For Ben's sake, he needed that.

He ran and ran, but the mist distorted the sounds of the fight. One moment the gunshots seemed to be a hundred yards ahead of him and then they were way off to his right. Then to his left.

He kept running, tripping over roots, slipping on moss, fighting his way forward until something huge and dark loomed above him out of the mist. Lawrence slid to a stop and raised his weapon, but the shape was too tall, too solid.

With the rifle ready, he crept forward. A second giant form emerged from the swirling mist to his left, another to his right. And then Lawrence understood where he was and what he had found.

It was the ancient graveyard with its towering monuments. Somehow, lost in the mist, he had circled all the way around to the very edges of his own family estate. He had been here less than an hour ago. He realized with a queer jolt that his mother was buried in a mausoleum not half a mile from where he stood. How had he not remembered that earlier when he'd ridden through here on his horse? Now the idea drove cold spikes through his bowels.

Something moved in the mist on the far side of the cemetery, and Lawrence spun into a crouch, stretching out with his senses.

A small sound. A whimper.

"Boy!" he called softly.

Another whimper. Lawrence moved forward into the heart of the circle, fanning the twin barrels of the rifle back and forth.

The mist eddied and there, not ten feet from him, was the boy.

Alive!

"God almighty." The words were jolted out of him. He rushed to the child, bent down and caught him by one arm. "Are you hurt? Can you run?"

The child raised a terrified and tear-streaked face toward him, but there was no sign of comprehension on his face. Lawrence repeated his questions but the boy just shook his head dumbly and said something urgent in Romany.

"Dammit," Lawrence hissed. He hauled the boy to his feet and checked for wounds. There was blood on the child's clothes, but Lawrence didn't think that any of it was the boy's. He turned the boy into the spill of bright moonlight and gasped as something on the child's chest flashed bright silver.

The boy wore a medallion. The medal of St. Columbanus. Exactly like the one Ben had owned. The one that was now in his own pocket.

A thought reached into Lawrence's brain and froze

him in place. He had said to her: "It was found on my brother's body."

And her answer had been: "But he was not wearing it."

The old Gypsy woman had given him back the medal, but Lawrence had shoved it into a pocket. This boy *had* worn it, and even though the werewolf had carried him off the monster had done him no harm.

"No," Lawrence said, wanting to scoff at the absurdity of the superstition, but everything that had happened in the last hour mocked his disbelief.

He straightened and took the gun in both hands.

"Boy," he said quietly and the child looked up, responding to Lawrence's tone even if he didn't understand the words. "Run."

But the child had been through too much, had endured too much. He stared at Lawrence with the innocent expectation of any child who expects adults to solve all problems, to chase away all monsters.

"God," Lawrence mumbled as he scooped the child up, hugged him against one hip and began creeping toward the edge of the nearest cluster of monuments. Above them the moon was huge and powerful, dominating the sky, and Lawrence realized with sinking dread that this was the Goddess of the Hunt, come to watch the slaughter here in this most ancient of arenas.

Lawrence began moving toward the edge of the circle, but out of the corner of his eye he sensed movement and he spun. There was nothing but a hole torn in the mist. He did not have to ask what it was. He knew. So did the boy, who whimpered and clung to him.

There was a sound, a scrape of a claw on rock and Lawrence turned again. Once more there was nothing but the mist, the vapor swirling as if something had been there and had fled the second before he turned.

It was here. He knew it.

And it was toying with him.

His heart was beating so hard he wondered why it didn't make the stones tremble. The boy was heavy; so was the gun. If he could run to where the Gypsies were beating the woods then he wouldn't need to shoot. But if he stayed, if he was forced to fight here in this place, he could not use the big rifle one-handed.

With a heavy heart he lowered the boy to the ground. The child tried to cling but Lawrence pushed him away, knowing that the separation would hurt the child, that it would feel like abandonment . . . and Lawrence knew what that felt like, how it scarred.

He backed away from the wall of mist, trying to guess where the creature was, trying to *be* it in his mind so he could predict the angle of attack. He moved backward until his shoulders were pressed hard against the cold slab of upright granite. It could only come at him from the front but then his heart slammed to a frozen halt in his chest.

He could hear it. The deep, quick breath of the beast.

On the other side of the slab.

Behind him.

Icy sweat ran down his face and stung his eyes. It felt like tears.

He licked his lips and slipped his finger into the trigger guard. There was a chance. Just a chance. If he spun around the stone and backed up, if he did it right, then he could open up with both barrels from point-blank range. It was his best chance. His only chance. But dear God it terrified him. He almost sobbed with the fear of what he was about to do.

God help me, he cried in his mind. *God . . . if you exist, if you're there . . . if you give a fuck . . . help me!*

He drew a breath and moved!

Lawrence spun off the stone and wheeled to his left, backpedaling five feet as he brought up the rifle. He pulled one of the triggers and the blast knocked him backward even farther as the bullet punched a big hole through nothing at all.

The werewolf was gone.

Lawrence stood there, flat-footed, shocked.

How could he have been wrong? He'd *heard* it.

Lawrence turned in a full circle, sweeping the smoking gun around, urging the creature to step out of the mist.

But it wasn't in the mist.

He heard the growl. Low, sneaky, hungry.

Above him.

Lawrence looked up and there, standing atop the pillar, immensely powerful against the white splendor of the goddess moon, was the beast.

He tried to bring the gun up. He was fast. It was faster.

The werewolf pounced on him, reaching for him with its taloned hands and smashing him down onto the damp earth so hard that breath and blood flew from Lawrence's mouth. His clutching finger jerked the second trigger but the bullet blew past the monster's head and struck fire from the stone before speeding off uselessly into the woods.

The werewolf hissed with fury as it raked him with its claws. Only the thick fabric of his greatcoat saved him from being eviscerated, but even so he felt lines of burning pain across his chest and the whole front of his coat disintegrated into ribbons.

Lawrence fought. This was the last moment of his life

and he knew it, but still he fought. With all of his fury and all of his hate, he fought. For Benjamin and the others who had died today, he fought. For his own soul, he fought. He punched at the thing, smashing his fists into its throat and mouth and eyes. He could feel its bones grind and he could feel his knuckles splinter. He smashed at it and drove his knee up to try and dislodge it. He even bit at it, tearing away a chunk of flesh and fur. He fought and fought and fought.

And then the werewolf swatted his hands away as if they were nothing and with a growl of dark hunger it lunged forward and buried its fangs into his shoulder.

The pain was so vast, so monstrous, that Lawrence was thrust into a world of red hot insanity. The creature shook its head, worrying at him, gnawing on him until finally it reared back and ripped flesh and muscle from Lawrence's shoulder. Blood sprayed the monster's face and blinded Lawrence. It splashed into Lawrence's mouth and he tasted it—hot and salty, smelling of copper and fear.

The creature swallowed the meat and prepared for the final bite. The killing bite that would end all of this pain and madness.

Then—*BANG!*

Something struck the werewolf and knocked it to one side. Lawrence, dazed beyond thought, could hear it scream—more in anger than pain. There was another bang, and another. More. A volley of gunfire.

Shouts. Men yelling in a language he didn't know.

More gunfire.

And then crushing weight of the beast was gone. It leaped from him and ran into the mist as bullets burned and buzzed like hornets and knocked chips from the stones.

Lawrence lifted his head and saw shapes filling the circle. Men. Gypsies. Many of them. Some of them still shooting into the mist. One of them lifted the little boy and kissed his face, his eyes, his brow, his cheeks. Others came to him and crowded around. They touched him. Were they helping? Were they killing him? . . .

Lawrence was losing touch with reality. The mist was spreading, filling his eyes, filling his head. Lawrence looked up into the sky and the huge white face of the Goddess of the Hunt filled his eyes, dominated his mind . . . and then it, too, faded to mist and darkness.

But before his mind collapsed into the great well of shadows he heard the voice of the creature rise above the forest with a single, long howl. Not of pain, not of defeat, but of ferocious triumph.

Lawrence Talbot sank beneath that sound and plummeted into a darkness that had no end.

CHAPTER TWENTY-TWO

The man should be dead. His wound was terrible. The ground beneath where he'd lain was soaked with blood, and the bandages the men from the camp had put on him were already drenched.

Maleva lit a cigarillo and studied the face of Lawrence Talbot, who lay on a pair of wooden cases that had been lashed together and covered with a clean blanket. His features were drawn, his skin gray and streaked with sweat and gore, his eyelids fluttering open every now and then but there was no sense or understanding in his eyes. The man was dying—should *be* dead—but Maleva knew better. And it broke her ancient heart.

The men of the camp had come back with the boy, who was unhurt but deeply traumatized by his ordeal. They brought the boy to her first, and though they had all seen the medal around his neck, they wanted reassurance from her. She checked the child over and then kissed his forehead.

"Fate has been kind to this little one," she told them, speaking in the Romany dialect of their tribe. "Even if she has been so cruel to so many others."

The dead of the tribe had been laid out in a row. Six men of the camp; three women. One child. And the five men from the town—the four with shotguns and the policeman. All of them lying in a row, their broken bodies covered with cloths. Some were missing arms and legs. The Rom scoured the woods to find the missing pieces, but even when this grisly task had been completed what had been assembled did not add up to ten of her people. The beast had fed as it killed.

The man on the makeshift table groaned and in his delirium he tried to move, but he had lifted his wounded arm no more than an inch when pain exploded through every nerve . . . and he screamed. His eyes opened wide and Maleva saw that the pain had awakened his mind. He stared at her with clear comprehension of what had happened, and the reality of it was close to unhinging his mind.

She motioned for her apprentice, a lovely woman who was not yet twenty-one but who was already deep in the practice of the healing arts.

"Hold him, Saskia," ordered Maleva. "But have a care."

Lawrence was thrashing and screaming, but the young woman pressed Lawrence gently but firmly down, whispering soothing words in Romany. Lawrence jabbered at her in nearly incoherent English, which the woman did not understand. His panic was like a storm in the narrow confines of the vardo. Maleva stepped close and took a bowl of mingled herbs, struck a match and dropped it into the bowl. Instantly, blue smoke coiled upward, filling the wagon with a powerful scent.

"Hold your breath," said Maleva, and Saskia did as ordered; then the old woman held the smoking bowl under Lawrence's nose and with each desperate panting breath he drew the herb smoke into his lungs. Within seconds his screams died to a confused moan and his eyes lost their focus. In half a minute he sagged back against the blanket and was still except for his labored breathing, but soon that slowed, too. Maleva opened the door and dumped the burning herbs into the dirt, and then opened the windows so that the cold night air swept the drugged smoke away.

Maleva and Saskia let out their pent-up breaths, each of them desperate for air. For a time they did nothing but breathe. Maleva was the first to move, and she opened a chest that contained the tools of her healing craft. She selected a needle and threaded it with gut and handed it to Saskia. Then Maleva fished in Lawrence's pocket for the St. Columbanus medal and looped the chain over the dying man's head. She placed the medal over Lawrence's heart, and shortly his breathing came more regularly.

The young woman looked at the wound and then raised her eyes to Maleva.

"Why do you save him?" asked Saskia. The sounds of weeping and grief still filled the camp. She knew everyone who had died, and grief was a knife in her heart.

"He risked his life for one of ours. For a child that he did not even know."

"He has been bitten! If you have compassion for this man, then you should end his misery before it begins."

Maleva shook her head. "You would make me a sinner?"

Saskia set aside the needle and took Maleva's hands in hers. "There is no sin in killing a beast."

The old woman stroked Saskia's hair. "Is there not?" she asked. "What of killing a man?"

"It's not the same."

"Where does one begin and the other end?"

Saskia pulled back, her face clouded with doubt. She picked up the needle and turned to address the gaping wound. The needle went into the flesh easily and

Saskia's quick, clever fingers began the process of sewing the wound shut. It was a huge wound and it would take a lot of time. As she worked she kept shaking her head.

"Speak your mind, girl," said Maleva gently.

"Many will suffer for this."

Maleva watched in silence for a long time before she answered, and when she spoke her voice was as soft as a heartbroken whisper. "Sometimes Fate's way is a cruel one. But she seeks a greater end."

Saskia looked up from her work, clearly troubled, but the old woman touched her cheek.

"Always?" Saskia asked.

"Always," said Maleva, though she did not meet Saskia's eyes when she said it.

CHAPTER TWENTY-THREE

aleva's one-horse cart was small, just enough to carry bags of vegetables or stacks of pelts for trade in the towns. She sat perched on the bench seat, her traveling cloak pulled around her, her face lit by a tiny lantern that swung from the canopy by a rusty chain. Before her, Talbot Hall rose like a dark fortress, but all of its windows were ablaze with light.

The front door opened as she pulled the cart to a stop at the base of the broad stone stairs, and a tall Sikh stepped out. He held a big oil lamp in one hand and a wicked-looking knife in the other.

"What is your business?" he demanded. "There is trouble abroad tonight and you have no—"

Her voice cut through his protests. "I bring grief to the house of sorrow." And with that she reached back and pulled away the blanket that covered the body that was strapped to boards in the cart.

Singh cried out in Urdu and then in English. But Sir John, looking exhausted and disheveled in his leopard-trimmed dressing gown, was right behind him. He rubbed his tired eyes and then became instantly still as he stared past Singh at the body on the cart.

"Lawrence!" The name was torn from him and he shoved Singh aside and bolted down the steps. The Sikh was at his heels. They crowded around the body, examining him by lantern light.

"He's alive," Singh gasped.

Sir John closed his eyes for a moment as he gripped the sides of the stretcher boards. "Thank God . . ."

On her perch, Maleva watched as the two men carried Lawrence up the stairs and into the hall. The door closed with a crash and the courtyard was bathed in darkness and silence.

"May Fate protect you," she murmured. "May Fate protect us all."

She turned the cart around and let the horse find its way back to her people.

Chapter Twenty-four

For Lawrence time had lost all meaning. There was no sense of its passing. He did not know when it was—neither the day nor the hour—and only vaguely grasped where he was. He swam for what seemed like centuries in a sea of darkness that had no up or down. He was like one of those blind creatures who lived in the lightless depths of the ocean, moving through eternal nothingness, with no destination and no purpose. The only sound was that of his own breathing, which was low and deep and steady, and when he listened to it his consciousness faded back into sleep.

One time he opened his eyes to see an empty room and the slanting golden light of afternoon sun.

When he blinked it was night and only the light of a single candle lit the room. A form slept in a chair but he could not tell if it was real or if it was a heap of old coats. He did not—could not—care, and let his eyes drift closed again.

Another blink and Gwen Conliffe was there, seated in a chair by the window, sunlight on her face, a Bible open on her lap. Gwen? Why was she here? Lawrence struggled to even remember who she was, but the harder he tried the more elusive the answer became. He saw her stir and turn toward him, but he was already slipping into darkness again. If she saw him, or spoke his name, he did not know it.

A couple of times he saw men in the room. Sir John, standing by the window, hands clasped behind his back, his body rigid with tension as other men spoke words that Lawrence was unable to process. He saw Singh once or twice, and he had the vague memory of a damp cloth being pressed to his forehead. Was it Singh who did that? Or his father? Or Gwen? Or was it a dream?

After a while he stopped trying to figure it out. He liked the darkness. It was better down there, swimming in the sea of nothingness, and so he stayed there as often as he could. There was no pain down there. There were no memories down there. And nothing hunted him through those shadows.

Lawrence swam through dreams as the hours melted into days and the days melted into weeks.

SIR JOHN TALBOT sipped whiskey from a glass and set it on the stone railing of his observation deck. He had stopped the pretense of going inside to covertly re-fill the glass from the decanter and the bottle stood next to the glass with barely an inch of golden liquid left at the bottom.

It was a cold morning with the ozone bite of coming frost in the air, but if the cold was somehow able to bite him through the whiskey burn in his system, then none of it showed on his face.

As he stood there, looking out over the fields and the roads of the estate, watching waves of leaves pushed by the wind, he saw something dark moving in the distance. He turned his telescope and bent to the lens. A line of

Gypsy vardos stood in silhouette on the far horizon, diminishing in size and clarity as they rolled away from Blackmoor.

Sir John stood, eyes narrowed and lip curled in a hard sneer. He picked up his glass, splashed the last of the whiskey into it, and stood sipping the scotch as the cold wind blew past him.

THE DRIVER OF the carriage reined the horses to a stop at the edge of the village of Blackmoor and twisted in his seat as the door opened and a passenger stepped out.

"You sure this is where you want to get out, sir?"

The man straightened and placed his bowler hat on his head. He was tall, with a heavy mustache and sideburns, a nose that had been broken at least twice, a stern mouth, and the look of a man who had spent more than a little time on the hard streets of London. He brushed the wrinkles out of his long tan coat and looked around slowly, taking in the gray sadness of the village and the dreary vista of the landscape.

"Sir? . . ."

"This'll do fine," said the tall man. He reached into the carriage and removed a heavy valise.

The driver gave him a doubtful look and cast a cautious eye at the village. He'd heard of this place. The London papers had been filled with strange stories of mass killings barely a month ago. Some kind of wild animal. He glanced at the sky, judging the number of hours left in the day, and wasted no further time clicking his tongue for the horses who immediately started forward as if they, too, were happy to be quit of this place.

The tall man stood by the side of the road and watched them go. He put his hands in his coat pockets, strolled to the far side of the road, and then mounted a slight rise so that he could have a better view of the land beyond the village. With the autumn trees stripped of most of their leaves he could see for miles. He could see all the way across the valley to the weed-choked fields that surrounded Talbot Hall.

He removed a cigar from his inner pocket, lit it, and stood smoking on the hill as he studied the Hall. His blue eyes were as sharp and cold as diamonds.

He smiled to himself, then turned and walked without haste toward the town.

SINGH CREPT QUIETLY along the hallway. Silence had become a habit over the last few weeks. Both the doctor from town and the specialists Sir John had brought in had insisted that rest and quiet were crucial to any chance of recovery. No noise, no shocks, no surprises. Just rest so that Lawrence's ruined body would have some hope of recovering.

Singh balanced a tray with a pitcher of water and a fresh towel on one hand while with the other he gently turned the handle of the bedroom. After the first day, he had made sure to oil the tumblers so that the lock turned soundlessly. He eased the door open, first seeing Miss Conliffe in her usual post, asleep in the chair by the window, a book open on her lap. Poor lass had been here every day since the Gypsies brought Lawrence home. She'd stayed up until all hours of the night, watching over Lawrence, wracked with guilt because it had been she who had sent a letter to London to obtain his help in finding Ben. And she had approved of

Lawrence's decision to hunt the monster who had slaughtered him.

It made Singh's heart hurt to think of these things. He had known Benjamin and Lawrence as children. He'd wept when Sir John had committed Lawrence to the asylum and then shipped him off to America. He and Sir John had fought bitterly about it, but in the end Singh was the servant and Sir John the master of this house. But Ben . . . he'd seen that poor lad grow up, had loved him like his own son. The heartache and bitterness over Ben's death was as strong in him now as it had been when he'd been killed. And now it looked like Lawrence would die as well. Three weeks in a coma, no sign of comprehension, no sign of recovery.

This was a cursed place, he told himself for the ten thousandth time.

He entered the room and crossed to the side table used for the supplies necessary to maintain a comatose patient. Light streamed into the room through the sheers and Singh cut a quick glance at the bed to see if the bandages were still—

Singh jolted to a stop and stared wide-eyed at what he saw on the bed. The tray toppled from his hand and struck the floor, the metal pitcher ringing like a bell and water splashing everywhere.

The sudden din startled Gwen Conliffe, who snapped awake and leaped to her feet, equally shocked and confused. She and Singh stood gaping.

"Lawrence? . . ." she murmured.

Lawrence Talbot sat on the side of the bed. Gray, sweating, terribly drawn and haggard. But very much awake and alive.

Chapter Twenty-five

Gwen flew across the room to Lawrence's side.

"I'll fetch the doctor," Singh said and bolted from the room.

Lawrence felt more than half dead. His eyes were sunken into dark pits, his hair greasy and pasted to his skull, his lips rubbery and slack. There was a foul taste in his mouth and an ache that was sunken deep into the core of every muscle and bone in his entire body. He hung his head and shook it slowly back and forth like a sick bear, trying to clear his brain of the layers of fog and cobwebs.

He heard the rustle of cloth, felt cool hands touch his, and he raised his head and turned to see Gwen seated next to him on the bed. Gwen? That made no sense. And she was no longer wearing her black funeral dress.

"I . . . thought you were leaving," he mumbled. "You'll miss your train."

Gwen laughed and sniffed and wiped tears from her blue eyes. "It seems this place is impossible to escape."

Lawrence frowned, not catching her meaning. He looked out of the window. The trees were mostly bare.

"Was there a storm?"

"Yes," she said with a hitch in her voice. "Yes . . . there was a very bad storm."

But Lawrence was asleep again.

DR. LLOYD ARRIVED within the half hour. He arrived to find Sir John standing at the foot of the sick bed and Gwen hovering solicitously by Lawrence's side. The doctor had become used to the strained silence between Sir John and the young woman from London, and privately he was happy for her that she hadn't married into the Talbot family. Not as long as Sir John was the master of the house. Cold, stiff-backed old bastard, Lloyd thought. Never got over his wife's suicide, as if his own heart had stopped beating when Solana's had, and Sir John had not been the warmest of men before that. Now with one son dead and the other polishing the hinges on death's door . . . well, he thought, Miss Conliffe must have the patience of a saint to have put up with Sir John all this time.

These thoughts ran through his head but he wisely kept them off his face.

He pulled a chair close and carefully unwound the blood-encrusted bandages. Lawrence Talbot's shoulder, chest and back looked like a map of a train yard. Lines of black sutures crossed and crisscrossed the bruised flesh. The doctor grunted and sat back for a moment, staring at the wounds. The wounds were remarkably well knitted, the lips of each laceration showing tight seals with almost no swelling. He bent to sniff the dressing and found nothing amiss. The wounds had been infected for a while but there was no telltale smell of suppuration. He held the back of his hand over the gashes—no heat, either.

"How is the pain?" he asked.

"It's . . . ," Lawrence began and trailed off. His face wore a quizzical expression. "It barely hurts at all. More of a dull ache. You're too good a doctor for a small town like this."

Dr. Lloyd grunted again. "Make a fist." Lawrence slowly curled his fingers into a fist. Lloyd's eyebrows rose. He held out a finger. "Squeeze my finger."

"I feel weak as a baby," Lawrence protested, but he grasped the doctor's finger and squeezed. His efforts brought a wince, but it was on the doctor's face.

Sir John shifted closer, watching with great interest. Lawrence noticed him and looked up.

"Father, what did the Gypsies say?"

A small smile curled the edges of the old man's lips. "That the Devil has come to Blackmoor."

The doctor withdrew his hand from Lawrence and quietly redressed the wounds. He met no one's eyes as he did so. As soon as he was finished, he shoved his instruments into his bag and rose.

"What's wrong," Gwen asked. "Is there infection or—?"

Dr. Lloyd shook his head and finally met Lawrence's eyes. "This is . . . remarkable. A week ago I would have said that you'd never use that arm again."

"And now?" asked Gwen.

The doctor looked steadily at her. "He was missing his entire tendon and most of the muscle. It seems . . . um . . . to have healed."

" 'Healed?' " echoed Sir John.

"It's truly remarkable." He turned back to Lawrence, but almost at once his eyes shifted away. "Remarkable." He straightened his shoulders. "I'll be back to check on you at the end of the week."

Lawrence said, "Doctor . . . thank you. You're a miracle worker."

"Not I," said Dr. Lloyd, and he still did not meet Lawrence's gaze as he turned and left. Singh ushered him out.

ONCE THE DOCTOR was gone, Gwen plumped Lawrence's pillows and Sir John came and stood by the foot of the bed.

"Miss Conliffe," he said softly, "thank you for staying with us during this difficult time. Perhaps if there was any sense of filial obedience in this house we wouldn't have inconvenienced you so."

Gwen stiffened and Lawrence looked from her to his father, sensing tension and rightly guessing that this was another round in an argument that had played out over the last few weeks, and her words confirmed his guess.

"Lawrence was just trying to find out what killed Ben," she said with frost, "as you well know. What he did was heroic, and he did it out of love."

" 'Love'?" repeated Sir John, shaking his head. "No, my dear, I think there was some stronger motivation. It is seldom love that compels a hunter to enter the forest."

Lawrence said nothing. There were many things about that night he couldn't remember, but the burning hatred and towering rage—those things he remembered with perfect clarity. But he did not want to side with his father against Gwen.

"Call it what you will," insisted Gwen, "but Lawrence was not being a willful child. He's a man." Her voice faltered for a moment. "A fine man . . . and he's suffered terribly."

"To no good purpose," Sir John countered.

"No? We know that Ben's murder wasn't the random act of some madman passing through the region. Wasn't that one of your theories? Well, this was no lunatic who attacked the Gypsy camp."

"No," he said, "but we don't know *what* it is, do we?"

"No . . . but now we know that whatever it is—it's still out there."

Chapter Twenty-six

D r. Lloyd had left a sleeping draught for him and despite his protests Singh had all but forced it down his throat. Lawrence vanished down a black hole. He wasn't sure if it was for hours or days. The act of waking, of confronting the reality of what had happened, of being poked and prodded by Dr. Lloyd, interrogated by his father, watched like a hawk by Singh and comforted by Gwen—all of this was too much for Lawrence, and he drifted back into an exhausted sleep. But it was sleep, not coma.

When he woke it was in the depths of night. Gwen was no longer in her chair. Lawrence had some vague memory of Sir John insisting that she take a night in the bed that had been provided for her across the hall, a bed she had barely used since the attack. Although he would have liked to speak with her here in the quiet privacy of the night, he was equally pleased to be alone.

His shoulder throbbed strangely. Not quite pain, but not a comfortable feeling. It was a strange sensation, as if things were moving beneath his skin. Lawrence had read about surgeons placing maggots on infected wounds because the little vermin ate only necrotic tissue and would not eat healthy flesh. Whereas he could understand the scientific logic of that, it nevertheless profoundly disgusted him and he hoped to God that there were no wriggling grubs beneath his bandages.

He swung his legs out of bed and placed them on the carpet, and for a moment he distracted himself by flexing his toes in the thick nap. But the strange sensation continued. He experimented with his grip by opening and closing the hand of his injured arm. Earlier that hand had been stiff and unresponsive, but now the fingers moved and the muscles worked correctly as he clenched and unclenched his fist. The action comforted him, but it made his shoulder throb and itch.

"So far so good," he said aloud, aware that his voice was a rusty croak from disuse. He'd nearly burned his throat raw recounting the whole story of the attack earlier in the day, and had said very little since. Singh had brought him endless cups of tea and honey, and Gwen had spoon-fed him soothing broth.

Standing was a challenge and Lawrence took hold of the bedpost and used his good arm to pull himself slowly to his feet. The room did a drunken jig for several nauseating seconds, but it settled down more quickly than he thought. Even so, he stood still for a full minute before he tried a step.

His muscles felt weak, but not as weak as he expected from nearly a month in bed. He tottered slowly across the floor to the window and looked out at the night. The sky was a velvet black with a gibbous moon washing the landscape with pale silver.

There was a tall dressing mirror nearby and he walked carefully to it and examined his drawn face and peered into his own dark eyes.

"Who are you, you old beggar?" he said, barely recognizing the face. His shoulder throbbed again and

Lawrence drew a breath as he made a very hard decision. He knew that at some point he was going to have to confront the truth about how badly damaged he was. No matter what nonsense the doctor had said about his tendons regrowing, Lawrence knew that he was likely to be at least a partial cripple. He was already wondering how the limitation of his mangled arm would impact his performance on stage. Shakespeare was a demonstrative playwright and, though subtlety of voice was important, gestures and physical performance were crucial.

"There's always Richard the Third," he told his skeptical reflection.

Steeling himself, he unbelted his robe and let it fall to the floor, and then with great care and caution he began to remove the bandages. The doctor had used what seemed like miles of gauze, and Lawrence unwound many turns of it, letting the cloth fall to the floor. But a perverse part of his mind noted that the lengths of gauze piled at his feet looked more like ghostly entrails. He cursed his own imagination for conjuring that image. The itching sensation was nearly maddening and he wanted to tear off the rest of the bandages and scratch like a madman, but that would be foolish. Dr. Lloyd had said that between what the Gypsies had done for him and his own work, there were hundreds of sutures holding his flesh together. God. Hundreds.

He removed several layers and now he was down to it. One large section of thick padding lay between him and the reality of what he would have to live with for the rest of his life. What horrors would he encounter? And, more importantly, would he be able to face the truth? He thought he would, but now at the moment of commission his certainty was faltering.

"Come on, you coward," he scolded himself.

He lifted the padding away, and the sight indeed turned a knife in his bowels. His skin was a mad patchwork of crusted scabs that ran from shoulder blade to nipple and from sternum to armpit. The blood was crusted and hard and it itched worse than ever.

"Son of a bitch," he swore as he poked experimentally at one of the scabs. The pressure didn't hurt as much as he thought it would and when he pulled his finger back some of the scab stuck to his fingertip and pulled clear of the wound.

Only there wasn't a wound beneath. He bit his lip, hoping that maybe the wounds were less widespread than they looked. Maybe a lot of the scabbing was just smeared blood that had dried on his skin.

He scratched lightly at the edge of one of the scabs. It resisted for a moment and then flaked away. Lawrence frowned. His shoulder itched terribly and he used his nails to crack more and more of the scabbing, scratching as much to satisfy the itch as to reveal the extent of his injuries. The scabs fell away, and stuck into them were bits of catgut and medical sutures. He kept at it, the action quickly becoming obsessive as more and more of his wound was revealed.

Only it wasn't his wound.

As the scabs fell away all that he could find were thin white lines to show where the long and terrible slashes had healed. There were no open wounds. No lines of stitches, no patchwork of ruined flesh. All he found was a network of pale scars that barely marked the places where teeth and claws and tried to tear the life out of him.

"God . . ." he breathed, shocked at what he saw, though he suspected, deep in his heart, that God had little to do with this.

CHAPTER TWENTY-SEVEN

Later that day—and against the insistent warnings of Gwen Conliffe—Lawrence Talbot went downstairs. He called it "rejoining the world."

"But your shoulder!" she stressed.

"It hardly hurts," he soothed; that was a lie. His shoulder did not hurt at all, but he had not shared this with anyone. He had not yet sorted out what he thought about the miracle, if "miracle" was a word that could be applied to this. "But . . . if you'd let me lean on you I'm sure I'll manage not to trip down the stairs."

He said it with a smile, the kind of harmless flirtation a convalescent can get away with, but Gwen blushed all the same. Even so, she offered her arm and Lawrence made it down to the sitting room, and he was glad he had her there. The arm may have healed but he was still far from steady on his feet.

When they paused on the landing, Lawrence took a few seconds to catch his breath. "When did father have those extra five hundred steps installed?"

"I told you this was too soon."

"Don't scold me, Gwen," he said, not yet letting go of her arm. "I couldn't take being confined in that room another minute. I've been restless all morning. . . ."

She gave his arm a small squeeze and was about to

say something when Sir John stepped into the hall. He saw their interlaced arms and said, "Well, well."

Gwen blushed a deeper shade of red and disentangled her arm from Lawrence. "He needed help on the stairs," she said defensively.

"I daresay."

Lawrence did not like the cold accusation in his father's tone, but he understood it. Gwen had been engaged to Ben. Any show of affection that he might show to Gwen might be construed as bad form, and too soon. To rescue the moment he said, "Well, you kept me from doing a series of pratfalls that would have done nothing for my reputation . . . but I think I can manage from here." He turned to the Ming urn set between the staircases and spotted the silver walking stick the old Frenchman had given him. The wolf's head seemed to snarl at him and as he reached for it he felt a wave of revulsion, but he snatched it up regardless and leaned on it. "This will do fine."

Sir John grunted and indicated the drawing room with a sideways tic of his chin. "If you're up to it, we have company."

"I—"

"An inspector down from London." Sir John stepped closer. "He wants to ask questions, Lawrence."

"No!" protested Gwen. "Lawrence isn't nearly up to an interrogation."

"No he isn't," agreed Sir John. "So let's make sure that's not what it becomes."

Lawrence said, "It'll be fine, Gwen. I'll do anything to help."

Sir John studied his face. "Very well then."

INSPECTOR ABERLINE WAS a cool customer; Lawrence could see that much right off. He had the easygoing mannerisms of a common laborer overlaid with a veneer of education, but Lawrence wasn't fooled. And despite the blue twinkle of his eyes Lawrence could see the calculating mind of a hunter. Under other circumstances Lawrence would have liked to play cards with this man. You can learn so much about a man from the way he played cards.

The inspector sat comfortably in an armchair. A cup of tea steamed in a china mug on the table beside him. Sir John stood beside the big globe, spinning it slowly though his eyes were fixed on Aberline.

"He was quite seriously injured, Inspector," said Sir John. "Quite grievously injured, and his memory seems affected. I don't know what use he can be to you."

"Certainly there will be a more advantageous time," agreed Gwen.

"I completely understand," said Aberline diffidently. "Only . . . if I could have just a few words with him. A completely unofficial interview . . ."

"No, no," said Sir John, his jaw set and eyes hard. "No."

"Even the briefest exchange," insisted Aberline, "could be infinitely helpful to us."

"No!" said Sir John and Gwen as one.

"Yes," said Lawrence, and everyone turned to him in surprise.

"Lawrence," Gwen began, "don't let—"

"It's all right. I'd like to understand what happened, too."

"It's foolishness," snapped his father. "You're clearly unwell. This is an outrageous imposition on your convalescence."

Lawrence nodded, although his eyes were fixed on Aberline, whose smile did not reach as high as his eyes; however, Lawrence thought he understood this man. Sir John's rant trailed off as he watched the exchange between the inspector and his son. He sighed.

"Oh, very well, damn it."

"Thank you—" Aberline began, but Sir John cut him off.

"If you push my son, Inspector . . . if you cause him distress in any way, then official papers or not, I'll throw you out. Your intrusion is taxing my civility."

As he said this Singh stepped into Aberline's line of vision and stood, heavy arms folded, behind Lawrence.

Aberline looked faintly amused, but he inclined his head. "I understand, Sir John. I will not abuse your generosity." With that he turned to face Lawrence. "Francis Aberline, Scotland Yard. It's an honor to meet you, Mr. Talbot. I'm an enormous fan of your work. It was my very good fortune to see your performance of *Othello* in Edinburgh some years ago. I agree with the critics who said that you have redefined Iago for the modern stage. Bravo, sir."

"That was on my first European tour," said Lawrence, surprised at the praise and the fact that Aberline had seen his work. "I suppose an inspector would appreciate a well-turned villain."

Aberline smiled. "Indeed I do, sir. And I was delighted to have caught you as Hamlet. Let me just say that I'm sorry to hear of your troubles. I hope they won't impede your return to the stage."

"Thank you." Lawrence was listening to Aberline's tone as much as his words, and he noted the ever-so-slight stress on the words 'caught you.' A slip? A trick? In either case Lawrence felt himself retreat a pace mentally. For his part, Aberline appeared to be trying to read Lawrence's face. *Well,* he thought, *let him.* He knew that police were good at reading lies and half-truths, but Lawrence had nothing to hide and even if he had . . . his whole life was built around deliberate inflection, to conveying only what his interpretation of the script demanded and nothing more. Let the man look.

Aberline must have realized that Lawrence had caught him in his assessment and he covered it with a laugh. "Forgive me for staring. I really can't impress upon you how much I am moved by your melancholy Dane. Are you certain you are feeling well enough for a few words?"

"Yes," Lawrence said. "Tell me, have you caught the beast?"

This bold counter was intended to throw Aberline off his game, and Lawrence saw the inspector flicker for only the tiniest second.

"I'm afraid not," said Aberline.

"What have you accomplished?"

Aberline looked around the room. "Mr. Talbot, I would very much appreciate if we could speak candidly and confidentially." He gestured to the door to the hall. "In your portrait gallery perhaps? Just outside. Would you mind?"

"I damn well would," snapped Sir John.

Lawrence waved him off. "Father, if this will help then it's all right. I won't let him bully me." He said this with a smile but the look he gave Aberline was challenging. The inspector bowed.

LAWRENCE LEANED ON his walking stick even though he felt he no longer needed it. With every second the weakness was fading, but even so his instinct told him to play this role until the end of the act. Aberline offered his arm, but Lawrence declined with a gracious smile. As they entered the spacious portrait gallery the inspector closed the sitting room door and spent a moment or two staring up at the long rows of handsome Talbot men and women.

"I'm grateful that Scotland Yard has taken the case," said Lawrence.

Aberline smiled thinly. "A series of vicious murders tends to pique our interest," the inspector said dryly. "Mr. Talbot, I'm told you suffered a savage attack. I must say you seem quite well."

Lawrence saw the trap and had no intention of putting a foot in it. "I have been very fortunate."

"Indeed. Did you get a good look at your assailant?"

A thousand answers fanned out before Lawrence's mind like playing cards. Which to pick? He could deny the truth and construct a believable lie. He knew he could pull that off so easily because the truth was so unbelievable. A werewolf? Lawrence had barely allowed himself to think of that word let alone let the creature fill his mind. He could also play amnesia convincingly. He had relied on that over the last two days rather than tell his father and Gwen that a supernatural monster had killed Ben. His father had committed him to an asylum once—a story like that would have Sir John calling for the men with the straight waistcoats and the black carriage. No thanks.

Trauma was the easiest role to play, and since waking from his coma he had to give that version of the truth at least a nod because the story *was* so fantastic. Monsters belong in fairy stories and penny dreadfuls. Lawrence was only slightly more than half convinced that his memories were, in fact, memories and not the lingering ghosts of fevered dreams. The Gypsies' dancing bear could well have slashed him up and everything beyond that attack could be a sideshow of phantasms.

All of this flashed through Lawrence's mind in an instant.

"It was some sort of beast," he said flatly. "I . . . don't know what kind. It was dark."

Aberline frowned. "You're certain it was an animal?"

"Oh yes," said Lawrence. "A large one."

"Hmm. A great mystery it is, given that there are no natural predators on the moors capable of inflicting such horrific injuries." The inspector clasped his hands behind his back and pursed his mouth judiciously.

"There are no bears on the moors, either," said Lawrence, "and yet one travels with the Gypsies. It doesn't take a great deal of wit to imagine how almost any kind of animal could be here, Inspector."

"There have been no other reports—"

"There were other witnesses," Lawrence cut in. "No doubt they had as good a look as me. Better, perhaps. Did you ask the Gypsies?"

"They are a suspicious lot. They talk only of devils and demons," Aberline said. "What I wonder is, is it possible that in fact you were attacked by a man? The savagery of the attack would *suggest* the action of an animal . . . compounded by the darkness . . ."

"No." Lawrence's answer was flat and hard. "What attacked us that night was in no way a man."

"Not just any man. A lunatic perhaps? Someone with a history of mental disturbance, who had spent time in an asylum? And who may have suffered injuries at the hands of his own victims? . . ."

That hung in the air between them, and with sinking

horror Lawrence realized that Aberline had to know of his own incarceration in an asylum.

"What are you suggesting, Inspector?"

"I find it strange that all the murders, including your estranged brother's, occurred near your ancestral home. And while you were in England with your acting company."

Lawrence could feel the inference jab him in the stomach but he would be damned if he let it show on his face. Damn the arrogance of this fool.

"Inspector Aberline," he said with care, "you are clearly aware of my personal history, as I believe I am aware of yours."

"Oh?"

"Weren't you in charge of the Ripper case a couple of years back?"

Aberline's face became wooden. "Yes. A sorry business that."

"I should say. So . . . is this a demotion, or have you come all the way out here because you have something to prove?"

The inspector's face underwent a process of change. His air of affability dropped from his face like a discarded veil and the face Lawrence now saw was harder, humorless and devoid of compassion. "Very well. You are a direct man, so I will be equally direct with you. I'm not your enemy, Mr. Talbot. But I've seen your Hamlet, Macbeth, Richard the Third . . . all in that same face. When you step on stage you become a different person. Every movement, every personal tic, every aspect of your personality undergo a disturbingly genuine transformation. A prudent man would ask who else might be living inside that head of yours. I'm sure you understand."

"What I understand now," Lawrence said bitterly, "is

why you never caught the Ripper. I would have hoped for more from Scotland Yard. In America the Yard is legendary, but I suppose that's the nature of reviews. You can never trust them for accuracy."

He stood up and Aberline rose more slowly, his eyes as cold as a cobra's.

"But hear me on this, Aberline," said Lawrence. "My brother was killed by that thing. I was in London. I can act the part of other men, but I can't separate myself into separate bodies that can be in two places at one time."

"Yes. That does seem to be the case." Aberline did not appear to be defeated by Lawrence's reply. "So you won't mind if I establish your whereabouts during all of your performances in London . . . and since."

"You would be doing your own case a disservice," Lawrence said. "But considering how the Ripper case was mishandled I can infer that this is the way you like to proceed. While you're at it you might want to establish my whereabouts on September twenty-eight of this year. Perhaps Herman Melville's death was no accident. Could have been me. Oh, and I was in Toronto in early June when the Canadian Prime Minister died. Better check to make sure he hadn't been savaged by an actor."

"This is hardly the time for jokes, Mr. Talbot."

"No, it isn't . . . nor is it the time for absurd accusations. If you want people to believe that you are an inspector worthy of that title, then I would suggest that you devote your time looking for whatever *thing* committed these atrocities rather than squandering your resources by harassing the victims." Lawrence's voice had steadily risen to a shout and the gallery door opened sharply as Sir John stepped in looking fierce.

"That's enough of this nonsense," snarled the old

man. "My son has answered your questions and he's been too accommodating by half."

"Sir John, I—"

"Get out," said Sir John in a voice that brooked no discussion and no refusal.

Aberline bowed stiffly and left, with Singh dogging him all the way to the door.

Chapter Twenty-eight

Lawrence spent the rest of the afternoon in the portrait gallery. Singh brought him food, but he had no appetite. He pulled on a brocade dressing gown and slippers, secured his cane from the urn, and walked out into the garden, then took the path that led to the lake. The sun was high and bright and it sparkled like jewels on the gently rippling water. The refracted light was intense, hard to look at, but Lawrence stared at it for as long as he could bear, imagining on some deep level that there were answers there if he could only discern them.

"Lawrence!"

He turned to see Gwen Conliffe hurrying toward him down the path.

"I looked for you and couldn't find you," she said.

"Has something happened?"

"No," she said, and almost blushed. "I . . . just wanted to talk with you." She stopped near him, the sunlight turning the blue of her eyes to a crystal paleness. "What did Inspector Aberline have to say? You both seemed so angry."

Lawrence was a long time deciding how to answer her question. He turned and began walking along the edge of the lake and she took his arm and strolled with him. "He's of no help," he said.

She nodded, then said, "I'm sorry."

"Sorry? For what?"

Gwen shook his head. "I . . . can't help feeling responsible for what's happened to you. If I hadn't sent that letter . . ."

"No," he said firmly. "It was right that I came back."

They stopped by a stand of bulrushes. Lawrence leaned his cane against a shrub, bent to pick up a stone, hefted it for a moment, and then skipped it across the lake. It caught the tips of half a dozen wavelets before sinking. He smiled and bent for a handful of stones, making thoughtful selections.

"So," Gwen said, "tell me about New York. I've often imagined what it's like."

He handed her a stone and watched her throw. It sank as soon as it hit the water.

"You must come and visit me there someday and see for yourself."

He gave her another rock.

"Anything is possible," she said and threw the stone. This time it hit, skipped, hit and skittered deep into the lake.

Lawrence began to laugh, then froze, his head cocked to listen. He turned and scanned the fields, the paths, the forest.

"Did you hear that?" he said.

"Hear what?"

He held up a finger and strained to hear, and there it was. Horses on the road. Still miles away, but coming toward the Hall. It was a wonder he'd heard them at all.

"Go tell my father we have company," he said as he bent to retrieve his sword cane.

"What's happening?"

"Go now," Lawrence urged.

She hesitated for just a moment, then hurried off.

CHAPTER TWENTY-NINE

Lawrence walked along the path that circled the house and entered the front yard just as a line of men on horses cantered up to the front steps. The riders saw him and their faces hardened and they angled their horses toward him. Fear bit into Lawrence as he saw the angry determination written on the features of each man. He recognized some of them. Pastor Fisk was at the front, leading the others in a grim congregation; Squire Strickland was on his left flank and Colonel Montford on his right. Dr. Lloyd, looking nervous and ashamed, hung to the back of the group. The rest of the men were strangers, but Lawrence knew that he had no friends here. He stopped and his fingers traced the silver collar of the walking stick. If this got nasty he could at least draw the rapier within. The sight of the blade might bring these fools to their senses.

Or it might encourage them to shoot him down.

"Hello, Doctor," Lawrence said, forcing faux good humor into his voice. "I thought my checkup wasn't till Friday."

Squire Strickland gave Lawrence a haughty look. "Come with us, Talbot."

Lawrence smiled. "Where are we going?"

Strickland began to speak but Pastor Fisk blurted, "It's nearly the full moon!"

"Yes," Lawrence drawled. "And what of it?"

The vicar pointed an accusing finger at him. "You were bitten by the beast. Don't deny it! You bear his mark now."

Lawrence burst out laughing. He couldn't help it. Of all the stupid rural foolishness he had ever heard, this was the most absurd. Even if he could believe his own memories that it had been a monster that had attacked him, it was the height of nonsense to think that *he* was a damned creature. He'd fought the creature, chased it, nearly been killed by it. But these men must have believed the vicar's nonsense. At least a few had the good sense to look embarrassed to be here. Dr. Lloyd looked thoroughly ashamed and he could not meet Lawrence's eye.

But Colonel Montford pitched his voice above the laughter.

"Come, Talbot . . . show us your wound."

"What for?"

"Because," fired back Pastor Fisk, his face alight with righteous anger, "we are told that it heals in an unnatural way."

Lawrence looked at Dr. Lloyd, who lowered his head to study the grain of his saddle horn.

Montford nudged his horse with his knee, urging it forward to crowd and intimidate Lawrence. The horse was a heavy-shouldered brute that stood at least three hands taller than the others, but when it was four feet from Lawrence the horse suddenly whinnied and shied back, shaking its big head side to side despite Montford's strong hand on the taut reins.

The moment seemed to freeze around Lawrence. The horse had been spooked, but by *what*? He half smiled. It almost seemed as if the horse had been frightened by Lawrence . . . but that was absurd.

None of the riders were smiling, and even Dr. Lloyd was attentive now. Every eye was on Lawrence. Montford nodded darkly and snapped his fingers. Three bull-shouldered men slid from their saddles and closed on Lawrence. The moment was so bizarre that by the time Lawrence realized what they were actually preparing to do he had lost his advantage. The cane was torn from his grasp before he could twist the handle to release the sword, and rough hands grabbed his arms.

"Let go of me, you bastards!" He struggled as hard as he could, but these men were brutes, their hands like iron.

"Open his shirt," ordered Montford.

Panic flared in Lawrence as the men began pawing at the folds of his robe and the sleeping shirt beneath. He yelled and kicked at them, trying to break free.

"You see?" demanded Pastor Fisk. "He tries to conceal it!"

Lawrence kneed one man in the crotch, but one of the others cuffed him above the ear and another punched him in the mouth. Lawrence's lip burst against his teeth and hot blood poured over his chin as iron fingers tore at his clothing.

"He will turn with the moon," shrieked Fisk, completely caught up in the passion of his belief. "Will you let him murder your wives and children?"

"Hold him, dammit," Montford growled as he slid smoothly from the saddle. He snatched the rope from one of the mounted riders and handed it to the men holding Lawrence. They immediately began looping it around him.

There was a deafening blast and the head of a garden statue exploded, showering Montford with jagged marble shards. The colonel reeled back, clutching the side of his face as bright blood ran freely from between his fingers. His eyes bled tears of blood from the stinging stone dust.

Everyone turned to see Sir John Talbot walking across the lawn. He looked composed, even calm as he broke open his big elephant gun and thumbed in a fresh cartridge. The rifle closed with a solid *thunk* and Sir John aimed the heavy weapon from the hip.

Montford stared at him in rage and disbelief, his face a mask of blood. "Talbot—damn you . . . *my eyes!*"

The other men began reaching for their weapons, but Sir John brought his rifle up to his shoulder.

"Sorry, Colonel," Sir John said with a small genial smile. "It was your brainpan I was aiming for. He pointed his rifle past Montford at Strickland, who was white-faced with shock. "Seems I'm not the marksman I used to be."

Lawrence was the first to recover from the shock and he tried to pull away from the men, but they held fast. Dr. Lloyd scrambled down from his horse and hurried toward Montford, who was bleeding badly.

"Leave him," snapped Sir John in a voice that brooked no argument. Dr. Lloyd stopped in his tracks. "Untie my son."

"He's cursed," said Pastor Fisk with such fervor that spit flecked his chin. "God has forsaken him."

Sir John sneered. "Well he can join the club then, can't he?"

"You know what he means," growled Strickland. "John . . . I know this is hard for you, but let us deal with him."

"Perhaps I am being unclear," said Sir John softly. "Untie my son or I'll kill you."

"You can't be serious," Strickland said. "You have two bullets. We have—"

"My Sikh manservant is on the roof above us, and you well know that he's a crack shot with a Martini-Henry. He'll kill the next five of you before he has to reload."

The lynch mob looked up at the sprawling mansion. They saw nothing but even the densest of them could tell that there were a dozen places a sniper could hide. They looked to Strickland, who in turned looked to Fisk. The vicar licked his lips as he weighed the moment in his mind. He gave the men a single curt nod.

It was Dr. Lloyd who finally stepped forward, removed the ropes, and gave Lawrence a weak conciliatory smile. Lawrence wanted to knock his teeth down his throat, but he was afraid that if he started hitting the fool he wouldn't be able to stop. Rage had become a feral thing in his chest and his knotted fists trembled with the desire to kill every single man among them. He kept his mouth clamped shut for fear that anything he would say would be a roar of uncontrollable fury.

Sir John walked over to Montford and studied the colonel's gory face. He smiled.

"Now get off my land," he said quietly. "And the next time any of you trespass this way I won't be so civil."

With that Sir John lowered his rifle and took Lawrence by the arm to help him. Gwen Conliffe came running from the house and took Lawrence's other arm. None of them looked back at the mob, but before they had even closed the garden doors there was the sound of hooves on the road.

INSIDE, GWEN AND Sir John helped Lawrence into a chair. In truth the encounter and struggle had taken a lot out of him, far more than he thought, and as the anger wore off it left him spent and weak, and the trembling in his limbs did not abate when he unclenched his hands.

Once Lawrence was in the chair, Sir John called for Samson and the massive wolfhound came bounding down the stairs. Sir John opened the door and made a clicking sound with his tongue. The hound snarled and raced outside to harass the lynch mob. Lawrence could hear his deep-chested bray even after Sir John had closed and barred the doors.

"Should we get Singh?" Gwen asked.

Sir John shrugged. "Can't. He's in town with the blacksmith."

Gwen stared slack-jawed at him, but Lawrence burst out laughing. He had never admired his father more than he did at that moment. Sir John chuckled, clearly pleased at his son's delight.

"Guess you're not the only one in the family who can act," he said.

"Bravo, sir," Lawrence said between horselaughs, "Bravo!"

Gwen knelt by Lawrence and as his laughter abated she pressed him back onto the settee and used a handkerchief to sponge away the blood from his torn lip. Lawrence recoiled at first, but her touch was gentle and soothing and there was a look in her eyes that was as unnerving as it was wonderful.

"I don't understand how they could think it possible that you are a threat to them," Gwen said.

"I'm not," said Lawrence.

"He's a stranger, Miss Conliffe," observed Sir John. He had his back to her and his son and neither could see how cold his eyes had become after he had seen the look Gwen had in her eyes as she tended to Lawrence, and the look in his son's eyes when he noticed it. He kept his tone light, but his face had become stone. "He's a stranger, and that suffices in Blackmoor."

With that he left the room and closed the door behind him. If it was a little too hard, neither Gwen nor Lawrence took particular notice.

Chapter Thirty

Evening fell softly over Talbot Hall. The mob from the town did not return, and Sir John predicted that they would not.

"How can you be sure?" asked Gwen.

Sir John smiled thinly. "They were led by a fool on a fool's errand, and things ended badly for them. Most of them probably went along because they were drunk—no doubt Strickland or that idiot Montford plied them with ale before leading the charge out here. Once they've sobered up I believe they'll realize how foolish their crusade was, and how absurd Fisk's argument is."

"You make it sound like this is something you've seen before," observed Lawrence.

"I've met a legion of fools over the years," said Sir John. "In the end they're just like bullies. Scratch the gruff exterior and you find cowards."

"But they could have killed Lawrence," insisted Gwen. "The rope—"

"Well, it didn't happen, did it?" said Sir John. His eyes were cold. "We've wasted enough of the day on this. Let it be."

"Father . . . ," began Lawrence.

Sir John had begun to mount the steps, but he turned and looked down at his son. "What is it?"

"Thank you. For today."

Sir John looked at Lawrence for a long moment, then without a comment he turned and mounted the stairs.

AFTER THEY HEARD his door close upstairs, Gwen touched Lawrence's arm. "Lawrence . . . may I ask a favor of you?"

Her face was soft and open, her eyes searching his.

"I owe you so much," he said. "You may ask me anything. Is this about Ben?"

"No. I . . . when you are up to it, when you're more healed and rested . . . would you tell me about what happened between you and your father? Ben didn't tell me much. Just some vague references to what happened after your mother . . ."

"After my mother killed herself?" Lawrence said bitterly.

"Yes."

"What do you want to know?" he asked. "And, why?"

"Because I want to understand."

"Understand what? Why our family disintegrated? Why my father and I can barely maintain a civil conversation longer than a few sentences? Why Ben and I barely wrote and never knew each other as adults? What is it you want to know?"

His voice was quiet but harsh, yet Gwen did not flinch away from it. Instead she stepped closer, placing her hands on his chest.

"I want to understand you, Lawrence," she said, and then flushed a deep scarlet. "Your lip is still bleeding," she said hastily as she removed her jacket and folded it too neatly. She picked up the basin, wrung out the cloth and dabbed at his lip.

Lawrence allowed her to fuss without comment. In truth he was feeling odd. He was sweating and his pulse was racing. He pawed the moisture from his forehead.

Gwen bent close to examine the wound. Lawrence could smell her perfume. And her skin. The scent of her was so lovely, so compelling that he could almost taste it. More sweat beaded his face.

"That doesn't seem so bad," she said. "The bleeding has almost stopped. I think you'll live . . ."

She said more but Lawrence was having trouble concentrating on her words. All of a sudden they had become noise without meaning, while everything else about her became so incredibly clear. He saw her pupils dilate, the blush on her cheeks fade; he could hear each of her breaths as if her mouth were an inch from his ear. He could hear and separate the rustle of every bit of cloth that covered her body. It came at him in a rush, maddening, overwhelming.

". . . this might sting . . ."

She blotted some phenol from a small bottle and pressed it to his lip—

And then with incredible speed he caught her wrist, his hand moving like a blur. He felt her skin within his hand, felt the softness of the flesh, the fragility of the bones, felt the sudden jump in the rapidity of her pulse.

Her eyes met his and the moment slammed to a stop, frozen in an impossibility of sensory inrush. He looked into her eyes and for a moment he felt as if he was falling forward and she toward him. Colliding with her, engulfing her, devouring her . . .

With a gasp Lawrence released her hand and staggered up from the settee. He backed away from her, breaking the contact, gasping for air.

"Lawrence?" she said, leaping to her feet. Her face was flushed, the exposed skin of chest above the swell of her breasts was as red as fire. "Is something wrong?"

It was an absurd question, and Lawrence almost laughed, but he knew that if he did he might never stop. He could feel the screams and shouts of insanity jabbering inside his skull. He felt other things, too. Hungers of all kinds, the need to satisfy appetites that he did not know he possessed.

"Excuse me," he said in a choked voice. He waved her back and staggered out of the room, searching for air, needing to be away from the moment. Needing not to feel those appetites as he looked at her.

Needing.

Needing.

Chapter Thirty-one

Once he was upstairs he felt calmer, though by no means calm. The sense of urgency, of panic, of *hunger*, seemed to have diminished. Like a fire that has been banked but not extinguished. He walked through the cold and drafty corridors of the second floor, peering into empty rooms, looking for something that he could not name, while at the same time knowing that what he sought was not here.

Suddenly he heard something. A deep-chested grunt, a soft footfall with the thin sound of nails scraping on floorboards. Lawrence crouched and turned. Whatever it was—the thing was just around the next turning. The sword cane was downstairs. He had only his fists to fight—

A hulking shape rounded the corner, moving through shadows toward him. Yellow eyes burned in the darkness.

Then the thing moved from shadows into a spill of candlelight.

Samson.

The monstrous wolfhound padded toward him. Lawrence shrank back from Samson as the dog approached.

The moment their eyes met, the dog froze in place. So did Lawrence. The awareness of each other was immediate and deep and *different*.

This was not the open hostility of their first meeting weeks ago, nor was it the guarded dislike they'd shared since. Samson always positioned himself between Lawrence and Sir John, occasionally baring his teeth or growling quietly until Sir John cowed him with a sharp word. Now, however, the dog stared with penetrating interest into Lawrence's eyes, and Lawrence met and matched that stare, sharing a moment of awareness that was unlike anything he could remember having with another human or beast. It was as if communication flowed back and forth between them on some primal level too far below the conscious mind's ability to eavesdrop.

Lawrence saw the muscles begin to tense all along the dog's shoulders and he felt his own muscles growing taut in response.

Then Samson flopped onto the ground and rolled onto his back like a puppy. Tail wagging, tongue lolling, belly completely exposed. The brute of a dog whined and wriggled right at Lawrence's feet.

Lawrence was stunned.

Not just because the action was so unexpected . . . but because on some level of awareness, he *understood it.* Not with his rational mind, but instinctively. This was right. And it was so very, very wrong.

That frightened him more than anything that had happened today. It frightened him more than mobs and guns and a hangman's noose.

He backed away, and then he turned and fled.

LAWRENCE DID NOT know what to do or where to go. He could not discuss things with his father, and to mention his fears to Gwen would surely result in her fleeing the house. Especially after the last moment they'd shared.

He felt terribly alone. . . .

And then he realized that there was someone whom he trusted and who could be counted on for a cool head and a closed mouth. He hurried down the darkened corridors, seeking some splinter of refuge.

LAWRENCE STOOD IN the open doorway to Singh's quarters for a long few minutes until Singh became aware of him and looked up with a start.

"You should be asleep, Lawrence."

"So should you."

He stepped into the room, which was like stepping through a hole in the world. On one side of the doorway it was Northumbria, on the other it was a Moghul palace. The large sitting room was lit only by a few candles and the air scented by rich incense. Beautiful and ornate carpets were hung on the walls, many of them depicting battles of great historical significance. There were swords and spears mounted on the wall as well, but the entire room was not a shrine to combat. Interspersed with the weapons were beautiful pieces of artwork from various eras of Indian culture. In the center of the room was a low brass table surrounded by dozens of brightly colored brocade cushions.

"Is there anything I can get for you? You look . . . worn."

"Tea?" Lawrence asked hopefully. "And a place to be."

Singh brewed tea for both of them while Lawrence sank to the carpeted floor and leaned comfortably on a pile of pillows. The incense and the familiar room were tonics to his nerves and he could feel the dreadful tension leaking away. Singh handed him a steaming cup. Lawrence nodded his thanks and sipped the tea. Hot and sweet, flavored with lemon and peppermint. Lawrence gestured with his cup to the heavy *kirpan* knife thrust through the Sikh's sash.

"Still the same knife. You've carried it since I can remember."

Singh nodded soberly. "Of course. Since Guru Gobind Singh, the tenth Guru of Sikhism, decreed it be so, every baptized Sikh wears the *kirpan*."

Lawrence looked around and saw rifles and pistols laid out for cleaning, and several knives arranged neatly by a whetstone.

"Are you expecting a war?"

"A Sikh is a soldier of God. As long as evil exists in the world we are technically at war, and we must always be armed against evil." He touched the hilt of the sacred dagger he wore. "But this is not a weapon of attack. The *kirpan* is a defensive weapon that embodies *ahimsa* or nonviolence. It is our way to prevent violence, not to simply stand by idly while violence is being done. This cannot be done without the right tools." He drew the blade and turned it so that it caught the fire from the many candles that surrounded them.

"It's silver."

Singh ran his thumb along the ornate sheath. "Yes," he said. "It is." He smiled grimly. "I am a *Khalsa* Sikh, which translates badly as a Saint-Soldier. And, no . . . I don't have magical powers, but my faith makes me strong and my dedication to God keeps me focused in my fight against evil. We are always vigilant because evil abounds."

"And yet you haven't gone hunting for the thing that killed Ben."

Singh shook his head. "Under no circumstance is a Sikh allowed to use force in aggression. This is part of our faith, and sometimes I struggle with that limitation for I, like all men, am a weak human tempted to sin. Vengeance would be too dangerous a path."

Lawrence sipped his tea. The large tapestry behind Singh depicted complex scenes from the Upanishads. It looked to be from the same weavers who made the one that hung between the double staircases.

"Do you believe in curses?" Lawrence asked.

Singh smiled sadly. "This house has had its fair share of sorrow. Your mother. Your brother . . . Yes, Lawrence. I believe in curses."

"How could you stand it here all these years? You didn't have to stay."

The Sikh refilled his cup. "Sir John isn't an easy man. But he is righteous. He is not what people think he is."

That provoked a grunt from Lawrence. "I don't know what anyone is anymore."

"This house, this place . . . mysteries are built into the brick and mortar."

Lawrence said nothing for a time, working things through. Finally he said, "Singh . . . I know what I saw that night."

"Yes."

"What I saw was not a man. And it wasn't an animal. Not an 'animal' in the way a sane man would use that word. Do you understand?"

Instead of answering Singh reached inside his shirt and drew out a key on a leather thong. He held it in his fingers for Lawrence to see.

"This will tell you what I understand."

With that he rose and crossed the room to an ornate

traveling chest and unlocked the bottom drawer. He pulled the drawer out and carried it back to the table. There, fitted into cushioned slots, were dozens of bullets of different calibers and sizes. The metal was brighter and paler than lead.

Lawrence felt as if the room was becoming unhinged from the world.

"Silver bullets? I didn't know you and father hunted monsters." He reached out and closed the lid.

"We didn't," said Singh. "But it is a sad truth that sometimes the monsters hunt you."

Lawrence walked away from him and stopped by the ornate mirror that covered one wall. His reflection looked worn and wild and not at all like the man who had stepped onto the London stage a few weeks ago. The deep sadness he saw in his own eyes nearly broke him.

He said, "I'm cursed, aren't I?"

When Singh took too long to answer, Lawrence turned and walked to the door and out into the cold shadows of the hall.

CHAPTER THIRTY-TWO

The mirror in his room was no kinder than the one in Singh's quarters, but Lawrence stood before it, shirtless, barefoot, hair wild, fists clenched at his sides. He looked into his reflected eyes, rarely blinking, and it seemed to him that he could see through those eyes, that they were windows instead of mirrored reflections. Beyond those windows was the barren landscape of some alien world. Nothing there was natural, nothing was suited to the needs or desires of the human experience. It was foreign territory across which dark shapes hunted and howled.

"God," Lawrence said softly, his voice weak and desperate.

With slow, trembling fingers he undid the knots on the bandages, unwound them turn upon turn. The white cotton coiled around his ankles like pale snakes.

As the last of the gauze fell silently to the floor, Lawrence stared at his shoulder, at the evidence of the savage attack.

And saw nothing.

No scabbing, no faint lines of healed scars, no pucker of missing muscle. There was no mark of any kind to show that he had ever been attacked.

Lawrence stared with naked accusation into his own eyes. Or were they still his eyes? Had the color changed?

Paled? Were there now hints of yellow there? Splinters of red?

"No!" he snarled and suddenly smashed his fist into the mirror, which exploded into a thousand shards.

"God save my soul . . ." he breathed.

But he feared that his plea to a forgotten deity and the renewal of his own discarded faith had come far too late. He stared down at the mirror fragments scattered around him on the floor. Each one seemed to reflect its own perverse distortion of him. One image was Lawrence the boy, lying in his mother's arms. Another was the boy in bondage in the asylum, his mouth opened to scream at the night—just as he had every night for years. Another fragment was the boy aboard ship to America, discarded, sent away by a father who could no longer bear to look at him. Another was the predator man he had become, striding the world's stages, sliding in and out of beds, descending into opium dreams in a vain attempt to replace nightmares with drugged hallucinations.

And one fragment, a sliver no wider than a knife blade and equally as sharp, lay on the floor between his bare feet and when Lawrence looked down at his reflection he did not see a man, or a boy. He saw the snarling face of a monster.

Lawrence closed his eyes and beat the sides of his temples with his fists. "Please," he begged. "Please . . ."

But all that answered him was the dark.

In the sky above the Hall the Goddess of the Hunt was rising in all her wicked white splendor.

Chapter Thirty-three

Lawrence pounded furiously on the door to Ben's old room. When there was no immediate response he knocked again and again until Gwen opened it a handsbreadth, her hair disheveled, eyes puffy from sleep, her nightclothes pulled around her. She held a brass candleholder and a match still smoked in the tray.

"What's wrong?" she asked.

Lawrence pushed the door wider and stepped halfway into the room.

"Gwen, listen to me," he said in a voice that was breathless with urgency. "You have to leave. Now. Right away. Grab only what you must take with you and return to London."

"Leave?" She half-smiled, as if expecting this to be some kind of prank, but that smile faded at once. "It's the middle of the night, Lawrence."

"I've sent for a coach. It will take you straight to the train station and the driver will wait until the train arrives."

"What is this?"

"It's not safe here. Please!"

She raised the candle and the expression cut into his features made her gasp. "Lawrence . . . what has happened? Have the villagers returned to—"

He shook his head and dug into his pocket for

something that flashed silver in the candlelight. He pressed it into her hand.

Gwen stared at it, her mouth open to form a perfect "O" of surprise.

"Ben's medal. . . ."

"You must wear it," Lawrence insisted. "You must wear it *now*. Around your neck."

"But, Lawrence, how did you get this?"

"You must wear it at all times. Promise me!"

She took the medal but did not put it on. Instead she reached out her hand and touched his chest, the medal swinging from between her fingers to brush his shirt right above his heart. Her blue eyes, even in the weak light of the single candle, were as bright as hope and promise, and as beautiful as all of the spring mornings in the world. Lawrence looked into those eyes and he could feel his self-control fracture like a diamond that a jeweler had struck the wrong way. Her fingers were warm where she touched him, and in the cold autumn of Lawrence's heart the weeds were withering as something fresh and wonderful struggled to bloom.

He closed his eyes and prayed to God that this moment, this feeling, could be real, could be true, and that it could chase away all of the shadows in his soul. His heart hurt worse than if he had been stabbed.

"Lawrence," she said very softly, "if there is something you need to say . . ."

"Is there something you need to say to me?"

In the darkness inside his mind he felt something stir. Something that was not love, not passion. Something ancient and dreadful and hungry. The thing in his mind whispered to him.

Take her! Smell her flesh . . . smell her blood! Take her now.

"No!" he said and staggered back from their point of contact, forcing his hands to close into fists. Not as weapons, but to keep his fingers from reaching for her. He took a step toward her and she involuntarily stepped back. She hadn't meant to do it, but the reflex was too fast for her to control. If she had slapped him it could not have hurt more deeply. Yet it was very correct, very safe, and in a strange way it steadied him.

"Gwen . . . if anything ever happened to you," he began, his voice thick with emotion. "I'd never forgive myself. Never."

Those words should have made her take another defensive step away, but Gwen looked up into his eyes, her brows knitting with concern. "Lawrence . . . what are you afraid of?"

He backed away one pace, then another.

"Please get dressed," he said. "You must return to London tonight."

He dared not say anything else, dared not *do* anything more. He whirled and stalked down the hallway toward the stairs.

FIFTEEN MINUTES LATER she came downstairs with her bag. Lawrence fairly snatched it from her and caught her wrist with the other hand and pulled her out the door and down the steps to where a coach was waiting. Several times Gwen tried to make eye contact with Lawrence. She could feel the heat of whatever passion drove him to such actions, but he would not meet her gaze.

The driver hopped down, placed her bag inside, and stood by the open carriage door.

Gwen wheeled around and forced Lawrence to look at her. His eyes were fever bright.

"I don't want to go, Lawrence."

She said it softly, without challenge. A plea . . . and the tone drained some of the madness out of Lawrence's eyes, leaving only sadness.

"You *must* go," he said softly. "Please . . . you must go now, Gwen."

"I—"

He turned away, his head low between hunched shoulders. "Pray for us."

Gwen reached out a hand, almost touching him.

"Everything will be alright, Lawrence," she said.

Lawrence whirled on her and Gwen gasped. He seemed larger, broader, a towering figure against the white façade of Talbot Hall. The wind whipped his dark hair and the open folds of his half-buttoned shirt. His eyes smoldered with hungers that touched secret places in her body and soul. She *felt* him as if he was somehow inside her every nerve, as if his breath whispered secrets against her secret flesh.

"Go!" he snarled, and he shoved her into the coach, his hands too strong to resist. He slammed the door and then leaned toward the driver so fiercely that the man backed away until his back thumbed into the corner of the carriage. Lawrence dug a heavy coin out of his pocket and slapped it into the driver's hand.

"Take this. Don't let her out of your sight until the train disappears. Do you *hear* me?"

"Yes!" the driver quailed.

Gwen leaned out of the window and called Lawrence's name, but Lawrence turned his back on her.

CHAPTER THIRTY-FOUR

Darkness had come to the village of Blackmoor long before the setting of the sun. For a month now the people had lived and worked and moved in a state somewhere between grief and dread. Everyone felt it; no one escaped the gloom and the anxiety.

Inspector Aberline, though a stranger to this region, was sharp enough to see that the current mood was not the usual atmosphere of the town, but something new. It had begun on the night that Ben Talbot and two other men had been murdered, and since the massacre at the gypsy camp the town was as dismal and sick as if the Black Plague had returned. No one smiled. Children did not play in the streets. No one walked unaccompanied, and every man above the age of ten carried a weapon of some kind, be it an axe, pitchfork or firearm.

Aberline walked the town, taking its measure, and with every step he felt his own mood darken.

He passed a house where a father and his two half-grown daughters worked with reckless haste to nail boards across their windows. Aberline paused to look down the row and he saw that every house was either shuttered or boarded.

He stopped into the big church and stood for several minutes in the back, listening as Pastor Fisk hurled fire and brimstone from the pulpit. It was a Tuesday evening and there was no saint's feast day that he knew of, but most of the pews were filled.

"There are those who doubt the power of Satan!" Fisk's voice was hushed and threatening. "The power of Satan to change men into beasts. Yet the ancient pagans did not doubt. Nor did the prophets."

Blimey, thought Aberline, *he's barking mad*.

"Did not Daniel warn Nebuchadnezzar that Pride goeth before destruction? A haughty spirit before the fall?"

The parishioners murmured agreement.

"But the proud king did not heed Daniel, and so, as the Bible says, he was made unto a wolf and cast out from men." He paused and his face was alight with holy purpose. "A beast has come among us."

LAWRENCE WAS GLAD Gwen was gone, though it broke his heart to have been so rude to her and to see that hurt in her blue eyes. However, he knew that on this dreadful night, hurt was the kindest thing he could offer her.

After the carriage had clattered away down the road, Lawrence turned and began walking. Not toward the house, but down the garden path that led to the woods. He needed to think things through, to decide how to act, and the house was too claustrophobic. He needed to be out in the wind.

His footsteps carried him down through the first patch of woods and to the rocky shelf that looked out over the gorge. Even in the failing light the vista was beautiful. The sun was swollen to an unnatural size and as it fell behind the distant line of trees it seemed as if the whole world was ablaze.

Lawrence watched the sun fall, dreading it and all that it meant. He turned away from it and continued walking toward the dense black shadows under the trees. Back to the Hall.

ON THE OTHER side of the ancient forest that edged the Talbot lands stood the crumbling and vine-shrouded ruins of an old abbey. Only parts of the thick walls still stood and trees grew between the cracked and displaced flagstones. Colonel Montford stood with Dr. Lloyd, heavy-bore hunting rifles cradled over their arms, their faces grim and set. Montford's face was crisscrossed with sticking plasters and discolored by bruises; the doctor's face was flushed with fear and hypertension. A few yards away MacQueen and a pair of stout lads from the squire's estate worked to position a sturdy stake and pound it deep into a cleft between two of the broken flagstones. MacQueen gripped the shaft and gave it a shake to assure himself that it was solidly placed.

He nodded to Montford and Lloyd. "This'll do 'er fine." Then he crooked a finger to the squire's men, who went to a wagon where a stag was tied. They loosened the tether and led the animal to the post, and Mac-Queen knelt and tied it firmly in place. MacQueen produced a knife from his belt, and with a deft flick of the wrist he opened a long but shallow cut on the stag's flank. The animal screamed and bucked as hot blood flowed down its side.

MacQueen wiped his knife clean on his trousers and stalked over to Montford. "The breeze will carry that scent for miles."

Dr. Lloyd mopped his face with a cloth. "Shouldn't we get back to town?"

Colonel Montford and MacQueen looked into the sky. The full moon was nearly over the horizon.

"Get indoors if ye want to," muttered MacQueen. He unslung the hunting rifle and checked that it was loaded. "I'll go home when this bastard's dead."

WHEN LAWRENCE ENTERED the foyer his father stepped out of the Great Hall, his face dark with fury. "What have you done?" Sir John demanded. "Miss Conliffe has left Blackmoor. Explain yourself."

Lawrence did not bother to ask how his father knew of this. He could not manage a single new complication.

"This place is cursed, Father," he said weakly. "I sent her away. She's back in London by now."

His father went very still and his eyes were hard as fists.

"You're a fool," hissed Sir John as he briskly pushed past Lawrence and vanished into the empty heart of the Hall.

PASTOR FISK WAS warming to his rant, his voice rising to a bellow of righteous fury. "But God will defend His faithful. With His right hand, He will smite the foul demon!"

The congregation said nothing, but everyone was bent forward, hanging on the vicar's every word.

"I say to you, the Enemy's ploy is a devious one. Twisting the accursed into beasts, he seeks to bring us low. Make us as animals. Teach us self-loathing, so we forget that we are made in the image of Almighty God!"

That brought murmurs of angry protest from the crowd.

"You ask me, brothers and sisters, why does God tolerate this mockery?" Fisk stared around at his flock and beat upon the pulpit with his fist. "Because we have sinned against Him! Because our crimes reek to Heaven. And our sins demand vengeance."

As another pair of congregants entered the church, Aberline slipped outside. He was not a churchgoing man. He had some faith, but it was rusty from disuse, and even as an idealistic lad he had never had much use for all the talk about hell and damnation. Aberline placed a much higher stock in crime and punishment, and in the growing police practice of scientific investigation. Evidence and analysis. The devil, he mused, was truly in the details.

He walked past the blacksmith's shop, surprised to see it open for trade this late. A small crowd of villagers were gathered in the doorway and Aberline joined them, looking over the heads of a pair of boys to where the blacksmith's assistants were taking silver plates and bowls and spoons and dropping them into a big iron pot that was so hot the metal began melting at once. Another assistant scooped the melted metal out with a stone ladle and poured it into a set of heavy molds. Aberline frowned and shifted so he could see what the blacksmith himself was doing at the far end of this production line. The big metalworker, wearing only trousers and a leather apron in the inferno heat of the workshop, held an old-fashioned bullet mold in his big hands. As Aberline watched, the blacksmith dumped a batch of bullets into a bucket of water and then scooped them out with a ladle before handing them to another assistant who checked them for burrs and smoothed their edges and finally stacked them with the dozens of others that had already been cast.

Aberline shook his head. Beyond the blacksmith were several bullet molds that had been discarded, and he had little wonder. Silver had a much higher melting point than lead and it probably ruined the molds after only a few castings. This nonsense was costing the blacksmith a lot of money and very likely going to result in him having a shop filled with useless junk instead of instruments of his craft. And yet . . . these people were all here with their precious silver—family heirlooms, wedding dowries, keepsakes—all to acquire bullets for something that didn't exist.

He hid a smile as he turned away and continued his stroll through the town. It was all madness. But maybe amid the madness some truth would be revealed, and then he would make his move.

He lit a cigar and kept his eyes and ears open.

TWICE LAWRENCE TRIED to go back to bed, to lose himself in sleep. Each time he was out of bed within a few minutes, pacing his room with nervous energy, sometimes muttering to himself. Fear was a clawing thing that tore at the walls of his chest.

He thought about the box of bullets Singh had shown him. Should he go there, ask for some cartridges?

Maybe, he thought, *but why? Defense or escape?*

He still did not know which option was his to take. Maybe it would be better if Colonel Montford and his lackeys succeeded in their murderous plans. It might be the best way for this madness to end.

He stood in the emptiness of his room and tried to decide what to do. He wished he had an opium pipe. Losing himself in the velvet dreams would help, but the last train to London had already passed through town, taking Gwen Conliffe with it.

Whiskey, he thought. A lot of whiskey might do the trick, and so he hurried downstairs to the Great Hall, filled a tumbler to the brim with his father's scotch and gulped half of it down. He choked and coughed, but the warm burn inside his chest felt good. He took a second gulp, and a third, then refilled his glass and went back to his room, but as he entered he heard voices. Outside. He crept to his window and peered out. Below, half hidden in the shadows of the garden, he saw his father and Singh. Sir John was uncharacteristically ruffled, his face haggard and distressed. He held a shielded lantern in one hand. The big Sikh looked frightened, and he stood with his right hand resting on the hilt of his silver *kirpan*.

"Please," urged Singh, "you must let me help him."

"He doesn't need your help," snapped Sir John. "Give me the keys, Singh."

"No, Sir John—"

Sir John set the lantern down and as fast as a snake grabbed Singh's left wrist and pried something from between his fingers. Even from that far above Lawrence could hear the dull metal clank of keys. Sir John stepped back, snatched up his lantern, and pointed a warning finger at Singh.

"Don't follow me," he ordered harshly.

ABERLINE LEFT THE dismal streets of Blackmoor and stepped into the tavern for a wet. He shrugged out of his coat and hung it near the door, loosened his tie, and was about to call for the barman when he realized

187

that the entire establishment had gone quiet. He turned. Every eye in the place was on him, and in every eye there was suspicion and fear.

Bloody superstitious fools, he thought and hung his hat next to his coat. He saw a young man—Cramer, the bar-back—coming toward him, but Aberline sank into a seat and unfolded the London paper. He was already engrossed in the paper when someone stopped in front of his table.

"Pint of bitters, please. And if you have any steak and kidney pie I—" He stopped talking as he glanced up and saw that it was not Cramer but rather the publican's wife, Mrs. Kirk, who stood there, fists on hips, her face harsh with disapproval.

"Good evening, Mrs. Kirk," said Aberline.

"Why aren't you out with MacQueen trying to catch that thing what killed my husband?"

Aberline leaned back in his seat and appraised the widow. When he spoke he pitched his voice loud enough for the other patrons of the tavern to hear what he had to say. "Seeing as I don't know where the lunatic will strike, it seems the most practical thing to do is stay as near as possible to the potential victims. And seeing that two hundred and fourteen of the three hundred and eleven residents of Blackmoor live within five hundred yards of this tavern, I was planning to spend the evening here."

He glanced around and every face was a study in doubt and fear. Only Mrs. Kirk held her ground and kept her scowl in place.

"Here? Not Talbot Hall?"

Aberline studied her. "Interesting. Why would you say that?"

"They're cursed," said Mrs. Kirk. "All of them."

Around the room, other people nodded or grunted agreement with the widow's statement. Aberline managed to keep a smile off his face.

"'Cursed.' Yes, well, unfortunately 'cursed' does not get me a bench warrant to wander around Sir John's estate at night. Rules, rules, rules." He leaned forward and put a spooky tone in his voice. "It's all that keeps us from a dog-eat-dog world, you know."

Even Mrs. Kirk had no answer to that. The people in the tavern leaned their heads together and murmured. A few knocked wood and fingered crosses strung around their necks on silver chains.

Rustic buffoons, Aberline thought. Aloud he said, "And now, Missus . . . a pint of bitters, please."

OUTSIDE THE MOON rose into the sky with regal grace and the inevitability of death. It was huge and beautiful. The Goddess the Hunt reached down with claws of silver moonlight to take the village of Blackmoor by the throat.

CHAPTER THIRTY-FIVE

Lawrence finished his whiskey and watched Sir John head down the path toward the forest and the gorge. Without thinking, without even knowing why he was doing it, Lawrence left his room, ran down the stairs, and followed. He did not bother to take a lantern of his own. The moonlight was very bright even though the moon had not yet risen to its full height. Lawrence followed the path his father had taken, and it wound down into the woods, and then the forest floor split as one section continued its descent into a thickly wooded valley and the other skirted the banks of a rocky pool and rose to form a line of jagged cliffs. There was a narrow path choked with young saplings that grew in the shadows of ancient yews.

Lawrence followed the lower path until it vanished into a shadowy tunnel formed by the outstretched arms of the trees. Once inside, the roof of the tunnel rose in a gentle slope and Lawrence could straighten to his full height. He moved forward quickly but quietly, all the while wondering why he did not just call out for his father. But each time he opened his mouth he closed it again. Instinct, perhaps, or the lingering sting of his father's last words to him.

The corridor of yews opened into a clearing and Lawrence saw the lantern for just a moment, far ahead. Moving with even greater stealth, he crept forward, knowing now where this path led and where his father was going.

When the ancient stone wall of the family mausoleum materialized out of the gloom, Lawrence knew that his guess was correct.

The door stood ajar.

Lawrence licked his dry lips and pulled the door open all the way. The creak of the ancient hinges seemed horribly loud and he paused, waiting for a sharp rebuke from his father . . . but there was no sound from within.

The place held a superstitious dread for Lawrence. His mother was buried here. And Ben. Would their ghosts welcome his intrusion? If he was truly cursed, would the sacred stone of this place allow him entry?

God, he thought, *can I do this?*

He stepped inside.

There was a short entrance foyer and then a set of wide steps led down into a large circular chamber that was bigger than Lawrence expected. Mist clung to the floor and moss grew from the cracks in the stone walls. There were sconces on the walls and candles guttered in several of them. His father's work, he knew . . . but why?

Movement from within startled him to stillness. Hidden in shadow, Lawrence watched as Sir John moved across the chamber and stopped by a large sarcophagus. On the day of Ben's funeral this tomb had been draped in black cloth, but now it stood revealed in the light of Sir John's lantern. The old man stood beside it, looking down at the likeness carved on the ponderous marble cover. Then he bent and tenderly kissed the cold stone.

Then Sir John straightened and brushed at his face.

He looked around, drew a heavy breath, and then moved across the chamber and vanished into a narrow corridor.

Lawrence waited for a full minute to be sure that his father was not coming back, and then he came into the chamber, moving silently, drawn to the central sarcophagus. He could not take his eyes off of it. It was made from creamy marble, a masterwork of the stonecutter's art. A woman in regal dress, her hands clasped upon her chest, fingers curled around the stem of a rose. A beautiful face in eternal repose, eyes closed, lips slightly parted. So real, so peaceful.

"Mother? . . ." he whispered and nearly fell to his knees.

Here she was, her likeness in stone so real that his crumbling mind thought for a moment that it *was* her, that a kiss would awaken her. Not a lover's kiss, but one from her loving son. The son who, as a young boy, had stood by and watched with impossible horror while her lifeblood drained away in the rain on that terrible night a lifetime ago.

Tears burned in Lawrence's eyes and he did not wipe them away, letting them fall like the rain that had fallen upon his mother that night.

"Mama," he said, and for a moment his voice was that of an even younger child. A baby learning its first words, expressing its most basic needs and reaching out to establish its first connection with the world. He placed his hand gently atop the clasped hands. "Mama . . . I miss you," said Lawrence Talbot.

Then a sound echoed faintly from behind him and Lawrence came instantly back to himself. He turned and searched the room with his eyes for the source of the sound, and then found it. On the far side of the chamber, half hidden at the back of a niche that held a statue of a nameless saint, was a small door. It was open and the steady glow of lantern light shone within.

Lawrence hurried over and knelt down so he could peer inside. His father's lantern stood just inside and its glow revealed a set of stone stairs that spiraled downward into the bedrock. His father must have gone that way.

Did Sir John know he was being followed? Did he leave the lantern as an invitation? Or did he have some other source of light down there and the lantern was merely there to help him find his way back?

"Father?" Lawrence called softly, but there was no answer.

He picked up the lantern and slipped into the walls of the mausoleum. The spiral staircase was narrow and shallow and Lawrence had to be careful not to slip. He held the lantern in front of him and its constantly advancing light gave the eerie illusion that the shadows below were slyly retreating step by step as he descended.

The stairway widened out at the base and Lawrence held the lantern high to reveal the cobbled walls of an ancient catacomb that stretched far into the darkness. There were many niches cut into the walls, each one containing a life-sized statue with arms crossed and eyes closed, and between each niche was an earthen burial chamber with carved sarcophagi. These were more than the remains of all the Talbots who had ever lived here, Lawrence knew. This crypt was vastly old and God only knew who or what had been buried down here over the centuries.

Lawrence steeled himself and began moving down the long hall of the dead, and again the movement of the lantern light transformed the shadows into capering creatures that darted out of the way as he passed. He did not stop to examine the statues or the burial chambers. At the far end of the corridor there was a pale flickering light and all of his attention was drawn to it.

And so he never saw the eyes of one of the statues in a darkened niche open as he passed. The figure stepped out into the corridor without making a sound and when Lawrence was far enough ahead, the figure followed.

Lawrence reached the end of the hall and found another door left ajar. This one was very heavy, made from oak timbers and heavily reinforced with studded iron bands and massive hinges bolted into the unyielding rock. It had a single small window set with thick iron bars.

Lawrence took a breath and then stepped inside.

The chamber was a large vault but it was not a tomb. Instead of a sarcophagus there was a massive iron chair fixed to the floor. There were no other furnishings, but the entire chamber was littered with garbage—bits of food, empty wine bottles, waxed paper wrappers, chicken bones and other filth.

But what drew Lawrence's attention—drew it and locked it—was a little alcove cut into the wall facing the chair. A pair of candles had been lit and their glow revealed many bunches of old roses—some withered nearly to dust—and a small portrait of *Solana Talbot*.

Lawrence stared at it, unable to look away, barely able to breathe.

"She was a magnificent woman," said his father from right behind him.

Lawrence cried out in surprise and alarm and jumped to one side, turning to face Sir John. Lawrence had not heard his father enter the chamber.

"What . . . ," stammered Lawrence, "what *is* this place?"

Sir John did not look at him. His eyes were focused on the portrait and he was smiling a strange, sad smile.

"She was beautiful. I know losing her wounded you deeply. It is monstrous, a young boy seeing his mother like that." He shook his head and began pacing around the chamber.

Lawrence recoiled from his father as he passed. There was something strange, something repellent about the way in which his father moved. It was not the gait of an old man, not even the sturdy step of a man whose fitness belied his years. No, this was something else. Sir John moved with an unnatural vitality that chilled Lawrence to the marrow.

"I would've given my life that you had not found us that night." His eyes now fell upon Lawrence and they were hot and alien in their intensity. "You don't believe me? You should, my boy. Some images are so terrible that we cannot forget them and as a consequence they rot the soul. I never wanted that for you."

As Sir John paced to and fro, Lawrence backed away until his shoulder banged against the open iron door. He shot a brief calculating look through the doorway and then back to his father.

"Yes . . . not a single day passes," continued Sir John, constantly moving between candlelight and shadows, "when I don't wish that my little boy had stayed asleep in his bed, safe and warm. You must believe me when I tell you this, Lawrence."

Sir John stopped his pacing and turned back to the shrine. As he did so Lawrence moved surreptitiously into the doorway.

"You do believe me, don't you?"

Lawrence said nothing.

Sir John's eyes were fixed on the picture of Solana. "I

loved her, that woman, I loved her with a passion like the burning of the sun. Her death finished me," he said. "And, yes, still I prowl the house at night . . . alone . . . I wander as before." He turned to Lawrence. "But I am dead all the same. Look into my eyes, Lawrence—you see I am quite dead."

Lawrence looked at his father, at the alcove and the dead flowers, at the iron chair and the debris . . . and finally at the walls. There were deep lines in the walls, from floor to ceiling. He turned to the section of wall closest to him and studied the marks. Sets of parallel lines torn into the rock. And then all of the doors in Lawrence's mind opened up and a realization struck him with such ferocity that he nearly screamed. He clamped his hand over his mouth and staggered sideways; if the doorway had not been there he would have collapsed onto the floor.

Sir John heard his muted cry and faced his son. He smiled and began walking toward Lawrence.

Lawrence stumbled backward out of the cell and finally the words were torn from him.

"My God! It's you!" he cried. "You're the monster."

Sir John kept moving toward him, slowly, a step at a time.

"Mother . . . she found out," Lawrence hissed. "She found out what you were and that's why she killed herself!"

Sir John was at the doorway now and his eyes burned into Lawrence.

"So much pain," he said . . . and then he moved with a blur of speed. Lawrence screamed and fell back, throwing his hands out to ward off the attack. But there was a heavy *clang!*

Lawrence stared at what had happened.

The cell door was shut.

He heard a key turn in a lock.

Sir John stared at him through the bars. Lawrence's mind could not process this. He turned and looked back down the corridor that led to the stairs and freedom. His escape was there, waiting.

Sir John leaned on the bars and spoke from inside the cell.

"I wish I could tell you, Lawrence, that the . . . tragedy that has been your lot in life was over . . ."

"Father . . . I don't . . ."

". . . but I'm afraid your darkest moments of hell lie before you . . ."

And then Lawrence understood. His father had not trapped himself inside the cell as a punishment. He had trapped Lawrence outside, unfettered, free. . . .

Lawrence sank to his knees as the full weight of what was happening landed on him.

"No . . . ," he whispered. "God, no . . ." He suddenly raised his eyes to his father and reached out his hand. "I'm going to . . . No!"

The pain that flared in his hand was so sudden, so unexpected, so intense, that it shocked him to silence. It was as if every nerve in his hand had exploded with fire, and as Lawrence watched with horrified eyes the shape of his hand *changed*.

"Father!" he screamed. "You're going to let them kill me!"

Sir John chuckled. "Oh, I doubt they'll kill you," he said. "No. But . . . I will let them blame you."

Agony rippled up Lawrence's arm, exploded through muscle and sinew.

"Why?" demanded Lawrence. Bloody tears began to roll down his cheeks.

Sir John turned away for a moment as if considering his answer. And as he turned back Lawrence felt a flare of hope ignite in him that his father could somehow change the moment, that he would have an answer. But as the candlelight bathed Sir John's face, Lawrence knew that there were no answers left.

Sir John's eyes were no longer human. They blazed with yellow fire and his smile revealed teeth that had suddenly grown long and sharp and hungry.

"The beast will have its day," Sir John said, but his words were mangled by a mouth that was not made for speech. "The beast will be out."

Those were the last words from that awful mouth. The rest was a vicious snarl of hatred and mockery that drove Lawrence to his feet and chased him down the hallway and away from that accursed place.

Chapter Thirty-six

For thousands of years the standing stones in the forest of Blackmoor had tracked the movements of the stars and planets and the moon. Now, as night consumed the town the rising moon spilled its light through the center of the heel stone to mark the precise moment when the full moon, in all her power, was above the horizon.

Archaeologists have long debated the need for early man to gauge so precisely the rising of the moon. Hundreds of papers and books have been written to explain how the phases of the moon predict tides and harvests and other aspects of the mundane and orderly world.

They have all been wrong.

Every one of them.

The flash of moonlight across the heel stone of the circle of monoliths did not mark a change of tides. It did not signal the start of a harvest. It marked the moment when the Goddess of the Hunt—and all of her full-blooded children scattered throughout the world—began their hunt.

It marked the hour of the wolf.

The ancients knew this and they, warned by their celestial clock, fled for shelter.

In the village of Blackmoor the people were, without knowing it, reenacting a ritual as old as the standing stones themselves. They were hiding, and arming themselves, and making peace with their gods, because in their hearts they knew that the night no longer belonged to them.

CHAPTER THIRTY-SEVEN

Lawrence crawled up the spiral stairs from the catacomb, grabbing the steps with fingers that were no longer his own, pulling himself up with hands that had become nightmare shapes, pushing with twisted and malformed feet.

"Mother . . . help me!" he begged, but his words came out as a twisted roar.

He collapsed inside the main chamber, falling to his knees before his mother's crypt. The light from the candles were far too bright, their meager glow somehow transformed in his eyes to sunbursts. He could feel his eyes changing, shifting. It was the most nauseating thing he had ever felt. And then it got worse.

His senses exploded as sights and sounds and tastes flooded in impossibly fast. In the span of a single second he saw grains of pollen—each as separate and distinct as planets orbiting the sun—floating on the breeze. A swarm of insects flashed into focus, and Lawrence could smell the traces of vegetable matter and animal blood on each proboscis, could count the minute hairs on their tiny legs, could discern each delicate lacy line of their gossamer wings. Water running in a brook became a torrent in his ears. His mind staggered under the sensory assault.

Lawrence could feel every separate bit of what was

happening to him. His flesh felt hot, as if every cell in his body had become a furnace. His respiration quickened until he was panting like an animal. The landscape of his brain shifted as new glands formed and pumped chemicals in combinations no human could endure and the old human processes faded and died away. Lawrence screamed and screamed. He could feel his body changing as bones bent to horrific new shapes and muscles tore apart and merged together in unnatural ways. Somehow his mass increased—perhaps drawing substance from Hell itself. His bones thickened to support the heavier muscle and corded ligaments. His skin burned and itched as new hair follicles formed and began sending stiff black shoots through the flesh.

His feet expanded and black claws tore through the leather as if it was paper. Lacings snapped like fiddle strings and the shoes fell away as his feet changed, the heel rising, the clawed toes digging into the rock of the mausoleum floor.

White hot pain flared in his jaw as his molars shifted forward to allow the growth of strong new carnassial teeth, and the incisors and canines became sharper and more pronounced.

Lawrence screamed his mother's name, but an animal's roar was what shook the room. There was no trace of a human voice in that roar. The sound was so loud that dust flew from the sarcophagi and old vases shattered. Insects crawling along the floor burst apart and cracks ran along the walls. The roar was as loud as all the pain and fury and despair in the world. It funneled out through the open iron door and tore at the night sky.

It was not the cry of a man.

In that moment, in that hour, that *form* of Lawrence Talbot no longer existed.

What remained—that thing that rose up on twisted legs and tore the air with monstrous claws—was no longer human. It was a monster from the oldest of legends. It burst from the mausoleum and stood in the cold wash of moonlight, and there, under the watchful eye of the Goddess of the Hunt, the Wolfman threw back its head and howled its fury at the night.

CHAPTER THIRTY-EIGHT

A mile away, on the far side of Talbot Hall, Singh sat alone in his room, his *kirpan* loosened in its scabbard and a heavy rifle resting across his thighs. He sat on the edge of his bed, staring at the door, which was closed and sealed with three heavy hasp locks. A pistol lay on the bedspread beside him and a silver-tipped hunting spear stood leaning against the bedpost.

Sweat and tears ran down his face.

The howl of the Wolfman burst from the forest and raced across the fields and invaded the house through every crack and loose board. That sound beat at Singh's ears. And he bowed his head and prayed.

IN THE CHURCH Pastor Fisk was still ranting about the power of Satan when an unearthly howl shook the building to its rafters. It was far away and yet the naked threat implied within its urgency seemed to breathe against the back of the vicar's neck. What little hair he had stood on end and gooseflesh pebbled his skin.

He left a passage from the Revelation of John unfinished and instead bent and blew out his candles.

The congregation stared at him in confusion and fear, their own candles trembling in their hands.

"Quickly!" he shouted. "No light . . . no sound!"

Everyone blew out their candles and for a long minute they sat in the darkness, safe within the church walls.

The creature howled again. Louder. Closer.

And suddenly the darkness in which they hid felt far less comforting.

INSPECTOR FRANCIS ABERLINE paused with his glass halfway to his lips as the howl cut through the din of the tavern and smashed everything to silence. The echo of the creature's call lingered in the smoky air for several seconds.

And then Aberline slammed down his glass and jumped to his feet. He grabbed his coat and hat from their pegs, patted his pockets to reassure himself of his whistle and pistol, and dashed out into the night.

The patrons stared at the open door for half a minute, and then Cramer raced over, slammed it and dropped the bar in place.

ABERLINE DASHED TO the stable, kicked open the door and saddled his horse with desperate haste. He barely had the girths buckled before he swung up into the saddle, kicked the horse in the flanks and headed out of town at a full gallop.

IN THE SHADOWS of the ruined abbey, the hunting party heard the howl and froze like rabbits. Colonel Montford cut a look at Strickland, who had gone as pale as the moon. Dr. Lloyd's face was bathed in icy sweat and he looked ready to collapse. Only MacQueen's face was neutral, though his jaw was set and he adjusted his grip on the heavy rifle.

MacQueen turned slowly and scanned the terrain, first checking to see that each of the other men were invisible in their hunting blinds among the ruins and then eyeing the stag to make sure it was standing in clear moonlight.

Everything looked perfect.

The howl came again, cutting through the air like a scythe.

"Did you hear that?" sputtered Dr. Lloyd.

"Of course we heard it you old fool," snapped Montford.

"Begging your pardon, sirs," said MacQueen quietly, "but it might be a good time to shut the hell up."

No one argued with him.

The howl tore at the night.

THE WOLFMAN MOVED like a ghost through the mist of the forest. Its huge feet made almost no noise as it ran along at a fast lope. It leapt gorges and ravines without effort, jumped atop fallen trees and ran their length before springing into the darkness. It never missed its footing. Where an owl might find the darkness and fog too gloomy, the eyes of the creature saw everything. Heard everything. Smelled everything. The woods withheld no secrets from it. If an insect wriggled beneath the loose bark of a sycamore three hundred yards down the slope, the creature heard it. If a fox two miles away sprayed a shrub to mark the edges of its territory, the Wolfman knew it. It could hear the thunder of their heartbeats, see the heat of their life force, smell the heady salt and sugar in their blood.

It smelled water and stopped, bending to drink—and then it paused, muscles tense, muzzle wrinkled in anger as something else leaned upward from the pond toward him. The Wolfman lashed out at it, raking claws across its eyes and slapping water high onto the banks. The image of the other monster wavered and then settled as the agitated waters stilled. The Wolfman eyed the reflection warily. With a low warning growl, it bent to drink.

Then all at once it was in motion again, running, leaping, moving at the speed of hate and hunger.

The moon bathed the creature with silver light, and in that light it was the most powerful thing under heaven. It feared nothing, hungered for *everything*.

It ran and ran and then stopped all at once, pressed up against the trunk of a tree, its claws digging into the bark, head raised to sniff.

There, on the wind.

Blood.

Fresh and hot. Exposed, naked to the breeze.

Drool fell from the creature's mouth onto the tatters of its shirt.

THE STAG COULD smell its own death out there in the shadows. It struggled against the ropes, throwing all of its weight against the restraints, crying out in the raw and strangled voice it only used in panic. Its eyes were wide and wild.

COLONEL MONTFORD PEERED down the length of his rifle barrel, sweat running down his bruised and lacerated face.

"Damn it, MacQueen," he whispered. "What's it waiting for?"

"Shhh," murmured the hunter.

THE STAG STOPPED its tortured cry and stood stock still, and the whole forest around it went quiet as well. To the watching eyes of the Wolfman the stag's blood was fire-bright and so hot and sweet. Though there were other prey in the forest, the bleeding stag was right here, its blood singing to the werewolf.

The Wolfman's muzzle wrinkled back in a silent snarl of unbearable hunger, and then it *moved*. Racing, running, its body a blur of impossible speed as it came out of the shadows and lunged for the bleeding stag. It leapt forward, a massive dive that cleared twenty feet so that it landed within inches of the deer.

And then the ground beneath it collapsed, without sense or substance, dragging the creature down into darkness. It fell and fell and landed with a huge crash into the stone-lined depths of the abbey's cellar.

Trapped.

Chapter Thirty-nine

The hunters rushed forward, opening fire in a haphazard barrage that tore chunks out of the ground and gouged trees. A half dozen whizzed past the stag, grazing its throat and chest and flanks and splashing it with blood, but none of the shots were fatal. The screaming stag lunged once more against its tethers and they finally snapped and it bolted into the darkness.

Montford fired and fired and fired, working the level on his rifle, sending his bullets down into the darkness without aim. The bullets struck fire from the stone walls of the cellar, ricochets pinged and wanged and buzzed through the shadows like furious hornets.

"Shit! Shit! Shit!" he cried as he fired, his eyes half mad with fear and murder. When his rifle clicked empty he drew his pistol and continued firing.

MacQueen materialized beside him and slapped the colonel's barrel up so that the last bullet blew a hole through layers of dried leaves overhead.

"Enough!" cried the hunter in a voice so loud and commanding that everyone came to their senses and took their trembling fingers off of their triggers. The air around them echoed with the thunder of the gunfire.

MacQueen crept to the edge of the cellar and peered down into the darkness. Below, the Wolfman screamed in fury and tore at the unyielding walls of its prison.

"Did I hit it?" demanded Montford breathlessly. He inched forward and dared a look down into the hole, but the bottom of the pit was black and half hidden by the remnants of the canvas screen they'd erected to hide the hole.

"Get a light!" MacQueen ordered, and Dr. Lloyd stumbled away from the trap to secure a lantern. He removed the blackout shades and suddenly yellow light flooded the clearing.

"I've got it," he called as he hurried back to rejoin the others.

"Bring it here," said MacQueen. "Let's see how bad we've hurt the bugger!"

Squire Strickland took the lantern and knelt by the edge. "I can't see it."

"Lower the lantern," ordered Montford. "A little more—"

Suddenly the Wolfman's taloned hand darted out of the shadows, closed around Strickland's face and ripped him down into the pit.

Immediately everyone screamed and stumbled backward, firing into the pit, firing wild into the trees, colliding with one another.

Something dark flew out of the pit and struck Montford in the chest. He looked down in dumb horror to see Strickland's torn and severed arm, the hand still clutching the pistol, finger hooked around the trigger.

"Good God . . ."

Then something else came hurtling up from the shadows. Something larger. Something alive.

The Wolfman crashed to the ground right in front of MacQueen. It landed hard on all fours facing away from him, and then rose slowly to its full, towering height. The hunter's eyes followed it as it rose, his mouth sag-

ging open with horror. But then he snapped his jaws
shut, flipped his rifle in his hands, and with a fierce two-
hand grip on the barrel swung it with all of his might,
turning shoulders and hips into the movement, slamming the heavy stock into the monster's back. The blow
was so powerful that the stock shattered and flew apart
and the impact staggered the creature. It should have
killed it, snapped its spine, but all it did was make the
werewolf take a single forward step.

The Wolfman whirled around just as MacQueen
flung the broken rifle aside and clawed for the heavy
pistol shoved into his belt. MacQueen was fast. But he
wasn't near fast enough. The Wolfman slashed at him
with both hands, the long claws cutting back and forth,
razoring through clothing and flesh, sinew and bone.
MacQueen seemed to disintegrate, to fly apart like a
house of cards in a strong breeze. The fury of the Wolfman's attack seeded the air with blood and for a moment
all that remained of MacQueen was a bloody mist and a
scattering of red debris.

One of the other hunters buried his pistol against the
creature's side and pulled the trigger. The blast was
muffled by the monster's thick fur, but the Wolfman
howled in anger and turned. The hunter backpedaled
away but the monster leapt atop him with such force that
bones snapped like firecrackers and blood gushed from
the man's mouth. The Wolfman's head darted down and
closed around the hunter's neck. Vertebrae crackled and
the man's scream was cut off with abrupt finality.

"Kill it!" bellowed Montford, and he swung his rifle
up and fired.

The Wolfman made a grab for Montford, but the colonel was backing away, firing as fast as he could work
the action. One of the other men swung around to bring

his gun to bear and Montford's next shot took his hand off at the wrist. The Wolfman grabbed the wounded man's arm and tore it out of its socket.

The other hunters scattered like sheep.

Dr. Lloyd and Colonel Montford among them.

MONTFORD SPLIT OFF from the pack. Let them draw the creature, he thought. Let them die.

He ran toward Talbot Hall. If he could make the house then he could barricade himself in. It was a tactical retreat, he told himself. He wasn't running away, he was regrouping.

He ran as fast as he could, trying to outpace the thunder of his own beating heart.

In the darkness and the mist he never saw the bog until his leading foot splashed down in it and he pitched forward onto his face. His rifle went spinning off out of sight; he didn't even hear it splash.

Screaming in fear and frustration, Montford scrambled to find footing in the wet mud, but the harder he thrashed the more the bog pulled at him.

And then he heard the thing. A growl and a splash and he knew that the werewolf had fallen into the bog as well. Montford righted himself and looked around and there it was! Not ten feet away, splashed with dark blood, its eyes as bright as the furnaces of Hell. Montford screeched in a high, shrill voice and sloshed backward away from it. The creature took a step toward him and sank to its knee, but with a huge wrench it pulled its leg free and took another step forward. And another.

"God . . ." Montford whispered and he felt heat spread down his thigh as his bladder failed.

The creature took another step, growling low in its throat as if it was enjoying the anticipation of what was to come.

Montford knew that he had no chance. He drew his pistol, but it would not stop this thing. The rifle had been loaded with silver bullets. The pistol was not.

"God save my soul," he prayed, then he shoved the barrel of his pistol under his jaw and closed his eyes as the Wolfman took a final step.

He pulled the trigger.

And nothing happened.

He pulled again, and again. A splinter of his mind remembered that he had not reloaded after the initial attack.

The Wolfman loomed above him, its face almost calm in its moment of triumph.

The screams of Colonel Montford frightened the night birds from the trees.

DR. LLOYD WAS alone in the woods. He could not run as fast as the remaining hunters and he had no sense of woodcraft. He staggered from tree to tree, seeking cover, wheezing, weeping, coughing, all but blind despite the moonlight. In his mind the image of the creature leaping out of the pit played again and again. Roots caught his feet and tripped him, branches whipped his face.

Dr. Lloyd finally collapsed with his back to an ancient elm. He clutched his rifle to his chest and rocked back and forth as he wept.

Then he heard a sound. Something moving through the woods.

He held his breath.

God . . . let it be Montford.

The sound came again, closer now. Stealthy, like a man sneaking through the brush.

Unless it wasn't a man.

Lloyd raised the rifle and turned to point it into the darkness behind him. Leaves rustled as something moved through the mist.

Please, let it be Montford.

Then he heard the growl.

It was so close.

Lloyd fired his rifle and in the split second of muzzle flash he saw the face of the beast. Not behind him; not in the line of fire.

It was right beside him.

INSPECTOR ABERLINE HEARD the howls and the gunfire and the screams and he spurred his horse into a full gallop. The horse's hooves kicked up ground mist so that the road appeared to catch fire and smoke behind him.

As he entered the woods he saw a shape rushing toward him out of the shadows and Aberline drew his pistol, but the animal that flashed past was only a stag. But it had a tether around its neck and its body was streaked with blood.

The sight of the animal and the smell of blood threw his horse into a panic and it suddenly reared up and Aberline was pitched out of the saddle. He fell hard onto the muddy ground, the air punched from his lungs and fireworks exploding in his eyes.

He lay there for several minutes, barely able to gasp in a full breath of air.

The forest around him grew still and quiet by slow

degrees, and by the time Aberline could stand everything was silent. A few shreds of cloud had drifted across the moon and the inspector stood in total darkness for a moment. He fished for matches but just as he found them the winds blew the clouds away and moonlight flooded the entire clearing. He saw that he was in what had once been the courtyard of an ancient abbey. Nearby was the black mouth of what had once been the cellar, behind him were the jagged teeth of broken walls hung with creeper vines. The last wisps of cloud trailed away so that the moonlight shone full and bright, illuminating everything.

What that cold white light revealed took his breath away more sharply and profoundly than the fall had done.

There were bodies everywhere. The hunters, the men from town. A dozen of them lay scattered around him, their limbs torn and broken. Aberline stood in a lake of blood with death all around him.

In the distance the howl of a wolf rose into the night sky and madness ruled the forests of Blackmoor.

CHAPTER FORTY

"**G**ood morning, Lawrence."

Lawrence Talbot heard the voice but his brain was too numb to process either meaning or identity. It took every bit of energy he had to open his eyes. The morning sunlight was like a fist in the face, and each glistening dewdrop on leaves and grass was as sharp as a splinter in his eyes. He could see someone standing over him but everything was a smear of shadows and light. Lawrence could feel dirt and tree roots under his buttocks and the gnarled bole of a big tree against his back, and as sense and focus came to him in slow degrees he realized that he was crammed into the hollow of a tree on a grassy slope.

"Can you hear me?" asked the voice. "Do you recognize me, Lawrence?"

There were other voices in the near distance, and the sound of horses blowing in the cold dawn air.

Lawrence blinked his eyes clear and what he saw tore an inarticulate cry from his throat. His hands . . . God almighty . . . his hands.

He held up his hands and for a desperate moment he thought he was wearing dark red gloves. But he was not. He looked down at his clothes. His shirt was torn to ribbons; the legs of his trousers slashed and ripped along the seams, his shoes gone. And everywhere he looked—his body, his clothes—there was blood. So much blood, caked on and ground into the cracks of his skin and under each nail. He touched his face and felt dried gore around his mouth, on his chin and throat.

He crawled to his knees and looked up at the figure standing just above him on the slope.

"What . . . ," he began, but how does one phrase the kind of question that was nailed to the walls of his heart? "What have I . . . I . . . ?"

Sir John Talbot stepped toward him and Lawrence stared up in horror at his father's blue eyes and white beard. Sir John's mouth wore the tiniest of smiles but his eyes were as cold as death.

"You have done terrible things, my boy," Sir John whispered. "Terrible things."

With a cry Lawrence staggered to his feet and recoiled from his father. He understood that smile and that coldness. The truth had hammered a fracture line in his soul. Lawrence turned to flee but there was Inspector Aberline not ten feet away. He wheeled and saw an entire posse of armed men, all of them big, all of them staring at him with equal measures of hostility and horror.

"No!" Lawrence shouted and bolted for a gap in the line of men, but the men shifted to block his way. He spun and tried to make a dash for the tree line but men on horses trotted toward him. Lawrence saw villagers from Blackmoor scattered among them, their faces taut with grief and devoid of all pity. Every man was armed with a gun or club.

In desperation Lawrence turned back to Sir John, who had not moved from where he stood on the slope.

"How does it feel?" asked his father in a voice too quiet for anyone but Lawrence to hear.

"No!" Lawrence cried. He backed away, pointing at Sir John. "Inspector . . . my father's a monster!"

Aberline drew closer, a rifle ready in one hand, and Sir John turned to him, a look of brokenhearted pity on his face. He gestured to Lawrence, and the inspector nodded as if all of this confirmed a discussion they had already had. Aberline raised his free hand to signal his men and immediately a half dozen burly officers closed on Lawrence, blocking all exits, crowding him, seizing him by the arms.

"Don't let him go," Lawrence begged. "Aberline, take me if you must, but for the love of God take him, too!"

Sir John's shoulders slumped and he looked old and defeated. "It is as you said."

Aberline looked wretched and he put a comforting hand on Sir John's shoulder. "I'm sorry, Sir John. Truly I am."

"Thank you," Sir John said brokenly.

Aberline turned away from him and nodded to his men.

"Bring him."

As the men began dragging Lawrence up the slope, Sir John stepped close and whispered, "Be strong, my son. Be strong."

Only Lawrence could see the humor behind this performance of grief, and he knew that his father— the true monster—would be free. Lawrence lunged at him, trying to grab his father's throat. He shrugged off two of the men and as they fell they collided with the others and suddenly Lawrence was free. He dove at his father, accepting his own death if this madness could all be stopped here and now.

Aberline stepped in and swung his rifle butt in a vicious jab that cracked against the back of Lawrence's head. Lawrence's fingers brushed his father's throat and then he was falling into a dark well.

CHAPTER FORTY-ONE

Lawrence had no awareness of being forced into a straightjacket, or of being chained to an iron seat in the back of an armored coach. He did not remember the ride to London, did not feel the rough hands of the white-jacketed orderlies who dragged him from the coach, stripped him and hosed him, dressed him in hospital clothes and then placed him in a restraining chair. All he knew was darkness and pain and dreams whose nature were so intensely awful that he fled deeper into his own unconscious to escape them.

But awareness did return. Slowly and at its own pace, and when Lawrence opened his eyes he knew where he was. And why.

Lambeth Asylum.

And here, more real even than the memories of last night, stood Dr. Hoenneger. The same man, the same madhouse from that terrible night after his mother's suicide. For a hopeful moment Lawrence thought that this was just another dream, but Hoenneger's face was older, thinner, with deeper lines cut through the pallid flesh. This was real, and this was now, and Lawrence's heart plummeted in his chest.

Hoenneger moved to stand directly in front of Lawrence and an orderly joined him. The orderly was huge, cadaverous, with dark eyes sunk deep into shadowy pits and an ugly smile filled with yellow teeth. Just behind them was a pool of water set into the stone floor.

"I *am* sorry to see you back with us, Lawrence," said Hoenneger gravely but without conviction. "Since you were here last, we have made enormous strides in the treatment of delusions such as yours."

The doctor's smile was anything but comforting. It was a prideful, boasting leer. "Ripler? . . ." he said, gesturing to the orderly.

Ripler reached for a big wooden lever and suddenly Lawrence understood what was happening. His chair was bolted to a thick plank mounted on a greased fulcrum and as Ripler pulled on the lever the board abruptly lowered Lawrence's chair so that he went face-forward into the icy pool of black water.

The water was so shockingly cold that it tore a scream out of Lawrence. Air burst from his nose and mouth, frigid water numbed his face and eyes. They could not be doing this . . . they could not leave him here to drown. His mind refused to accept it but as the seconds crawled past and the last bits of air in his chest began to burn his lungs, the lever moved again and he rose sputtering and choking back into the air. His seat landed with a bone-jarring thud and Ripler leaned close and exhaled foul breath in his face.

"Bracing," Ripler said, "ain't it, guv'ner?"

"Why are . . . you . . . doing . . ."

But before Lawrence could gasp out a question Ripler gave the lever another pull. The second impact with the water was far, far worse. It surged up his nose and drove icy needles into every inch of his face and throat. When the chair was pulled back Lawrence felt like he would rather die than go into that hellish water again.

Hoenneger's face bent toward him.

"We've made so many fascinating and promising advances in our science, Lawrence. You'll be amazed."

He raised his hand to show Lawrence the huge hypodermic needle he held. Lawrence's arms were strapped to the chair. He could not move, could not escape as the needle pierced his flesh and Hoenneger depressed the plunger. The drugs burst like fire in his veins and within seconds Lawrence could feel the substance of reality crack and peel away in layers. Even before his eyes drifted shut he saw the faces of Hoenneger and Ripler change into monstrous distortions of grinning ghouls who bent toward him to consume him with needle-sharp teeth. The drugs filled every part of his consciousness and tore him from sense and order. . . .

. . . LAWRENCE OPENED HIS eyes and he stood alone in a long hallway that stretched away into the shadows. He turned and saw the same stretch into dark infinity. Closed doors lined each side of the corridor. The carpet beneath his feet was the color of fresh blood, the sconces on the walls flickering with candles that burned with cold fire.

"Father!" he called, but his voice was an impotent whisper; he could barely hear it himself. "Gwen? . . ." he said, and this time his voice was insanely loud and echoes punched the walls and sent shockwaves back that staggered him.

He heard a sound behind him and turned to see a door open twenty feet from where he stood. The door swung wide by itself and Lawrence took a step toward it, but suddenly a child burst from the room and raced away from him into the shadows.

"Boy!" Lawrence called, but the child ran full tilt

away from him. He started walking after the boy, then began to trot and finally he, too, was running as hard as he could.

The boy abruptly turned and ran into the one of the rooms, and as Lawrence approached he saw that the room was the entrance to a dank cell. The floor was covered with straw and filth, the walls black with mildew, and the barred window looked out onto the gray pollution of the Thames. Without knowing how, he understood that this was his own cell, that this was where he had been brought by his father and Inspector Aberline. It was the same cell he had lived in for two years as a boy.

The child he had chased was here, naked, shivering, huddling in the corner between the bed and the wall.

"Boy . . . who are you?" Lawrence said, taking a tentative step into the room. "Why are you here?"

The boy shifted so that only one eye peered up at him from under a tangle of unwashed black hair. The child picked up something from under the bed and slowly raised it to show Lawrence. It was a skull. No, more than that it was the prop skull used in the London production of *Hamlet*. Lawrence's next words died on his tongue because now he recognized that eye.

It was his own eye . . . and this child was *him*, the tortured boy who had been sent to this hell hole all those years ago.

"My God," Lawrence whispered. He knelt down and reached a hand toward the child. "Don't be afraid."

He placed his hand on the child's thin shoulder and pulled gently. "Let me help you . . . I won't hurt you."

The child turned then. Not slow and tentative, but with unnatural speed and with a face that was not that of Lawrence the boy. This was the snarling, feral face of an animal. Yellow eyes flashed and it snarled with pernicious delight as it lunged at Lawrence, wicked teeth snapping . . .

. . . RIPLER WORKED THE lever again and Lawrence plunged back into the frigid water. The pain and shock were the same, but Lawrence could not tell if this moment was real or if it was part of the never-ending dream. . . .

. . . LAWRENCE TURNED OVER in his sleep.

And then was aware that he *was* sleeping. The ghouls and phantasms were gone, the child was gone. The cell was dark except for a thin spill of moonlight through the barred window.

There was a metallic click and Lawrence peered through the gloom to see the door handle turn and the door swing quietly open. Lawrence shied back, expecting Ripler and Dr. Hoénneger . . . but against all sanity it was someone who could not be here. Slender, dressed in gossamer, moving with delicate steps she entered his prison.

"Gwen? . . ."

It *was* her. She smiled at him with a gentleness and compassion that he had not expected to ever see again. Only his mother had ever looked at him with such love, but that had been so completely different than this. The moonlight made her gown translucent and Lawrence could see every beautiful curve of her. The breeze stirred her garments and he could see the graceful line of her hip as it flowed down to become her thigh. Her breasts bobbed as she moved, the dark nipples tenting the thin fabric.

"Thank God it's you," he said as he sat up. "I just had the most horrible dream."

She rushed to him, bending to place a finger against his lips. "Shhh . . . don't worry, Lawrence." She kissed his forehead and bent to his ear. "You're safe now. . . ."

Gwen showered him with a hundred quick kisses that were like the softest, most soothing rain on his face. Her hands caressed his face and throat and then her clever fingers were at the buttons of his shirt.

Lawrence pulled her to him and their lips met in a kiss of such intense erotic heat that his entire body felt as if it was suddenly released from some ancient bondage.

"I need you," he whispered. He slipped the gossamer from her shoulders and it fell away to reveal the alabaster perfection of her skin. Lawrence kissed the side of her throat and she moaned and moved against him, tearing at his shirt and trousers. Within seconds they were skin to skin, bathed in moonlight, their mouths hot and hungry, their bodies moving together in that perfect and timeless rhythm of true love and pure passion. When he entered her she arched her back and cried out, her breasts crushed against his chest. She locked her legs around him and pulled him deeper, her moans and cries filling the room.

"I love you," he said.

"I—" she began, but her words became another gasp of need.

Urgency sang in their nerves and with every heartbeat the cadence of their bodies built and built; Lawrence's breath rasped in and out of his lungs and Gwen's cries became sharper and louder with each thrust.

"Lawrence," she shrieked. "God . . . Lawrence . . ."

The intensity mounted and mounted as they soared toward that sweet precipice.

"Lawrence!" Her voice was sharper now, louder in his ear.

The bed banged against the wall, the springs squealing under their weight.

"Lawrence!"

Her tone changed and he lifted a hand to her face, to brush a strand of hair from her eyes . . . and the whole world changed to madness. His fingers were long and gnarled, coated with dark bristling hair, and at the end of each finger was a claw that tapered to a deadly point. And every claw was drenched with hot blood.

Lawrence arched off of her and stared in raw horror at Gwen's body. Every inch of her sacred flesh, from thighs to throat, was torn open. Blood welled from a hundred jagged gashes and her screams were now those of terrible agony. Gwen stared at him with hopeless eyes, her fingers scrabbled at him as if trying to make this reality into a fantasy, but with each beat of her heart blood spurted from her chest and mouth and . . .

. . . LAWRENCE WOKE IN rage and torment, screaming Gwen's name, cursing God Himself. He was crammed into a corner of his cell and he scrambled to get his feet under him so he could make a dash for the door, but he only made it two steps before something grabbed him by the throat and dragged him back. He grabbed at his throat and found the unyielding solidity of a cold iron collar clamped around his neck and a heavy length of chain leading from it to a massive ring set into the gray stone wall. He was chained like a dog.

And he was awake.

Somehow he knew that this was the real world, that everything else had been phantoms in his brain created by the drugs and the water torture. This . . . the chain, the hard stone under his bare feet . . . this was real.

Lawrence sank to his knees and beat the floor with his fist, cursing this place, cursing Heaven, cursing his own life. He bent his head until his skin was pressed against the moldy floor.

He remained there for a long time, sobbing, feeling totally lost and alone.

But he wasn't alone.

Someone was on his cot. It wasn't the feral boy. It wasn't Gwen.

Sir John sat there, one leg folded casually over the other, a coffee cup cradled between his palms, smiling the coldest smile Lawrence had ever seen.

CHAPTER FORTY-TWO

"Father," Lawrence pleaded, "*why?*"

"I contracted the disease in India," said Sir John quietly. "In the Hindu Kush. Singh and I had heard tales of a remote valley where no white man had ever set foot and where the game was as astonishing as the natural beauty of the place. After wasting many months on dead ends and expensive guides, we finally found our Shangri-La."

Lawrence shook his head. "I don't understand. Why are you telling me this?"

His father put a finger to his lips. "Shhh. Just listen, Lawrence. This is your real heritage." Sir John sipped his coffee and set the cup aside. "We bartered our way into the good graces of the native hunters. The valley was everything the tales spoke of. The game was exceptional, the country fantastic beyond words. And the locals . . . well there is no greater, more primal bond among men than that formed by hunting together. We swapped stories. Customs. Beliefs. Among theirs was the strange belief in a rite which would grant the devotee enormous powers. Powers of hunting, and of the sexual kind."

Sir John's eyes twinkled with a mischief that made Lawrence want to gag.

"No animal or woman could resist whoever partook of his black magic. None of the natives could boast having undergone the rite, as they viewed it the prospect would be too . . . fearsome."

" 'Rite'?" Lawrence echoed in a hollow voice.

Sir John laughed and waved a dismissive hand. "Of course I didn't believe a word of it, but nevertheless I was intrigued. So, the natives directed me to a cave high up in the mountains where, according to legend, lived a strange creature. After a great many days of climbing, searching, finally, I came upon it. I *found* it . . . the cave. And the strange creature that lived there."

Lawrence straightened. Even with the lingering effects of the drugs he now had every ounce of his being focused on his father.

"It was a boy." Sir John laughed and shook his head. "It was a wild, feral boy who attacked me."

"He . . . bit you?" Lawrence asked in a whisper.

"Oh yes. I was bitten. By him. I returned to my hunting companions thinking I had been made the butt of a joke." He cocked his head as if looking at the memory. His cold smile never wavered. "I soon learned otherwise."

Lawrence stared at him with a growing horror that was far bigger and more terrible than the story his father was telling. The revulsion and heartbreak threatened to tear open his chest.

"My mother . . ." he breathed.

Sir John waited.

"She didn't kill herself . . . did she?"

Sir John Talbot's smile grew colder still. "No," he said. "I suppose I did."

Lawrence screamed . . .

. . . AND HE WAS back there, back in the rain on that dreadful night, back by the reflecting pool with the bleak walls of Talbot Hall looming above him. The clouds above were thinning, the rain slowing to a gentle fall like tears, and above it all the moon emerged like a predatory creature, watchful and hungry.

Lawrence Talbot stood twenty feet from the pool, dressed as he was in the Asylum. He knew that this was a dream, but somehow he had become a part of it, just as he knew that what he was seeing now was what truly happened all those years ago. He was a witness to his own memory, to something he had never been able to fully remember since the event blasted him into shock and madness.

He saw his mother lying sprawled in the arms of his father. They were in silhouette, Sir John's back to him. There was a cry in the night and Lawrence turned to see his own younger self, a frail boy of nine years old, standing in the doorway of the glasshouse garden. In the continuous flash of lightning young Lawrence's forehead was knitted in consternation and uncertainty.

"Mother?" whispered the boy, taking a tentative step outside.

A wail tore through the night, rising upward from the kneeling figure as Sir John raised his head and screamed to the storm. As he did so the body in his arms shifted and Lawrence—the child and the man—saw Solana's arm fall limply down, her hand striking the wet ground. The black rain flowed from her, from her arm, from her body, from her skin. A river of darkness that washed from her and across the flagstones toward Lawrence.

"Mother? . . ." young Lawrence said again, and this time his father heard his plaintive little voice. Sir John turned, still cradling Solana to his chest. As lightning flashed Lawrence could see the lines of terrible, impossible grief carved into his father's face. His father's eyes were dark, a red that was filled with grief and fury and rage and an impossible loss.

But that was not how it was. Not really, and Lawrence the man, standing now in this grand theater of memory, saw a different version of the scene play out.

Lightning flashed and Lawrence could see his mother's body. He looked for the wounds where she had slashed her wrists, but even as he looked Lawrence knew that those wounds would not be there. Other wounds would.

He stepped closer, standing right behind the boy, and as lightning flashed above them he saw his mother's lovely face. So pale and still. And he saw her throat. It was a red, torn ruin. The wounds on her chest and arms and legs were not the pristine cuts of a razor. They were bites. Savage and brutal.

Sir John threw his head back and screamed.

Only it wasn't a scream. It was a howl.

And it wasn't Sir John.

It was a werewolf.

The boy screamed.

Lawrence screamed, too. . . .

SIR JOHN PICKED up his coffee cup and took a sip, watching with icy interest as his son bent forward over the knot of pain in his heart and buried his face in his hands. The sound of his scream echoed off of the walls of the stone cell.

"You *bastard*!" growled Lawrence. He raised his head and spat at Sir John, but his father wiped the spittle from his jacket. "You said you loved her! You knew what you were and yet you . . . you . . ." He shook his head, trying to dislodge the truth. "You should have killed yourself."

Sir John grunted. "I cannot tell you how often I have considered it. I suppose you would have been a happy little family, just you and your brother and your mother. . . . Ah, but life is far too glorious, Lawrence. Especially to the cursed, the damned. Every night of the full moon, for many years, I've been locked away in that crypt. Singh does it. My faithful servant for twenty-five years . . . but then *she* came, didn't she?"

" 'She'? . . ."

Sir John's voice trembled. "Hot, burning like the face of the moon. Like your mother. Like your mother. And out of reach."

Lawrence gasped. "Gwen . . ."

"Yes," said Sir John gently. "Gwen. She would have taken your brother away and they would both have vanished into the night. And, although I was resigned to it, the beast in me was not. You understand that now, Lawrence, don't you?"

"What do you mean?" demanded Lawrence. "You talk about the beast as if it's not you."

"One can't control what it wants. What it does." Sir John paused. "The night Ben died we had a terrible quarrel. Terrible. It was a fight really. Ben, you understand, had come to tell me he was resolute in his decision to leave Talbot Hall for good. I got drunk and violent." He sighed. "Extremely violent. I even struck out at Singh, who was trying to restrain me. I knocked him out cold." He gave Lawrence a rueful smile. "Poor old Singh. I used to be a bare-knuckle prizefighter, back in the good old days . . . long time ago."

Sir John got up and walked across the cell and stared out of the tiny window.

"Yes . . . poor old Singh." He turned to face Lawrence. "Anyway, I knocked him unconscious, and as a consequence I waited too long . . . and by then I was *unable* to lock myself in the crypt that night."

"What did you do?" asked Lawrence, though he was dreadfully certain that he knew the next part of the tale.

"In the morning . . . after I became . . . I found your brother in a ditch . . . not far from the house. He'd been torn to pieces." He leaned one hand against the wall and hung his head.

"God damn you to hell," said Lawrence, but the grief was so sharp that the words came out as a weak whisper.

Sir John slapped the wall and turned sharply to face Lawrence. His face was hard, his eyes ablaze and all traces of heartache and remorse were gone.

"But now I understand!" he said triumphantly. "Now I know it was all a mistake, trying to lock up the beast. Twenty-five *years*, Lawrence. All those wasted years, all those years being ashamed of it . . . and I should not have been! I should have let nature run its course. Don't you think so, Lawrence? I should have let it run free . . . kill or be killed."

Lawrence lunged at him but once more the collar stopped him short. He reeled back, clawing at his throat, cursing and gagging. With a jolt he realized that his father had played him, that he had come to lean on the wall near him to provoke a gesture that would prove Lawrence's impotence. "If you dare touch Gwen . . ."

Sir John smiled. "Don't threaten me, boy. You don't have the fiber for it. You have a ways to go, my young pup, before you can tell me what to do. But . . . your chance is coming." He strolled over to the barred window. It was already late afternoon. "The Goddess will hunt the skies again . . . and she's full tonight."

"No!"

"Oh yes, Lawrence. But . . ." He dug into his coat pocket and removed a shaving razor. With a snap of his wrist he flicked out the blade. It was mirror bright and gleamed with argent fire.

"This is a small gift for you, Lawrence, in the event you don't find life as glorious as I find it to be . . . or 'not to be.'" He gave him a wink and reached close to tuck the razor under the thin mattress of Lawrence's cot. Lawrence did not move. And when his father bent and kissed him gently, lovingly on the head, tears broke from Lawrence's eyes.

"Sleep now, my boy," murmured Sir John. "Rest. I do love you. If that can make sense after all this."

With that he called for the turnkey and left Lawrence alone with his despair and the horror of the truth. Lawrence curled into a ball against the wall and wept.

CHAPTER FORTY-THREE

R ipler, the evil-faced orderly, came for him an hour later. He and two muscular goons forced him to dress in a crisp white shirt and clean britches, then they manhandled Lawrence into a straightjacket, then threw him down into a wheelchair and lashed him tight with leather bands.

"What . . . what is this?"

"Shut up," growled Ripler.

"I need to speak to Inspector Aberline," Lawrence implored. "Please, if I could just—"

Ripler cuffed him with a vicious backhand that rocked Lawrence's head and sent the world into a sickening spin. Then the orderly grabbed a handful of Lawrence's hair and bent so close that when he spoke the sour vapor of his breath was inescapable.

"Listen to me, guv'nor," hissed the orderly. "You mind your manners and 'old your tongue or me an' the lads will 'ave a go with you before we take you to see the doctor. Lafferty there's an old pro. 'E can bust your ribs without leaving a mark. And Strunk here is a right nasty lad. 'E should probably be in 'ere rather than working 'ere, ain't that right, Strunk?"

Strunk grinned to show a line of cracked and crooked teeth. "I'm a product of a troubled 'ousehold is what I am. Doctor 'Oenneger says so." His leer was an eloquent threat.

Ripler gave Lawrence's head a vicious shake and then released the handful of hair. He patted Lawrence on the cheek, and Lafferty stepped up to push the wheelchair as Ripler led the way through a series of long stone corridors. They passed dozens of barred doors through which Lawrence could see all manner of madness, from screaming lunatics who banged their heads on the walls to destroyed people who sat huddled in catatonic isolation. This was a familiar hell that he had thought himself permanently separated from, but Fate was more cruel than he had ever guessed.

They came to a set of double doors and Ripler and Strunk held them open as Lafferty pushed Lawrence into a large room that was filled with people. In the center of the room was a reinforced chair fitted out with straps and buckles, and nearby were tables laden with medical instruments of such arcane design that to Lawrence they looked like tools of the torture trade. The rest of the room was given over to bleachers that rose like in a stadium—or, to Lawrence's view—the seats at the Roman Coliseum. The seats were packed with scores of what Lawrence guessed to be medical doctors and scientists. He had heard about Hoenneger's theatrics even when he'd been here as a boy.

"What is this? . . ." Lawrence began, but before he could complete the question Ripler and his mates began unstrapping him from the wheelchair so they could wrestle him into the reinforced chair that was the centerpiece of the room. Lawrence struggled wildly but the men were much stronger, and when he opened his mouth to shout Ripler covertly punched him in the groin while Strunk simultaneously drove his knuckles into Lawrence's kidneys. It was so fast and smooth that it had the feel of a tactic these men had used many a time before, and never for any wholesome reason.

Voiceless with pain, Lawrence was helpless as they sat him down and fitted all of the restraints into place. When they were done all he could move was his head, and that lolled in a painful stupor for several minutes. Ripler bent toward Lawrence, ostensibly to make a last check of the restraints, but as he did so he gave Lawrence a final warning: "You behave yourself, mate, or you won't like what 'appens when you get back to your cell. No, indeed, my buck, you won't like that at all."

Lawrence raised his head and met the orderly's eyes. "Damn you to hell."

"Probably already am."

Lawrence mustered the energy to sneer. "Tell you what, friend," he whispered. "Wait until the moon rises and then come visit my cell."

Ripler just grinned and shook his head. "Bloody madmen," he said to his mates. "Always entertaining."

The orderly rose and waved his two cronies away. Dr. Hoenneger appeared next to him.

Ripler walked over to the double doors, locked them, and then returned to hand the keys to Hoenneger. "Everything's secure, sir," he said.

The doctor nodded, gave Lawrence only a fleeting glance, and then turned to his audience. Lawrence could tell that this was a show to Hoenneger, a performance.

"My friends and colleagues," Hoenneger began, "gentlemen of the press, representatives of Scotland Yard, and esteemed members of the public, I welcome you to Lambeth Asylum." His orator's voice was deeper and louder than his speaking voice and it filled the surgical theater. "We are here tonight to illustrate conclusively that your fears are quite irrational."

Hoenneger nodded to a second doctor, who walked across the hall to the far wall, took hold of a braided cord and pulled on it to draw back the sets of heavy drapes that covered the windows. The windows looked out over the crooked skyline of London and revealed a large expanse of the night sky in which a few pale clouds drifted across the lush white expanse of the fully risen moon.

Lawrence almost screamed.

"What . . . what are you doing?" he stammered and wrenched at the leather bands that held him in place. "You're insane. . . ."

Hoenneger turned from the vista of the full moon to face Lawrence, but he still pitched his voice to be heard by all. "We are going to remain in this room together all night. And once you've witnessed that the full moon holds no sway over you . . . that you remain a perfectly ordinary human being . . ."

". . . My God . . ." breathed Lawrence.

". . . you will have taken your first small step down the long road to recovery."

Lawrence stared at him in shock, unable to believe the dangerous insanity of this. He looked at the crowd, hoping to see a familiar face, someone to whom he could appeal, and there, far up in the stands, was Inspector Aberline.

"Aberline!" he cried. "You can't do this . . . you can't! Get everyone out!"

The inspector said nothing, even when those around him turned to him and a buzz of conversation rippled through the audience. Aberline's eyes were so hard and intense that Lawrence knew he had no ally there.

"Lycanthropy," pronounced Hoenneger, "is a disease of the mind, existing somewhere in the deep recesses of your thoughts. Yes, Mr. Talbot, I know that to you it seems very real."

"It is real! God in heaven, you have to believe me."

The doctor gave a small sad shake of his head. "You've suffered quite traumatic personal experiences, Mr. Talbot, we're all aware. You hate your father. Your mother committed suicide. Therefore your father must be to blame for her death . . ."

Once again Lawrence threw all of his weight and muscle against the leather straps, but though the leather creaked and the wooden chair rattled, escape was far beyond his powers.

"You witnessed your mother's self-mutilation. Your young mind, unable to accept it, created a fantastical truth: that your father is literally a monster."

Lawrence sagged against the straps, breathing hard, weakened by the chemicals, in pain from the abuse Ripler and his men had given him, defeated by his own human limitations.

"But, your *father* is not a werewolf," said Hoenneger, and there was a ripple of laughter from the audience. The doctor held up his hand to silence the crowd. "You were not *bitten* by a werewolf."

He turned dramatically toward the open window and the full moon.

"And you will not *become* a werewolf any more than I will sprout wings and fly out of that window."

This time Hoenneger allowed the laughter from his audience.

MILES AWAY, IN the old forest at the edge of the Talbot estate, moonlight bathed the circle of ancient standing stones. As the Goddess of the Hunt rode across the sky her pale light slid across the stones one by one until it caressed the heel stone. The light intensified as the moon swung toward the center point of the great celestial clock.

"TONIGHT," HOENNEGER SAID, "we will sit and watch the evening passing uneventfully."

"Damn you for a fool," Lawrence snapped. "Tonight you will sit and watch me become a werewolf . . . and then I will kill *all* of you!"

Hoenneger gave him a tolerant smile. "I believe we are all safe from you, Mr. Talbot . . . and you will see that you, too, are safe from demons that exist only in your mind."

"Please, Doctor," Lawrence implored, "listen to me. Even if you don't believe me then at least, for pity's sake, sedate me. Lock me up."

"You are quite well secured—"

"With chains and bars, damn it! Lock me up or . . . kill me. Please, that would be a mercy. Kill me!"

"Be at peace, Mr. Talbot. Soon you'll see that this is all in your mind."

Lawrence felt stabs of pain in his hands and he looked down to see the veins on the backs of his hands begin to throb as if huge amounts of blood were suddenly being forced through them. He watched in growing horror as his pores widened and black hairs began to sprout on his fingers and wrists.

"God . . . no," he said, and then to Hoenneger he cried: "It's *happening*!"

Hoenneger did not bother to look at him. He turned a knowing smile to the audience. Over his shoulder he said, "It's your imagination, Mr. Talbot. All in your vivid imagina—"

Lawrence screamed as a wave of pain hit him that was so enormous that he felt like his body was exploding. His limbs trembled with the onset of convulsions and he threw his head back as screams were ripped from him.

"Get . . . out! . . ."

Hoenneger saw the front rank of the audience suddenly leap to its feet and he turned, still smiling . . . but the smile died on his face. As he stood there and watched, Lawrence Talbot's eyes changed from brown to orange to a fiery yellow. Hoenneger's brain seemed to freeze. He stood, openedmouthed, watching as the teeth in Lawrence's screaming mouth lengthened and thickened, tearing the gums as they swelled to dagger-like points, and then the whole jaw *shifted*, expanding to allow more teeth to tear through. The flesh of Lawrence's hands and feet rippled as the bones broke and reformed into new shapes. Blood spurted from each fingertip as black claws tore through the flesh.

Hoenneger's mind was spinning toward darkness. For a moment a detached part of him thought that this was a forced manifestation, like the stigmata appearing on the wrists and feet of religious fanatics, but even as he thought that, the horrible truth of what he was seeing smashed that fantasy to fragments. This was happening, and it was happening right here. Inches away.

In the bleachers Inspector Aberline leaped to his feet, unable to see what was happening over the heads of the people in the rows ahead of him. He craned his neck for a better look and what he saw smashed into his mind like a bullet.

Lawrence tried to warn them all to run, but his mouth was no longer made for human speech and his mind was losing its ability to frame cohesive thought. The room was becoming brighter and his last conscious thought was the realization that he could *see* the blood glowing in the bodies of everyone in the room. And then everything that defined Lawrence Talbot as a human being was torn apart by what he was becoming.

The creature's body began expanding as its muscles swelled and its chest grew more massive. The seams on the heavy canvas straightjacket burst apart. The strap across his chest was forced outward so sharply that the metal of the buckle twisted and snapped.

People were screaming now and the crowd was shrinking back from this impossible spectacle.

"Get the needle!" Hoenneger shouted, but the assistant doctors were rooted to the floor by shock.

With an ear-shattering scream of rage the Wolfman surged up from the chair as leather straps ruptured and wood splintered. It rose to its full height, towering over Hoenneger and his staff. One doctor grabbed a metal tray and swung it at the creature's head, but the impact did nothing to the monster, except to anger it.

The Wolfman spun toward the doctor and struck him with a backhand that caught the man across the chin so fast and hard that his head spun more than halfway around. His neck snapped with a sound like knuckles cracking, and he fell dead to the floor.

Hoenneger grabbed a syringe and held it like a

weapon as he began backing away from the creature. The monster seemed momentarily confused, distracted by all of the people in the room. It was not afraid; rather the insatiable greed of its appetites pulled it in too many directions at once. The blood sang to him.

Inspector Aberline stood stock still on the stands, unable to process what he was seeing, unable to believe it, the pistol in his pocket forgotten in the insanity of the moment.

The Wolfman sensed movement near him and turned to see Dr. Hoenneger backing away. The creature did not possess human thoughts, could not access Lawrence Talbot's memories, but on some primal level it understood that this man was the enemy. Not just food, but a rival predator.

The creature bent forward, head low between its massive shoulders, and snarled a challenge.

But then it saw someone else that it hated even more. Ripler was making a dash for the doors. The Wolfman saw that man, remembered his smell, and equated it with attack and pain. With a snarl it leapt from the ruins of the restraining chair and cleared twenty feet in a single jump, landing on the stones ten feet from Ripler. The man screamed and grabbed for the door handles, forgetting that he had locked them and given the keys to Hoenneger.

He spun around as the Wolfman stalked toward him. The big, muscular orderly dropped to his knees and began weeping like a baby, begging for mercy. But as he had proven so many times to the helpless inmates in his charge, there was no mercy within these walls. The Wolfman grabbed him with its massive clawed hands, raised him over its head, and then threw Ripler at the wall forty feet away. The orderly hit with an impact that shattered bones. He collapsed to the floor, broken but alive, and the quirks of a merciless god kept him awake even as the Wolfman buried its snout in the orderly's stomach and began to feed.

"Jesus Christ!" someone shouted, and the yell somehow jolted Aberline out of his stupor. He shook his head and then raced down the rows of bleachers toward the monster.

Hoenneger and his assistant edged toward the locked doors. Hoenneger had the keys in one hand and the syringe in the other.

"Hurry, Doctor," hissed his assistant. "Hurry!"

Everywhere in the room there was panic as the crowd surged toward the various exit doors, all of which were locked.

"I got it," Hoenneger said breathlessly as he jammed the key into the lock and gave it a violent turn, but in his haste he used far too much force. The slender key bent . . . and broke.

"Oh God!"

The Wolfman raised its head, smelling a new flavor of fear. He turned and again saw Hoenneger, but this time the man was screaming and pounding on the locked door.

OUTSIDE THE ROOM, Lafferty and Strunk heard the commotion and tried to work the handles, but the door was solidly locked. The door's small circular window was opaque and they couldn't see what was happening, but as they watched, someone began beating his fists on the glass. The glass cracked and shattered and the two bruisers stared in surprise as Dr. Hoenneger pressed his face against the jagged opening.

"*Help*! Let me out! Oh, Lord . . . someone please open this—"

Strunk patted his pockets. "Right, sir. I'll just pop 'round to the works office and get the key. Won't take a—"

"You bleeding imbecile!" screamed Hoenneger. "Open this door—"

And then something huge and dark appeared behind the doctor and yanked him backward and out of sight. A split second later the broken window was sprayed with blood. The sound of screams from inside was drowned by the roar of something immeasurably strong and unnatural.

Lafferty looked at the bloody window and then turned to Strunk.

Without a word they bolted down the hallway, running as fast as they could. Another custodian ran past them, heading toward the mad din in the examination theater. Strunk and Lafferty watched him go.

"Think we should have told Roger not to—?"

"Not our concern, lad."

They tore down stairways and skidded around turns until they burst out of the Asylum's front door.

"What the bleedin' 'ell is 'appening back there?" demanded Lafferty.

"God if I know," said Strunk. "And I don't want to know."

They heard a crash and looked up as the big picture window of the surgical theater six stories above exploded outward. Something red and twisted came hurtling into the night and the men lingered just a second too long in shocked surprise. As they turned to run glass rained down on them and Dr. Hoenneger's body crashed onto the spikes of a wrought-iron fence that ran along the edge of the Lambeth grounds. The doctor had been ruined—torn and mangled—and much of him was missing, and he hung from the gate's spikes like some grisly trophy.

They stared at the corpse and then turned once more to look up.

The Wolfman, falling silently, was plummeting through the shadows toward them. It had a six-story fall to gather speed and the impact smashed both men into the cobblestones with so much force that their internal organs were pulped and blood exploded through their pores.

The fall jarred the Wolfman but it pitched forward onto the grass beside the cobbled walkway and crouched there, waiting as broken bones reformed and torn muscle tissue was made whole within seconds. It threw back its head and howled for the sheer joy of the fresh meat in its belly and the power of its life force.

There was a sharp *crack* and sparks leapt from a guardrail a yard away. The Wolfman craned its neck upward to see a man leaning out of the window. There was another crack and fire leapt from the man's hand. A bullet tore through the Wolfman's shoulder, passing through flesh and nicking bone before burying itself in the dirt. But before the man could fire his third shot the wound was gone as if it had never existed.

The Wolfman roared at the figure in the high window and then turned and dropped forward, running on all fours faster than any wolf ever did . . . faster than any animal that the natural world ever produced ever could. It leapt over railings and hedges, springing high into the air without effort, reveling in the power that coursed through its muscles. People—men and women—screamed and fled before it. Horses reared and kicked and shied away; mongrel dogs whined and rolled onto their backs as it passed.

The creature jumped onto a low wall that led to a shed rooftop, then climbed a drainpipe more nimbly than an ape. At the top of a tall building it stopped and paused to look around. It feared nothing. It hungered for everything. There was a line of statues perched on the edge of the roof and the Wolfman climbed onto the largest, a massive stone griffin. There it lingered, staring down at the city, at its playground, at its hunting fields. He could smell the sweat and fear and blood. He knew that everything down there that was aware of him feared him.

And he, in turn, hungered for all of them.

CHAPTER FORTY-FOUR

Inspector Aberline burst from the Asylum's lower doors and skidded to a halt by the gate. The moon was on the other side of the building and the courtyard was in shadows, but Aberline could smell blood. He fumbled in his pockets for an electric torch and shined its light across the ground and then gasped at what the light revealed. Dr. Hoenneger's torn body hung limp and ragged from the spikes and the two orderlies lay in pools of blood on the walkway.

"Dear God in heaven . . ."

His mind felt disconnected from reality. He could *not* have seen the things he had seen. It was impossible, insane.

And yet . . .

He drew a steadying breath and squatted down to play the torchlight over the ground. A line of clawed footprints were dug into the soil of the verge. The trail ran for only a few steps and then a pair of deeper marks showed where the creature had leapt toward the row of hedges.

Aberline dug into his pocket for his whistle and he blew a high, shrill note, the note as shrill as the scream that might otherwise have burst from his chest. Once, twice . . . and then it was answered almost immediately by another whistle down the lane. And another far to his left.

With trembling fingers, Aberline reloaded his pistol. He was still trying to accept the facts as he knew them . . . and what they meant to his understanding of the world. His heart was beating like the hooves of a galloping horse and sweat ran down inside his clothes.

"Steady on," he muttered to himself as he pressed the shells into the chambers of the cylinder. He thought about the blacksmith in the village and the silver bullets. "Steady on . . ."

In the distance he heard the running feet of a squadron of constables.

But before they could arrive he heard a sound and turned to look up at the roof of the building on the far side of the hedges, and there, framed against a rounded curve of the moon, was the monster.

Every instinct told Aberline to run. He saw his death up there. He saw hell itself crouching atop a stone griffin, the Devil himself in true form. He wanted to run.

And he did run.

Toward the building.

THE WOLFMAN'S HUNGER was a furnace that could not be fed. It screamed within him, demanding meat, demanding blood.

It leaped from the back of the griffin and began running along the edges of the building, jumping from one rooftop to another with ease, sometimes dropping to all fours to spring faster than a racehorse, sometimes climbing, always moving, a blur of darkness against the smiling face of the Goddess of the Hunt.

Aberline ran as fast as he could, trying to keep pace with the monster. He saw it leap from a building and land badly, scrambling for purchase at the edge of the building across the way.

"Got you!" Aberline hissed. He stopped and stood with his legs braced, raised his pistol in both hands, closed one eye and fired.

The first bullet tore a chunk of brick and dust from the wall a foot from the monster's shoulder. Aberline drew a breath, corrected and fired again. And again. He could see the back of the creature's shirt puff with each impact. He fired and fired until the hammer clicked on an empty cylinder.

The Wolfman did not fall. It did not falter. It threw a growl over its shoulder and then hauled itself over the edge of the building and vanished.

Aberline cursed and kept running.

He had no idea what he would do, or could do. He had just used the last of his cartridges.

TWO BOBBIES ON horseback heard the bleat of whistles and then six spaced gunshots. They turned and tracked the echoes to the far side of the park.

"That's the Asylum," growled Pettit. "Jailers have let another madman slip out."

"Bloody loonies ought to be put down," answered Frost as he kicked his mount into a jump to clear a row of hedges. They angled toward the center of the park, the quickest route to the Asylum, but both horses suddenly cried out and reared as a wave of screaming people broke from under the shadows of the trees and surged toward them in a mass.

"What the bloody 'ell?" demanded Pettit.

"All the loonies have broken out," warned Frost as he drew his baton. But the crowd that surged toward them and past them were not inmates in straightjackets or prison pajamas. They were businessmen and clerks, ladies and street musicians, wealthy children and shabby beggars. The only thing that unified them was the absolute terror written onto each face.

The tide of shrieking, panicked people washed past them, spilling out into the streets, running away from the row of buildings near the Asylum.

The two bobbies stood up in the stirrups and looked beyond the trees at the buildings and at the thing that ran from rooftop to rooftop.

"Oh my God . . . ," they said in perfect chorus.

ABERLINE BROKE FROM the park and ran toward a knot of constables hurrying his way on foot.

"Are you armed?" he demanded.

Two of them produced pistols and one man in the back had a shotgun.

"Give me your gun," he demanded and the nearest officer handed over a heavy pistol. "And all your bullets. Come on, hurry, damn you."

The wave of panicking people were sweeping toward him, but Aberline crashed into them, shoving people roughly out of his way. The bobbies fanned out behind him in a muscular phalanx off of which the mob rebounded.

"There!" called one of the officers, and Aberline saw that the creature had changed direction, heading now toward the center of town. They pelted after him, racing down streets, cutting through alleys. When they ran down a shadowy street that proved to be a dead-ended mews, Aberline stopped, cursing in frustration.

Music floated through an open window to their left, and immediately Aberline ran that way. He didn't even pause at the door but crashed into it with two burly sergeants on either side. The door was ripped from its hinges and the officers pounded over it, crashing into the middle of a gathering of richly dressed toffs seated on sofas and ornate chairs as a string quartet played some pastoral confection. The music screeched to a sour halt and the gathered gentry cried out in shock and protest, but Aberline had no time for détente. He led his men through the house, kicked open the back door, and ran into the yard. He raised his pistol, expecting the monster to be leaping from that rooftop to the next, but there was no movement.

The monster had changed direction. They'd lost him.

BEYOND THE WALL were bright lights and the smell of meat. The Wolfman narrowed its yellow eyes and watched as people—scores of them—moved through the streets. Hot spittle dripped from its teeth as its muzzle wrinkled back in a hunting snarl.

It crept forward, selecting the perfect prey. . . .

ABERLINE RAN DOWN the alley and burst out into the street in time to see two of his best detectives, Carter and Adams, jumping down from an armored wagon.

"Carter! You got a pistol?"

"Yes, sir. We're both—"

"Good," Aberline snapped. "Follow me. The rest of

you men, find a way to get to the rooftops. Spread out and find this thing." But he paused and jabbed a finger into Adams' chest. "Telegraph the yard. Issue weapons to everyone. Now!"

Aberline slapped Carter on the shoulder and the two of them ran.

Between puffing breaths, Aberline asked, "Carter . . . does the Yard have any silver bullets?"

Carter ran ten steps before he replied. "Silver?"

THE WOLFMAN WAS blocks away, running along the rooftops, tracking the movement of the herds of prey below. The greed of its own appetite made it indecisive. Each new one he saw looked more enticing than the last. Drool flew from his mouth and spattered the slashed remains of Lawrence Talbot's white shirt.

AS ABERLINE AND Carter burst from the maze of alleys they saw a large group of bobbies running in a pack toward the commotion. When the officers saw Aberline they ran to meet him.

"Carter, take half of these men . . . gather whomever else you can and protect the streets. Who knows where this beast will strike. The rest of you come with me."

EIGHT BLOCKS AWAY a constable sat astride a bored horse in the center of Leicester Square trying impatiently to manage the flow of traffic. He had not yet gotten word of the escaped killer and the rush and bustle was irritating him. There was only an hour left of his shift and he liked things calm and quiet.

An old woman struggled across the square, moving with painful slowness on arthritic legs and blocking the flow of carriage traffic.

"Come on, come on," he barked. "Move along smartly!"

The lady looked up at him, startled at his rudeness, and then her eyes flared wider and wider and her mouth opened into a silent "O."

"What is it, you old—"

The bobby never saw the mass of muscle and claws that hurtled down at him from the rooftop of the nearby clock tower. He felt a sudden jolt and then the world seemed to be tumbling and spinning around him.

THE WOMAN WHO ran the flower cart heard a scream and the sound of an impact and turned just as a vast something smashed into her cart and something smaller and heavy hit her in the chest. She fell backward with the object resting on her skirts between her outstretched legs. She stared, unable to comprehend the severed head of the traffic constable. Her eyes met those of the bobby and there was still life there. Dazed, she turned and watched as the bobby's body, still sitting astride his horse, went galloping wildly down the street. Then she looked down at the head in her lap. Impossibly, the bobby opened his mouth and tried to scream. He could not.

So she screamed for both of them as a bloody thing rose from the wreckage of her cart and turned a drooling face toward her.

ABERLINE SAW THE lights of the local police station and cut across the street toward it. He blew his whistle as he ran and a cluster of officers scrambled down the stairs. A sergeant strode toward him, one hand up to stop him.

"What's all this then?" he demanded, but Aberline skidded to a halt and flashed his inspector's badge.

"Sergeant, telegraph the Yard. Issue weapons."

"What for, sir?"

As if in answer to the inquiry an unearthly howl split the night, the echoes bouncing off of the surrounding buildings as if a pack of monsters was descending on London.

"*Now!*" bellowed Aberline.

THE DEAD TRAFFIC officer's horse ran at a full gallop down the middle of the street, its headless passenger still mounted perversely in the saddle. The corpse's booted feet were jammed into the stirrups and the reins were knotted around one slack hand. It was a grisly sight, something out of a penny dreadful, and pedestrians—men and women alike—screamed and recoiled from it. The horse veered off toward the park, its shrill cries filled with panic.

And in its wake, running on all fours, the Wolfman followed.

When the crowd saw what pursued, they turned and fled, convinced that the gates of Hell itself had been thrown wide and devils walked the earth.

BRIGHT LIGHTS, MUSIC and the tinkling sound of laughter washed over the Wolfman's senses. It slowed, letting the headless horseman gallop away. The creature rose from all fours and stood erect, sniffing the air, smelling meat and blood, hearing pulses throbbing beneath fragile skin. The grizzled flesh of its muzzle wrinkled in pleasure and fresh, hot saliva boiled out of its gums and dripped onto the grass.

The Wolfman began stalking these new sounds, following the glow from beyond the trees.

Then it paused a dozen yards away from the glowing walls of glass that formed one side of the conservatory. Its eyes narrowed as it studied the terrain and calculated the best point of attack. But its stomach rumbled with hunger and as it began stalking slowly forward the Wolfman bent and licked the glistening red gore that coated its arms from claws to elbow. The blood was sweet but it was already growing cold. Hot, fresh blood was so much more delicious . . . and there was so much of it before him, confined, contained within those glowing glass walls.

The Wolfman smiled a predator's smile, filled with red delight.

ALL ACROSS LONDON the telegraph wires ignited with the news. Officers by the score grabbed pistols and shotguns and took to the streets. Aberline, still on foot, led his small party of men back into the park, drawn by a fresh wave of terrible screams. In the far distance, all the way on the other side of the vast park, he saw the lights of the conservatory and his heart sank. There was a masked ball tonight and half the nobility of London would be there.

As he ran his mind burned with a litany of pleas. *Oh, God . . . oh, God . . . let me be in time.*

But he knew that he would not be in time.

CHAPTER FORTY-FIVE

The glass-domed conservatory was decorated like a fairy kingdom, with hundreds of tiny candles hidden among the evergreen garland and colorful bunting. Tables were laden with food of every description: there were pot-bellied baskets of steaming chestnuts, pyramids of polished pears and apples, half a dozen varieties of fat grapes, silver trays laden with salmon and trout garnished with pineapple and lemon, a row of suckling pigs roasted to pink perfection, a dozen plump geese overflowing with sage and onion stuffing, and central to it all a huge roast of beef that was red and luscious.

Hundreds of people crowded the chamber, each of them in exotic costumes. A pirate with an eye patch and tricorn walked arm-in-arm with Cleopatra; a satyr stood talking politics with Apollo, King Henry VIII and Merlin. King Arthur and Sir Francis Drake vied for the attentions of Marie Antoinette, while Bacchus sat in a corner getting quietly drunk with Jack-of-the-Green and William Wallace. There were Greenmen and Celtic warlords, most of the Greek and Roman gods, and six separate Tam Lins, who each affected not to notice the others. The costumes were expensive and elaborate, some very specific, others more vague, but all were beautiful.

Threescore people sat in chairs arranged in front of a dais which was occupied by the orchestra. The rest walked in and out of doors, sat at small tables with plates of food, or stood huddled together in conversational groups that broke and reformed.

Wine flowed like the blood of heaven and applause rolled like thunder as the orchestra finished the *Clarinet Quintet in B Minor, Opus 115*, the latest piece by Johannes Brahms.

As the applause died down a young girl dressed like a fairy princess led a blind soprano to the center of the stage. The soprano was gorgeous, in an elegant gown of silk and lace, and her milky eyes seemed to possess an awareness that transcended the mundane world. The audience was excited for this performance, the centerpiece of the evening—Rowena's aria from *Ivanhoe*, accompanied only by the first violin. The violinist stepped up and bowed to the lady and to the audience and tucked his beautiful instrument under his chin.

The soprano drew a slow breath, waiting for the introductory note, and the musician delicately placed his bow on the strings and closed his eyes to immerse himself in the music that was about to flow through him. With a deft turn of his wrist the bow glided over the first string, coaxing out the whisper of the initial sweet note, and when the introduction had run its course the soprano began to sing.

The Wolfman stood in the rear doorway and watched as the colors moved and swirled around him. The music enchanted him and it caused his mind to vacillate between the urgency of the hunt and some other, more deeply hidden need. He entered the huge room but did not attack. He was confused by the prey. None of them feared him. A few wrinkled their noses at him, but he could sense no fear, could smell none of the scents of panic and flight that triggered his instinct to hunt and kill. When the soprano began to sing, the Wolfman turned his head toward her, picking out her voice from amid the din of laughter and conversation. The sound was like nothing else the creature had experienced, and almost immediately it lifted him above the hunger, above the input of its other senses.

The Wolfman took a step toward her, and another, drawn to the sound of her voice, and for a moment the hunt was forgotten.

As the creature moved among the revelers he brushed past a woman in a white gown. The woman gaped at the red smear that now glistened on the expensive fabric of her costume. She touched her fingers to it and sniffed. Her eyes widened. She had been on too many fox hunts not to recognize that unique coppery smell.

She screamed, but the cry was nearly lost beneath the weight of the music and other noise. The people around her glanced at her, and at the hairy thing moving among them, and smiled.

Robinson Crusoe leaned close to shout in the ear of Sir Galahad. "Bloody good costume, don't you think?"

Galahad, a city banker with a long nose, sniffed disdainfully. "Hardly looks real, does it?"

The Wolfman kept moving toward the stage, its eyes glazed with fascination. He bumped into people and pushed aside a waiter with a tray of canapés. When the entire tray of roast baby new potato with caviar and *crème fraîche* chive mash tumbled into the lap of the Third Earl of Rosse, everyone at his table leaped to their feet in outrage.

The Earl's nephew, a rich merchant, grabbed the Wolfman's arm.

"I do say, sir," he began with loud indignation, "your manners are quite disgus—"

That was the last thing he ever said. The moment the merchant touched the Wolfman's arm the spell of the music was broken. All at once the inner call vanished and was entirely replaced by the unyielding compulsion of the hunt. The Wolfman lashed out with incredible speed and ferocity, clamped his powerful hands on the merchant's upper arms and snatched him off the ground and then clamped his jaws around the man's head. Bones cracked, skin split and gore showered everyone around.

The screams this savage action invoked were not lost in the din, and they did not go unnoticed.

In his fury the Wolfman had bitten down so hard and so deeply that his fangs were locked into the hard bone of the merchant's skull. It snarled in frustration and rage, shaking the man's body to try and tear itself free. Despite the dreadful wound, the merchant was still alive, and he screamed and beat furiously at the monster, but each of his blows carried less force. The Third Earl gaped at the spectacle playing out inches from where he sat, his face spattered with hot blood.

The revelers scattered as fast as if a bomb had dropped in their midst, everyone running madly in every direction with the blind urgency to be anywhere but where they stood. Those who did not move fast enough were knocked down and trampled by lords and ladies as panic ruled the moment. People screamed in terror at what they had seen and in pain as they were buffeted and battered underfoot. Notable men shoved women out of the way; a visiting duchess yanked her daughter's

hair to clear the way for her own escape; a highly regarded Member of Parliament collapsed into a blub-
bering heap, too frightened even to flee.

The Wolfman, unable to tear its fangs free, bent
forward and bit down hard, crushing the bones in its
powerful jaws, and then it reared back and tore the entire crown of the merchant's skull off. The man collapsed to the ground, dead and limp, and the Wolfman
howled with triumph.

On the stage it was the same, as the orchestra flung
down their instruments and dashed for the edges of the
rostrum. One hearty cellist grabbed his instrument by
the neck and swung it like a war hammer so that it splintered across the monster's broad back, and a moment
later he was dead, his broken body discarded among
the abandoned instruments.

Alone and forgotten in the mad surge, the soprano held
her ground and tried to understand what her remaining
senses told her. She heard screams and the stampede of
people, and she heard a growl that sounded like a wild
animal. None of it made sense.

ABERLINE HEARD THE first screams a second before
the revelers began surging out of the conservatory in a
mad rush. He ran toward the entrance, but it was like
wading into a crashing tidal surge. Bodies buffeted
him, people tried to shove him back to clear a path for
their own escape, desperate women clawed at him in their
terror.

By the time Aberline and his men reached the doorway, the floor of the conservatory was already awash in
blood. Aberline stepped inside and raised his pistol,

trying for a clear shot, but there were so many damned people . . .

THE WOLFMAN TURNED in a slow circle, enjoying the flight of prey, but when it saw the soprano standing there it narrowed its eyes. This one was not acting like prey, and the Wolfman sniffed the air for the telltale scent of another predator. But no . . . all it smelled was fear and it growled quietly as it took a step toward her, its lips curling back from its teeth as it opened its mouth to take a bite.

Then suddenly it was knocked sideways by two hard punches to its shoulder. The Wolfman spun, snarling a challenge, but there was no enemy at hand. There was a loud *pop* and a third impact drilled fire into its chest and the creature saw a man standing twenty feet away. Fire erupted from the man's hand and there was more pain. The Wolfman recognized this enemy and it tensed to spring even as the four bullet wounds closed and vanished.

FRANCIS ABERLINE STOOD his ground and continued to fire at the monster even though he could see that the bullets were doing little real harm.

The bullets distracted the creature from the blind woman, but the creature did not fall. How in God's name did it not fall? Aberline fired his last shot as the creature tensed for a leap, and then the air was filled with the firecracker bursts of a dozen shots as a wave of bobbies came pelting into the conservatory.

"Kill the bloody thing!" bellowed Aberline as he dug fresh bullets out of his coat pocket.

A fusillade of bullets struck the Wolfman, driving it back from sheer impact and drenching its clothing with fresh blood, but it did not fall. It did not even flinch.

But it did not like the shrill bleat of the whistles.

The creature roared a challenge and then spun and leapt over the buffet tables and smashed through one of the glass walls. The exploding glass tore a thousand jagged cuts in the monster's hide and bullets tore the heaped food to fragments, but the monster was gone.

THE WOLFMAN LANDED on the sidewalk outside of the conservatory. It crouched low and stared around, momentarily overwhelmed by the noise and movement. There were hundreds of people on the streets. Gentlemen and their ladies out for an evening stroll, street vendors by the dozen, street urchins dashing in and out of the crowds, corner musicians, and others, crowding the London intersection. Scores of carriages and coaches rattled along the cobblestone streets, and a clunky steam-powered omnibus trundled along, every seat filled and people hanging onto side straps.

The noise was painful. Screeches and squeals and shouts. Women shrieked, horses whinnied in fear, men yelled in fright as the creature stalked slowly into the center of the square. A blind beggar pulled off his black glasses and stared at the monster, and then he turned and bolted faster than his own dog could follow.

The driver of the omnibus was the last person in the square to understand what was happening. People suddenly started running across the street, heedless of the big machine. The driver jerked the lanyard for the shrill steam whistle and he emphasized the warnings with a string of curses that would have shamed a dockhand. No one paid any attention to him and he swerved and swung the wheel to avoid committing mayhem.

And then something impossible reared up directly in front of the omnibus. A thing from a nightmare, with tall tufted ears and a face from Hell itself. The Wolfman hissed at the big machine and the driver jerked the wheel hard to one side, but in his panic he swung it too hard. Mass and momentum, and the weight of all the passengers, were against him and the omnibus canted sideways, two of its tires lifting off the ground. It paused for a moment, balanced on the other wheels, and then there was a loud *snap* as the front axle collapsed and the whole mass of it fell sideways even while the omnibus was still moving forward. It crashed down with a thunderclap and slid along the cobbles past the monster. A dozen passengers were crushed under the weight of the whole crowd falling sideways and down. Everyone screamed in confusion and pain, and the Wolfman had to leap atop the bus to avoid being crushed. It landed on a side window and before the bus had stopped sliding the creature began pressing its face against the cracked glass. It could smell the fear of the mass of writhing people inside. The window cracked more, dropping pieces inside. The Wolfman thrust its hand in through the jagged hole, ignoring the teeth of the broken glass, reaching, stretching to grab an arm or leg or throat.

Then suddenly the whole window caved in and the Wolfman pitched headlong down onto the wriggling tangle of trapped passengers. It landed with a howl of surprise and anger. This was not a hunt, this felt like a trap. Panic flared in its heart and the Wolfman scrabbled to right itself, inadvertently tearing flesh with its claws as it fought to get out of the confined space.

Then the bobbies burst from the park, Aberline at the forefront, all of them firing at the creature as it crawled out of the overturned bus. Whistle bleats filled the air. Still confused by the sudden confinement, the Wolfman turned and fled down an alley on the far side of the fallen omnibus.

ABERLINE GRABBED A burly sergeant. "Take ten men and block the alley. I'll take the rest and circle behind. We'll catch the bastard in a crossfire."

The sergeant gave him a curt nod and was calling out names as he headed into the alley. Aberline took the rest and raced to the corner as fast as he could.

IN THE ALLEY the Wolfman ran with incredible speed, occasionally dropping to all fours before springing over heaped garbage or tethered horses. The bobbies ran as fast as they could, all of them fit and tough, but the monster outpaced them with ease.

The sergeant, a fleet-footed Scot with a dark red mustache and the cold eye of an ex-soldier, aimed his pistol as he ran. He'd been in running fights before and he knew how to time breath and stride with the pull of the trigger so that he was a deadly marksman even at a full run. His pistol bucked in his hand and the bullet caught up with the fleeing monster. Blood pocked the back of the tattered white shirt. The sergeant grinned as he ran and put a second bullet into its back a handsbreadth from the other.

The creature slowed and stopped, and the sergeant shared a quick look with the bobby running next to him. They had the thing!

They raced toward it, still firing, wanting to tear the thing to pieces.

But the Wolfman had not stopped because of the sergeant's bullets. Or, not because of any injury they were intended to have made. It stopped because the bullets were not doing any harm at all. The predatory instincts understood this now, and the creature had not turned because it was at bay. It turned to attack.

With a howl of bloody delight it leaped at the policemen, and before they could realize that the trap had turned on them the Wolfman was among them.

WHEN INSPECTOR ABERLINE and his men flooded into the alley from the far side of the block they found nothing alive.

The creature had done its butchery and escaped.

Aberline stood amid the wreckage of sanity and order. His own clothes were as red-splashed as those of the dead officers who lay around him, his face as bloodless.

He looked down at the pistol he carried. It had been useless. Less than useless, like a toy gun against a tiger. All of the fight that was left in him drained away, leaving him empty. Spent.

Aberline was not a religious man. He had never held much stock in faith. But he whispered, "God help us."

And he meant it.

"God help us all."

CHAPTER FORTY-SIX

The Wolfman squatted for a long time in the inky shadows of the bridge. He tore a bite from a severed arm, chewed slowly, took another bite. When the flesh was gone he snapped the forearm and sucked out the marrow.

When there was no more to eat, he dropped the bones and gristle into the water and settled back against the moss-covered bricks. They were cool and soothing. The sound of whistles and people yelling had faded off to the north and soon died altogether.

The monster sniffed the air. There was no one near. A few rats, but nothing that he wanted to hunt, and nothing that was hunting him. In the east a pale rim of light was slowly defining the outlines of buildings.

The creature's eyes felt heavy. This spot felt safe. The hunt was over for now. It was time to rest.

Chapter Forty-seven

Lawrence did not want to open his eyes. He feared the light. He feared being awake. He feared everything.

He gradually became aware that he was awake, but his body felt somehow missing, as if he was only consciousness with no form. Lawrence hoped that he was dead, *prayed* that he was dead.

Then, bit by bit, his physical awareness returned. The first thing he felt was pain. It was vague, an amorphous mass of pain in which his consciousness seemed to float, but it gradually became specific. He felt his back, one aching vertebra at a time, as if someone ran a finger along and poked each throbbing edge of bone. His arms sent messages of inert agony, and then his legs. Lawrence had no idea how long the process took. An hour, a year.

When he finally mustered the courage to open his eyes he had to blink them clear. He stared straight up to see a blue sky framed by grimy brick walls. The walls were gouged with claw marks and splattered with blood. It did not surprise him, but it sickened him. He wished the walls would crumble and fall in to crush the life from him.

Smell returned next and the stink was horrendous. Spoiled meat, rotten fruit, foul water, sweat and human waste. Lawrence realized that he was lying in a heap of garbage under a bridge. He gagged, and the stench more than anything else made him move.

Lawrence sat up slowly. Nausea was a sick wash in his stomach and his eyes watered from the smell. He looked at his hands and what he saw made the sickness a thousand times worse. They were caked with dried blood.

His whole body and his clothes were nothing more than tattered streamers smeared with gore and filth. The cry of gulls was a chorus of accusations that flayed him.

"God, no . . ." he prayed.

He looked around and saw that he was in an alley that was heaped with rubbish. And he was not alone. A corpse—an old beggar in castoff clothes—lay three feet away. The man's face was a ruin, an arm was missing.

Lawrence buried his face in his bloody hands and wept.

LATER, DRESSED IN the dead man's clothes and smelling of garbage and death, Lawrence Talbot shambled along the streets of London. He walked like a zombie, head bowed, eyes staring blankly at the ground, feet barely lifting from the concrete. Passersby saw him and walked around him, shaking their heads in disgust. Women pulled their children to the opposite sides of the street. Even stray dogs growled warnings at him.

As he walked he mumbled the words, "Please, God . . . please, God . . ." over and over again, and the unspoken end of that plea echoed in his head.

Please God . . . let me die.

But he did not die and Lawrence cursed God for His bloody indifference.

When he reached Essington Lane he stopped and realized that he knew where he was going. The thought jolted him. Lawrence stared at the street sign, set into the plaster of the side of the near building, and he turned and looked across the street. He could not understand how he had managed to make his way here without knowing that he was heading anywhere, and to a place whose address he had only heard but had never visited.

Yet there it was, right across the street, its reality proclaimed on a painted sign: CONLIFFE APOTHECARY.

Lawrence licked his lips.

What would the Conliffes do? Would they bar the door against him? They should, even though tonight's moon would not be full. Would they call for the police? Half of him wished they would—and maybe he could contrive to get the police to shoot him down right there on the doorstep. Or would they shoot him down like the animal he had become? That would be justice . . . and perhaps a mercy. Throughout the morning, as Lawrence had staggered along the side streets and back alleys he heard the newsboys yelling the headlines. Mad killer on the loose, they all said.

Mad?

No . . . something far worse than mad.

He stared at the Conliffe's shop. It looked closed, but there were lights on in the rooms above. Gwen had said that she and her father lived above their store on Essington Lane, between a milliners and a flower shop.

He chewed his lip. If they chased him off would he go? *Could* he go? Or did the survival instinct of the wolf still rule his deepest mind?

With these doubts gnawing at the walls of his soul, Lawrence risked everything and stepped into the street, threaded his way through the traffic, and crept up to the door of the shop. It took more strength than he thought he possessed to raise his hand and ring the bell.

Silence was the only answer. The windows were dark and he cupped his hands to peer inside. The establishment looked empty and his heart sank, but then he saw someone move in the shadows at the back of the shop. A moment later the lock clicked and the door opened.

Gwen Conliffe looked at him and opened her mouth to dismiss the beggar at her door.

"Gwen . . ." said Lawrence, in a voice that was filled with all of the heartbreak and need in the world.

Her eyes widened as she saw past the grime and dried blood and agony.

"Oh my God! Lawrence!"

"I—" he began, but Gwen seized him by the arms and pulled him urgently into the shop. She closed the door and pulled the shade and then hurried over to draw the curtains across the picture window so that only a sliver of the cold morning light sliced through the brown shadows of the shop. Then she turned to him, her hand touching her throat.

"Lawrence? What are you doing here? How did you—?"

"Is your father here?"

"No. He's away on a buying trip in Paris. Oh God, please tell me what's going on."

Lawrence sagged back against the foyer wall and ran trembling fingers through the greasy tangle of his hair. "What's going on?" he mused and almost smiled. The attempt was ghastly. "Horrible things . . . and it's all true. All of it. Gwen . . . I am what they say I am."

"No . . ."

"And it's worse still than that."

She still stood by the curtained window, ten feet

away, and she did not move. "What do you mean? The things I've heard . . . what could be worse?"

Lawrence slid down the wall until he sat on the floor of the foyer, his head in his hands. "My father is . . . he's the same as me. And—God, how can I even make myself say this—I'm certain that Benjamin knew about it and tried to stop him. I think that's why he was in the forest that night." Lawrence wiped tears from his eyes. "And I'm just as certain that's how he was killed."

Gwen stood there, her face defined by the sliver of cold, hard light of day. Lawrence could see how his words tore into her, how the implications lacerated her heart and soul. Tears gathered in the corners of her eyes and dropped like silver rain down her cheeks. He expected her to scream. He expected her to throw him out into the street.

He did not expect her to cross the room and kneel down in front of him. She touched his face with gentle fingers.

"I'm so very sorry," she said.

Her words, her kindness, broke him. A huge sob hitched his chest and then he was crying uncontrollably. Gwen gathered him in her arms, and she, too, wept.

Chapter Forty-eight

Lawrence lay shirtless in a guest bedroom above the apothecary. His clothes had been burned in the furnace. He'd bathed for nearly two hours in a hot tub as Gwen brought endless pots of steaming water. He scrubbed his skin until it was nearly raw, and even though the gore and filth washed away he could not cleanse himself of the feel of it, and knew that he probably never would. Not if he lived for a century, and he doubted he would see the end of this year.

When he had first awakened in the alley and had stripped off his rags to clothe himself in the dead beggar's garments, Lawrence had been covered with scratches and cuts and the bites of a hundred insects. Now his skin was totally unmarked. Lawrence did not remark on this to Gwen, but he knew that his lack of scars was damning proof that he wore the Mark of Cain. The mark of the Wolf.

The clock was chiming seven o'clock in the evening when Gwen entered carrying a dinner tray. As she set it down Lawrence saw the folded newspaper lying beside the coffeepot. With great trepidation he took the paper and unfolded it. He feared what it would say, but what he saw was worse than he even imagined. There was a photograph of him that must have been taken shortly after his arrival at Lambeth Asylum. The face it showed was that of a crazed, wild-eyed madman. The headline, with huge letters, read:

ESCAPED LUNATIC AT LARGE
DOZENS KILLED BY MONSTER

" 'Dozens' . . ." he whispered and closed his eyes, and for the first time since his mother's death, he crossed himself.

Once again he looked at Gwen expecting to see horror and revulsion, but again all he saw was compassion and pity. Fresh tears glistened in her eyes.

"I can help you."

Lawrence threw down the paper and set the tray aside. He swung his legs off the bed and sat up. "There is no help for me," he said in a low, savage voice.

"Maybe there is," Gwen said as she held out her hand to him. Something silver glimmered in her palm. "Here."

He sat there, unable to move, so Gwen took the medal and looped the chain over his head so that the talisman lay over his heart. The medal was warm from her palm, but the warmth seemed to sink into his flesh and loosen the strictures around his heart, and for the first time all morning he found that he could take a deep breath.

"If such things are possible, Lawrence . . . is not all of it possible? Magic? The Devil?"

He looked up.

"Even . . . God?" she asked.

Lawrence touched the medal, and something like hope flickered within him. A weak flame flickering in the black breath of the wolf, but there nonetheless.

"Yes," he said softly. "It's all possible."

She knelt and took his hands, squeezing them with

surprising strength. "Then there *must* be a way to stop it, too!"

"No . . . ," he began, but the urgency in her eyes washed the protest from his lips. "Gwen, listen to me. I have to accept what I've done, and if there is a God then my doom is already certain. I'll burn in Hell for the pain I've caused."

"No! You were not yourself. Something *else* did that."

"*I* did those things, Gwen. Whether I was in control or not."

"Then it's like an infection. If you are sick and your sickness causes harm to others then it's not your fault." She stroked his cheek. "This morning, when you told me what happened at that horrible asylum, you told me you begged them to lock you up, to chain you, to *kill* you."

"Yes . . ."

"But they didn't! *They* did not. If they had done as you asked no one would have been hurt. If your father had warned you in time, if he had locked you up back in Blackmoor rather than locking you out, then you would have harmed no one. This is not your fault, Lawrence. You're a good, decent man."

He attempted another smile. "No one has ever accused me of decency before."

She shook her head fiercely. "This . . . disease or curse or whatever it is . . . this was done to you. Not by you."

"No one else will think that."

"I do," she insisted. "And you must."

"I don't know. I have no control over this . . . and I can't let this happen again. I can't bear the thought of the beast getting free again. I already have too much blood on my hands."

"Then don't let it," she said.

He stared at her. "What do you mean?"

"Sir John built himself a cage so that he could contain his beast. You can do that, too."

"Maybe," he said doubtfully. "I'm a fugitive, Gwen. Even if I manage to escape the police and flee the country, I'll have to live in hiding the rest of my life."

"It's a big world, Lawrence. Change your name, become someone else. Leave all your pain behind. It's better than becoming another victim of the monster, and that's what you'll be if you let this destroy you the way it destroyed Ben."

Lawrence stood up and paced the room. Her words were like a tonic—not a cure, but at least a respite from the cancer of hopelessness. Then he stopped and turned toward her. "I have to end this with my father," he said, his eyes hard. "I need to go back to Blackmoor. He may even be waiting for me to return. If I can stop him, then I'll need to disappear. Forever. I . . . I'll likely never see you again."

Gwen rose and crossed the room to him and put her hands on his shoulders.

"No!" she said, her blue eyes fierce. "Please . . . let me find a way to help you. You can't go into towns, you can't be seen . . . I can."

He did not know how to answer that. He wanted to insist that she stay away, but her strength, her sense, her beauty . . . were impossible to resist.

"Lawrence," she said, "there must be a cure."

He was intensely aware of the soft warmth of her hands on his naked shoulders, and he could see the moment when she became aware of it, too. And yet she did not move her hands.

"I must confess," Lawrence said softly, touching her

cheek, "I envy him. My brother. For the days he had with you. What joy he must have felt."

When she blushed he almost pulled away. "Forgive me," he said quickly.

"No . . ."

"I would have given anything to have known you in another life. And I can only pray that Ben forgives me. For . . . my feelings for you."

He bent and kissed her lightly on the mouth, without force but with heat. Then he pulled his head back. "God, I'm sorry—"

"No," said Gwen. "No . . ."

She pulled him to her and her kiss was filled with urgency and a passion unlike anything Lawrence had ever experienced. The intensity of it was fueled by the honesty and freedom with which the gift was offered, and he took her in his arms and the kiss became a scalding point of contact that spread its heat down through every other place at which their bodies touched—breasts and hands and hips and thighs moving toward each other, discovering the place where they fit and the ways in which they were welcomed. Their hands explored each other, running over bare flesh and pulling aside clothing to discover the reality of things seen and imagined. Lawrence began unfastening her gown as Gwen tore at the lacings of his trousers when—

Bang! Bang!

A heavy fist began pounding on the door downstairs and they froze together, clothing askew, eyes alert and afraid.

"Miss Conliffe!" a voice called from outside. Gwen disentangled herself and hurried to the window to peek out. Her gown was halfway off, one perfect breast exposed, the nipple swollen from his kisses. She appeared not to care about that, but instead peered carefully down through a slit in the curtain.

"My God!" she breathed. "It's Inspector Aberline."

They stared at each other for a long moment. Lawrence crossed to her and kissed her forehead and then bent to kiss her breast once more; then he gently lifted the strap of her gown and placed it on her shoulder.

"You had better let him in," he said softly.

CHAPTER FORTY-NINE

Gwen opened the door. Inspector Aberline stood on the doorstep, his eyes smudged from exhaustion and stress. Two of his bulky assistants waited on the pavement, their faces set and hard. One of them carried a shotgun, the other had a pistol poorly concealed beneath one flap of his jacket. A light rain had started to fall, but the men from Scotland Yard seemed not to care.

Aberline touched the brim of his rain-spattered bowler. "Miss Conliffe, good morning."

"Inspector," Gwen said with forced politeness.

He glanced past her into the foyer, which was lit by a single candle in a wall sconce. "May I ask if you're staying here on your own?"

"Yes. My father is away."

"May I impose?"

Gwen hesitated, but Aberline looked over his shoulder at the rain. She felt trapped by the moment and the demands of social graces. To refuse him entry under the circumstances would make him suspicious, so she nodded and stepped back and opened the door.

"Of course, Inspector, please come in."

Aberline nodded his thanks and once inside he removed his hat and looked past her into the darkened shop, but Gwen held her ground, keeping the encounter confined to the foyer. The inspector smiled faintly.

"Ma'am, I must ask you directly: have you seen Lawrence Talbot? I'm sure by now you've heard of his escape."

"Yes. I did take the news," she said neutrally. "But, no, I haven't seen him."

Even as she said it Gwen knew that she had pitched her voice the wrong way. Her denial sounded flat and as false as it was. She saw Aberline's tired eyes sharpen at once, and his gaze flicked quickly to the shop.

"I'm alarmed that your father allows you to remain here unaccompanied with a murderer on the loose. I would like you to come with me."

"That's entirely unnecessary, Inspector. However, I puzzle over why you think I may be in danger. Lawrence would never harm me."

"Miss," said Aberline firmly, "I cannot stress to you what mortal peril you are in." With that he produced a newspaper from his deep pocket and let it fall open on the counter. It was the same edition she had brought to Lawrence, with the same bold headlines and a photo that made him appear quite deranged. "What peril you would *be* in should you find yourself in his presence."

Aberline put his hand on her shoulder and gently pushed her to one side. She knew that if she had been a better liar he would never had taken such a liberty. The inspector entered the shop and began opening the doors to any closet or cupboard that was large enough to hide a man. When he found nothing he parted the curtains at the back of the shop and saw the set of stairs that led to the apartment above.

Gwen tried to insinuate herself between the inspector and the stairs. "Maybe you don't know the man as well as I."

"Maybe not. But I've seen the monster with my own eyes." Those eyes searched her face as he said it, looking to see how the words affected her, but Gwen forced her expression to remain placid. "And I can tell you, Miss Conliffe, it is worse than anything—*anything*—you can possibly imagine."

Instead of making her more afraid, Aberline's words made her angry, and that put iron into her resolve. "Thank you, Inspector; I will be careful should I see him."

Aberline sighed and turned away from the stairs, and then his eyes landed on something that stopped him in place. A small cabinet on the near wall stood ajar and on the end of the counter nearby was an open box of bandages and a bottle of antiseptic without its cap.

Aberline smiled thinly. "Miss Conliffe. I admire your noble intentions, truly I do. But you must listen to me now." He stepped closer. "You think you can save him . . . but you can't."

"I don't know what you—"

Aberline snaked out his hand and caught her by the wrist.

"Please!" he implored. "I must insist that you come with me."

"Insist?" she said sharply, hoping that outrage would work where outright lying did not. "Who do you think you are? What am I? Chattel?"

Gwen struggled, but Aberline's grip was iron-hard.

"Take your hand off me!"

Over his shoulder the inspector called, "Thompson!" Instantly a tall man with bull shoulders came hustling into the room.

Gwen started to scream. "Let go of—"

But then Thompson clamped a huge hand over her mouth. She tried to bite him, but the detective was too savvy for that and pressed her back against him, his lower fingers jamming her jaw painfully; at the same time he locked a thick arm around her waist. She was helpless in his grip, though she kicked and fought every inch of the way down the hall and out into the street.

Aberline leaned his head out into the rain, where a squad of heavily armed officers of the elite Special Police waited. "Now!"

The waiting officers surged into the house. Dozens and dozens of them, and everyone armed with a rifle, a fire axe or a heavy truncheon. Gwen tried to scream a warning. This was not an arrest . . . this was a hunt, and from the pitiless looks in the eyes of the men who barreled past her into the house, she knew that taking Lawrence alive was not their goal.

THE SPECIAL POLICE were the elite of Scotland Yard. To a man they were ex-military, hardened and seasoned by wars in every part of the globe, tough and resourceful. A squad of them would be enough to quell a riot. But the mass of them who thundered into the apothecary through the front and back doors and pounded up the steps was enough to stop *anything*.

Aberline passed Gwen Conliffe to his sergeant and, drawing his heavy pistol, he re-entered the shop and climbed the stairs at the head of the charge. The images from last night were burned into his brain and his hatred for the vicious monster was matched only by the terror that gripped him.

At the top of the stairs his men fanned out to kick

open doors and toss furniture aside. Aberline himself headed down the hall toward the rearmost room where the door was closed. Six men with rifles followed in close order. If that door opened then anyone or anything who stepped out would be blasted to rags.

When they were at the end of the hall, Aberline licked his lips, slipped his finger inside the trigger guard, and reached for the door handle. The six rifle barrels leveled out over his shoulders in the narrow confines of the hall.

As soon as the lock clicked open Aberline kicked the door in and they rushed the room. The room appeared to be empty, but almost at once Aberline saw a pair of legs standing motionless in the gray shadows behind the lower edge of a full-sized mirror. The feet did not look like human feet.

Sweat popped out on Aberline's forehead and his mouth went dry. He ticked his chin toward it and the other officers sighted their weapons on it. The inspector held a finger to his lips as he aimed his pistol at the center of the mirror and thumbed back the hammer. The click sounded unnaturally loud in the still room.

"Talbot!" he growled. "Raise your arms and step out where I can see you."

Talbot's feet did not move.

"Talbot . . . you have my word that you'll be treated humanely."

Nothing. Not so much as a twitch.

Very well, damn you, thought Aberline. With the six rifles fanned out on either side of him, he carefully approached the mirror and then with a sweep of his hand grabbed it and sent it hurtling onto its side. Wood and glass splintered.

Behind the mirror stood a full-size statue of the woodland god, Pan. Half man, half goat. All bronze.

Lawrence Talbot was gone.

Behind him the Special Officers let out a collective sigh. All of them had wanted to bag Talbot, but none of them had wanted to face the creature. Detective Adams pushed his way through the throng and looked from the statue to Aberline, who stood looking out of the windows at the endless rows of empty rooftops.

"There's some bad luck for you," Adams said.

Without turning, Aberline murmured, "It's bad luck for everyone."

CHAPTER FIFTY

Lawrence snuck back into the house in the gray bleakness before dawn. As he went silently to the top of the stairs, he heard muffled conversation downstairs. Men's voices. Aberline was smart and careful. That was fine. Lawrence knew that he could be smart and careful, too.

He wrapped his feet with towels and so did not make a sound as he prowled the upper floors for supplies. He found a small satchel with a shoulder strap and, in a bedroom on the third floor he surprised himself by finding a wardrobe filled with men's clothes. It was all too big for Gwen's father and when Lawrence checked them he found a tie with BT embroidered on it. BT . . . Benjamin Talbot. Ben must have used this room when visiting the city. Touching his brother's clothes gave him equally sharp pangs of grief and guilt. He could still remember the taste of Gwen's kisses, and the curve of her breast.

He closed his eyes for a moment, etching the memory into his soul. If he died then he would at least have had one perfect moment, and when he died he would recall that beauty so that it was the last thing he saw before darkness consumed him.

Then he opened his eyes and set to work, changing

his clothes and packing essentials for his escape from
London.

AN HOUR LATER he was on the streets walking
briskly away from Essington Lane. With the dawn the
newsboys took to their calling and began hawking the
day's headlines. He was still the running story.

Lawrence had a muffler wrapped around his mouth
and nose and a top hat pulled low so that only his eyes
showed. He lingered near a newsagent's stall just long
enough to see that his photograph was still on the front
page above the fold.

The newsboy shouted the headline: "Monster still on
the loose! Two weeks until the next full moon! Talbot
missing!"

Over and over again.

Lawrence fled from the sound of it.

"PUT THEM OVER here," Gwen said to the clerk from
the bookshop, and the young man tottered over to the
indicated table and set down his burden. It was the fifth
load of books he had delivered to this address, and each
of them on the strangest subjects. Medical reference
books of all kinds. Books on disorders of the mind. Books
on Gypsy magic. Books on mythology and legend. And
every text on the legends of werewolves and the mystery
of lycanthropy that his employer could find.

He lingered for his tip and knuckled his forehead
when she handed him some coins, then, as he turned
to leave, he paused and asked, "Pardon my insolence,
ma'am, but are you selling charms?"

Gwen looked puzzled. "Charms?"

"For the monster." The boy nodded to the apothecary shelves. "Is there some kind of potion or something you're making to ward off monsters? If so, my mum would like to—"

"No," said Gwen with a faint smile. "Nothing like that."

The clerk glanced at the stack of arcane books.

"Just indulging in a curiosity," Gwen said.

The clerk bobbed his head and left, but once he was outside he threw another long look at the apothecary. "'Indulging in a curiosity,'" he muttered. "Bloody mad as a hatter."

LAWRENCE HAD ALWAYS needed to shave twice a day, so thick was his beard, and now he was glad of it. Within three days his jaw was covered with a beard so dark that most men would have required a week to grow it; by the end of the second week the beard was a wild tangle. Even so, he drew some cautious glances from passersby, so he seldom made eye contact and kept to the shadows as much as he could. He had found money in Mister Conliffe's bedroom and booked a room in Limehouse, a squalid part of town where no one ever poked their noses into anyone else's business. If anyone gave him a moment's thought they probably guessed him to be a toff drawn to the whores and opium dens of the neighborhood.

He could not yet risk taking a train to Blackmoor. The stations would be closely watched. All he could do was wait for the hysteria and heat to die down, but every new day brought more screaming headlines and constant patrols by the police. Time ground on and each night Lawrence looked up at the sky to see the moon roll through its phases.

One evening, with the moon three-quarters full over the smog of London, he found a small church with a crooked steeple and he slipped inside. It was dark and empty and Lawrence hunkered down in a corner pew, but once he was there the faces of the saints and the bloody image of the crucified Christ were like cudgels that beat him down. He buried his face in his hands, unable to meet the eyes of the icons.

He heard a rustle and saw a small man sliding onto the other end of the pew. Lawrence raised his head and saw a kindly old face above a Roman collar.

"Hello, my son," said the minister. "What brings you here?"

Lawrence did not know how to answer that. He saw no hint of recognition on the minister's face. That, at least, was a blessing.

"I need to pray," Lawrence said.

"May I join you? As the Lord says, when two or more are gathered in My name . . ." He waited for a response; when he did not get one the minister cocked his head to one side and gave Lawrence an appraising look. "So . . . what are we praying for? Peace? Help? Forgiveness?"

Lawrence shook his head.

"Strength," he said wretchedly.

GWEN CONLIFFE BENT low over the ancient text, picking through the Latin slowly. She had learned the language from her father, who used it regularly as part of his trade, but some of the phrasing here was very dense and obscure. She spoke the English translation slowly as she read. ". . . buried deep within this terrible aspect the heart of the victim still beats. Though the werewolf is a monster of the Devil's creation . . . the immortal human soul still resides therein, trapped and helpless by the evil power of this unnatural transformation. . . ."

She looked up, tears glistening in her eyes.

"Lawrence," she said softly.

Then she took a steadying breath, brushed the tears angrily from her eyes and bent back to her work.

THE NEXT DAY Lawrence Talbot left London on foot. With his satchel of clothes slung over his shoulder and his back bent beneath the weight of loss and guilt he headed away from the gray sprawl that was the City. Perhaps once he was away from the scene of his crimes he could beg, borrow or even steal a ride. He needed to reach Talbot Hall while there was still time.

If, indeed, there was still time.

CHAPTER FIFTY-ONE

Lawrence waited for the stable lads to finish mucking out and head back to the main house and then he slipped from his hiding place in the hedges and crept toward the stables. If he could steal a horse then he might still make it home before the full moon. It was a ride of no more than twelve hours, but on foot it would take two full days.

The barn door was latched but not locked and he lifted the metal bar slowly, making no noise at all. The barn smelled of horse manure and fresh straw. Light slanted in from several small windows and the whole thing had a smoky, homey feel. It made Lawrence want to find a corner and curl up on a pile of straw. But that was a fantasy he knew he would never make real.

He slipped inside and looked down the row of horses. A dozen animals, all of them munching hay or oats. The nearest was a roan with strong legs. A horse that could take a heavy pace, or so he hoped. Lawrence scooped a handful of straw from a manger and held it out, speaking slowly and soothingly as he approached. He'd always been good with horses . . . but when he was ten feet from the animal it tossed its head and rolled an eye toward him. Lawrence froze. The horse suddenly shied backward, neighing in protest and fear.

"No!" called Lawrence. "Shhhhh, shhhh . . . it's all right . . ."

But the horse was panicking. It reared back and kicked at the stall door, which startled the horse in the adjoining stall. Within seconds all of the horses were crying out in fear. They bucked and kicked and bit the air in terror.

There were human shouts from outside.

"God damn it!" Lawrence swore; then he turned and fled.

IT WAS STILL early morning when the rear door of Conliffe Apothecary was opened slowly by a cautious hand. Gwen peered out, looked up and down the alley, and saw no one. She slipped outside and closed the door silently. Her father was busy in the shop and was convinced that Gwen, exhausted from her ordeal, was asleep. Fat chance. She may not be an actor like Lawrence, but there wasn't a woman deserving of the title who could not conjure tears on cue or playact a case of the vapors. She was a little surprised, though, that her father—who knew how strong and independent she was—fell for the drama anyway.

Gwen gathered some money and put a few things in an oversized purse, and once she was convinced the alley was clear she hurried along to the bystreet where she could catch a cab.

LAWRENCE TRUDGED ALONG the back roads, frequently cutting across country—both to shorten the trip and to avoid the main roads. He spent a night huddled in the lee of the remaining wall of an ancient Roman fortress whose name was forgotten even by historians of the region. In the morning, while digging a small hole to bury the remains of his meager breakfast, he found a Roman coin on which the profile of Caesar could still be seen. Lawrence pocketed the coin, telling himself that it was a lucky find, and he needed any luck he could take with him on this last leg of his journey.

He walked all day, cold and weary to the bone, his mind unable to let go of the image of last night's moon, which was nearly full and heavy with threat. Twice he saw mounted men riding in pairs across the fields and rightly guessed them to be police. Aberline was no fool, so it was reasonable that he would have men watching the roads leading to the Hall. Lawrence was glad of the warning and doubled his caution as he picked paths whose dirt and grass showed little or no signs of recent use. And as he walked these paths he stayed to the edges or just inside the edge of the forest so that he left no marks of his own. Like the wolf who howled within his blood, Lawrence had grown cautious. There was a wisdom that becomes apparent to those being hunted, and Lawrence let his mind work through the logic of cause and effect so that he made it all the way to Talbot Hall without once being sighted.

The forest path was the safest for the last part of the journey, and he walked along the pool at the base of the cliff that separated the old growth forest from the marshy downlands. He passed the circle of standing stones and stood for a long time glaring at the heel stone. Tonight the full moon would spill her light across the stone and the hour of the wolf would be here. Moonrise was only a few hours after sunset.

Lawrence had made a decision that if he could not

find and stop his father by moonrise, then he would throw himself off of the cliff wall into the jagged rocks of the shallow pool, or if not there then from the top of the house. He was not optimistic enough to believe that the fall would kill him, but if he did it while he was still human then maybe the injury plus the St. Columbanus medal would interfere with the transformation. Perhaps he might make it through the rest of the night unable to do harm.

The other option was Singh and his silver bullets. If the Sikh would not take a hand in the fight, then Lawrence would do it himself. A silver bullet in the thigh would surely disable him, possibly even prevent the transformation . . . and it would still give him his arms with which to shoot should his father finally come around.

On the other hand, if he found his father, then everything would need to be handled once and for all time. Lawrence no longer cared if he lived. Not unless a cure was guaranteed, and he was less optimistic about that than Gwen had been.

Gwen . . . Her name brought the memory of sweetness and hot kisses to his mind and he touched the medal beneath his shirt.

"God . . . whatever happens," he prayed as he walked, "please spare her more pain. Please God . . . spare her."

The cold wind blew past him and brought no answers and no promises.

GWEN RODE THE train to the stop before Blackmoor and then grabbed her bag and departed quickly, checking always to see if she was being followed. If there were any of Aberline's men on her trail then they were too subtle and sly for her to spot. Even so, she took every precaution she could manage.

She spent several hours asking questions, occasionally having to pay for reliable answers. In the early afternoon she hired a horse from a stable and headed quickly out into the country, following a series of directions scrawled on a slip of paper by a milkman who had sworn he had spotted the person for whom Gwen was searching. Just before two o'clock, Gwen spotted a wagon further along the road. A Gypsy vardo. Gwen kicked her horse into a trot and soon caught up with the wagon.

The driver was a fierce man with a scarred face and two daggers in his belt. He eyed Gwen suspiciously and leaned out to look up and down the road to see if this was part of some trap. A second man sat next to him, a rifle across his thighs.

"What do you want?" the first Gypsy demanded.

"I'm looking for a woman named Maleva," said Gwen. "Would you know her?"

The two men exchanged a look.

When they answered her it was in a long string of Romany. None of it sounded like directions where to find Maleva. Much of it sounded like threats.

Gwen almost snarled at them in frustration and kicked her horse again. When she looked back, the Gypsies were standing on the wagon, watching her.

LAWRENCE HUDDLED IN the lee of a disused barn, tearing at a cooked chicken he'd stolen from a farmhouse. It was meager, but he was so famished that he was grateful even for this.

Far above, the sun was carving a path toward twilight.

Lawrence did some math in his head and judged that there was nearly a full day left until he reached the Hall. The thought made his stomach clench and in disgust he threw the last of the chicken away. He was exhausted and he knew that if he didn't get sleep now he would never have the strength to do what he needed to do tomorrow.

Drawing his jacket tightly around him, he curled up on the cold ground. As he lay there, he thought of Ben and of his mother. He thought of his father. He thought of the horrific things that had been written with grotesque attention to detail in the newspapers.

But when he dreamed, he dreamed of Gwen.

CHAPTER FIFTY-TWO

Inspector Francis Aberline opened the carriage door and stepped down onto the cobbled high-street of Blackmoor. Adams and Carter alighted behind him. Aberline had hoped never to return to this benighted little town, and had sworn to himself on that last bloody night that he would not do so alone. That part of the promise he kept. The doors of the carriage behind his opened and a half dozen of the toughest and most experienced officers of the Special Police stepped out. They were grim-faced men, all ex-soldiers, all battle hardened. Every one of them wore a gunbelt and carried a shotgun or heavy hunting rifle.

The townsfolk saw the men, the guns and the unflinching determination in the eyes of these men, and they fled the streets. Doors were slammed and barred, windows shuttered. The church bell began to ring.

Aberline smiled at this, and it was no longer the mocking smile he'd worn before the terrible incident out at the ruined abbey. No, this was the grim smile of a hunter who knows his prey and also knows that he has brought with him the right hunters and the right weapons to do the job. Francis Aberline would be damned before he would allow another slaughter.

He led his men into the tavern and commandeered a long table. The men sat down and immediately took stock of their weapons and equipment. One man set a heavy ammunition box in the center of the table and flipped open the lid. Inside were rows upon rows of gleaming silver bullets.

Carter reached out and selected a bullet from the box and admired it in the candlelight.

"You're sure he'll come?" he asked.

"Quite," said Aberline. From an inside pocket he produced several maps on which names had been written and red crosses to indicate posts. As he handed them out he said, "Everyone knows their posts. Priory road, train depot, south lawn and the river. Adams . . . tell Sir John we're here, and then stay in close to the estate. But not too close. We want to trap Talbot, not scare him off."

"What do we do if we confront the suspect?" asked one of the officers.

Aberline's eyes were as hard as flint. "Don't engage him, don't be drawn into conversation. You are to shoot on sight. Shoot to kill. Does any man here have a problem with that?"

All of them had been in London during the massacre. The eyes that stared back at Aberline were as hard and cold as his own. No one had a problem at all.

DISHEVELED AND DEFEATED, Gwen returned to the tavern where she had booked a room. She dismounted outside and stretched her back, aching from hours in the saddle. Over the last twenty-four hours she had found a dozen Gypsies, but none of them had given so much as the time of day. If any of them knew Maleva they shared nothing with Gwen. However, before she had gone two paces a figure stepped out of the shadows of the stable that adjoined the tavern. Gwen gasped and retreated a step . . . but it was only an old woman.

A Gypsy woman. Instantly Gwen knew who this old woman was.

"Maleva," Gwen said, and the old woman nodded. Despite her years, the Gypsy woman's eyes were sharp and shrewd.

"What do you want from me?"

Gwen licked her dry lips. "Lawrence Talbot."

Maleva's eyes didn't flicker. She said nothing.

Gwen said, "You're the only one who truly understands what has happened to him. Please . . . help me. I must save him."

The old woman took a step closer and peered at Gwen.

"Do you love him?"

There should have been a denial on her lips, or at least a hesitation in her response, but Gwen said, "Yes. I do."

"Then," said Maleva, "leave him to his fate."

This was not what Gwen had searched all these miles to hear. She could feel her face flush with anger. "I will not! I've sought him for weeks. The moon is nearly on us." She stepped forward, softening her tone. "Please! I beg you . . . tell me what to do."

For just a moment the stern mask of the Gypsy woman softened and the eyes lost their harshness.

"You would risk your life to change what cannot be changed."

"I would risk everything for someone I love."

Maleva narrowed her eyes. "This love of yours. Is it selfish? Or is it fearless and true?"

It was an odd question, and a dangerous one, and Gwen found herself unable to sort through the jumble of emotions in her heart. "I don't understand."

"You will when the moment comes. You will have but one chance," said Maleva quietly. "Look closely for it. Only then will you know the truth of what I say." Then Maleva stepped closer and grabbed Gwen's arm in a surprisingly powerful grip. "The Devil walks among us. May the Saints protect you . . ."

The hand around Gwen's arm was painfully tight, the fingers like talons.

"May the Saints give you the strength to do what you must."

Their eyes were locked together and Gwen suddenly felt strange, as if the hand touching her and the eyes staring into her were more than just ordinary connections. She had the oddest sensation that something was passing from the old Gypsy woman and into her.

The Gypsy released her and staggered back, visibly weakened.

"Now go," she gasped. "Go to him. Save him from the beast."

"I—" Gwen began, but Maleva cut her off.

"Go!"

Gwen backed away and then spun, swung into the saddle, and headed out of town, riding hard toward Blackmoor.

NIGHT CAUGHT HIM on the road and flew ahead of his labored pace so that by the time he reached Talbot Hall the sun had burned away and darkness swept the world. Since the moon was still down, the sky was littered with a billion stars and by their light Lawrence emerged from the forest and beheld his ancestral home. No light shone in any of the windows. The walls looked cold and empty.

Lawrence dropped his traveling satchel and hurried across the fields toward the house, running through the woods parallel to the road. From a hundred yards out he could see that the huge front door stood ajar, and as he drew close and climbed the stairs he saw leaves and other debris scattered outside and in. The house looked abandoned.

As Lawrence reached to pull the door the rest of the way open a shiver of icy pain rippled up his back and he turned, thinking for a moment that he'd been struck. But he was alone.

On the far horizon, above the sloping hills, the first white curve of the moon began slicing its way into the sky.

"God . . ." he breathed.

ABERLINE STOOD AT the edge of town, holding the reins of his horse as he watched the edge of the moon begin to creep over the horizon. When he heard a second horse galloping up the road, he turned to see Adams coming from the south. The detective reined in.

"Carter hasn't reported. He's not at his post in front of the house."

"Maybe he's . . ." he trailed off as a second horse came up the same road. Aberline turned, expecting it to be Carter or one of the others, but it was not. "Bloody hell," he breathed.

GWEN CONLIFFE SAW Aberline and another standing at the edge of town, on the road that led to Talbot Hall.

"No!" she cried softly, and then set her jaw, jerked the reins hard to the left, and kicked her horse into a fast gallop down a side path. She knew every deer trail and walking path on the estate, but could she get to the Hall in time?

"MISS CONLIFFE?" CALLED Aberline, but the woman vanished in the gloom behind a row of trees. "Get the others!" he yelled as he swung into the saddle. Without waiting for a reply he spurred his horse and raced down the road to follow the woman.

Chapter Fifty-three

awrence pulled the door wide but did so carefully, making no sound. On cat feet he stepped into the foyer. When he was sure that he was alone, he moved deeper into the house.

The entrance hall was as still as a tomb, the floor littered with leaves and the droppings from small animals. He heard creatures scurry away on tiny clawed feet, and he knew that it was not the presence of a man that had scared them but the presence of a predator. The wolf in his blood was screaming for release, and Lawrence threw all of his will against it. He reached under his shirt and closed his fist around the medal, praying for protection, for some fragment of mercy.

Lawrence stopped at the foot of the stairs and listened to what the old house had to tell him. He was certain that Sir John was here . . . but *where*?

All he heard was the night wind whistling through gaps in doors and windows left ajar. The big grandfather clock stood still and silent, the key in place but unwound for days. He crossed to the Ming urn between the double staircases, but his sword cane was no longer there.

Then he heard a soft sound and turned toward the double doors that led to the Great Hall. Though the room beyond the opened doors was pitch-dark, he thought he saw the faint gleam of something red. Was it something crouched low to the ground?

Lawrence steeled himself and moved into the room, pausing beside the grand piano, momentarily using its bulk to act like a barrier between him and whatever might be waiting in the dark. His night vision was growing sharper with each moment, his muscles tensed to attack. Or to run.

He circled the piano and crept deeper into the Great Hall, his eyes fixed on that one hellish red eye.

Lawrence stopped abruptly as he realized what it was, and didn't know whether to laugh in relief or cringe in dread. It was a fading coal from a long that had nearly burned out. The soft sound was the log shifting. He saw the edge of his father's high-backed settee positioned in front of the fire, and moved silently into the room, angling in a wide circle to be able to see if Sir John was sitting there, waiting for him. It took more courage and effort than he thought to cross that room.

He crept closer and closer, his fists balled ready to fight, to lash out at the monster who had made him into a monster. Three steps away he saw a wineglass on the table within easy reach of the settee; at two steps he saw an overturned wine bottle that still dripped blood red wine onto the floor. Then he saw the curve of an elbow, the folds of dark cloth around an arm resting on the settee.

"Father? . . ." he whispered, but his throat was so dry that his voice was barely a whisper. There was no answer.

Lawrence took a breath and then jumped around the edge of the settee.

A man sat there.

But it was not Sir John.

A man he did not recognize, wearing a dark tweed suit with a police detective badge pinned to his chest, sat in the chair. His legs were crossed casually, his hands folded neatly in his lap, his eyes open. But the man's throat had been slit from ear to ear and blood had drenched the front of his clothes.

Lawrence cried out in shock and horror and backed away.

He ran to the wall and snatched down the big Holland & Holland elephant rifle that rested in brackets on the wall. Sir John must have done this. Even though the moon was not yet up, his father had to have done this. But *why*?

The hunting rifle was heavier than he expected and the stock rasped against one of the clips. Lawrence froze, waiting for a sound from somewhere in the house.

Nothing.

He broke open the rifle . . . but it was empty.

Lawrence was panting with tension now. He crossed to the cabinet beneath where the rifle had rested and quickly opened drawers until he found a box of shells. There was not enough light to tell if the heavy bullets were lead or silver. He selected one and tried to gouge it with a thumbnail. Lead was soft, silver was much harder. His nail left a clear line through the tip of the bullet.

"Damn it to hell!" he snarled. It meant that he would have to go to Singh's quarters and find his bullets. And he didn't have the key.

HE STAGGERED OUT into the entrance foyer, turned toward the grand double sweep of stairs and ran up the closest set, knowing that time was flying past him. His revulsion quickly gave way to fear as he could feel the strange itching begin beneath his skin. Not full, not yet. But there.

At the top of the stairs, however, he paused. Singh's room was at the back of the house, down and around the long hallway that was lined with the trophy heads of slaughtered animals. All of the candles in the sconces were dark and cold, but some faint brushstrokes of moonlight painted the carpet through the open doorways of disused bedrooms: His own, abandoned long ago. Ben's transformed by the savage hungers of their father into a chamber capable of holding only memories; guest rooms that had provided no comfort for travelers in decades. Lawrence tried to feel some echo of Gwen's warmth in this place, but the shadows held only threat and awful secrets.

The doors to each room had been left open, and as he passed each black doorway he took a frightened look inside. On one side of the hall, the rooms were completely dark; on the other, the moonlight seemed to grow brighter with each careful step. He listened for the smallest sound . . . and heard nothing. But he did not search the rooms. The fire downstairs had burned low; Lawrence hoped that meant that Sir John had done the sane and decent thing and left the house to lock himself and his appetites in the mausoleum.

Not that a single act of self-control on Sir John's part would change how this night would end. How it had to end. Even if Sir John was locked in his cell Lawrence had decided to do what had to be done. He was going to kill his father. No pleading, no lies, no clever manipulations would save that monster now. Not after Ben. Not after all of the hurt and harm Lawrence had inflicted after his father—his own *father*—had passed along this spiritual cancer. This unholy curse.

A single silver bullet to atone for the combined crimes of father and son, to wash away a river of blood.

As Lawrence passed Ben's room, he heard something and it froze him in place.

A sound.

Heavy breathing. Panting. Low and fierce.

An animal sound.

God! Was he here after all? . . .

Lawrence put the rifle to his shoulder and stepped slowly into the room. The chamber was awash with moonlight and in the mirror Lawrence could see the reflection of the nearly risen Goddess of the Hunt. He licked his lips. The panting was coming from the far side of the bed. Something was there, hunkered down out of sight. As he slowly rounded the foot of the bed, Lawrence turned the rifle around and held it like a club, ready to smash, to crush.

Let it end here, he prayed. *Let it end now . . .*

He took the last step as a jump and raised the gun high, setting his teeth as he prepared to kill his father.

Animal eyes stared up at him.

But not the eyes of a monster.

Samson, the great wolfhound, had worked itself into a narrow gap between bed and wall, and the massive dog shivered with terrible fear. It lay in a pool of its own urine, nervous drool flecking its muzzle, its eyes insane with a terror so profound that the animal looked near to death. Its breath steamed in the moonlight and when it saw Lawrence it simply closed its eyes and lowered its head as if expecting to die and willing to be killed without a fight.

The sight struck Lawrence deep in his heart. He lowered the gun and backed away, sorry for the dog that he had hated and feared. No animal should suffer as it suffered, though Lawrence understood its terror. Or thought he did.

Then, like the icy fingers of a ghost on the back of his neck, Lawrence felt an awareness touch him. Still holding the rifle like a war club, he whirled . . . but the room was empty. The doorway was empty, and when he stepped into the hall, it, too, was empty.

What had he felt? It was as if he knew that eyes were upon him, but there was no one else here. The shadows on both sides of him stretched to the ends of the hallway, and nothing lived within them.

THE FEELING GRADUALLY subsided, and it took Lawrence a dizzy moment to reorient himself. This once familiar house now felt like an alien landscape. The itching beneath his skin was maddening, and he snarled aloud in fury and frustration—and that cleared his head. The shapes and angles of the hallway regained their familiar form, and he staggered onward toward Singh's room.

The door was closed but not locked, and Lawrence burst through and into the Sikh's quarters. Moonlight fell jaggedly into the room, and Lawrence turned to see that the windows were broken, the remaining fragments of glass like broken teeth.

Lawrence turned slowly, seeing that the damage was not confined to the window. The whole room was a shambles. Furniture was broken, the heavy carpets torn from the walls, pillows gutted so that their stuffing spilled like pale entrails onto the littered floor. He looked for the parallel marks of savage claws but saw none. This room was a study in rage, but it was the rage of men.

Lawrence took an involuntary backward step, but

then the texture of the carpet beneath his shoes crackled strangely. He looked down to see that he was standing in a large puddle of some black, viscous fluid. He bent and touched it with his fingers.

Blood.

But it was dried, days old.

Lawrence looked up slowly, following the line of blood from the carpet to the baseboard and up the wall. Then all at once the weapon sagged in his hand and his mouth dropped open.

A dead man hung in the shadows of the wall behind him, his body impaled by a heavy silver-bladed knife that had been slammed through his chest. The man's head lolled backward, mouth thrown wide into an eternal scream.

"Singh!"

The sight nearly took the heart out of Lawrence. The gun fell from his nerveless fingers, and he backed away in mute terror.

"Oh my God . . . ," Lawrence whispered. Tears burned in his eyes.

Realization and understanding flooded into Lawrence. Singh had been the guardian of the family, the holy Sikh warrior of God who had dedicated himself to keeping the Talbots safe while at the same time protecting the world from the family's curse. Singh might have forgiven Sir John for the death of Ben. It had been a kind of accident that had allowed the beast to roam free that night. But there was no way that Singh could have been a party to what had happened beyond that. He would have been outraged when Sir John allowed the beast within Lawrence to roam free and to kill. He would have confronted Sir John about it. The state of Singh's room spoke to how that confrontation must have played out.

Singh had tried one last time to oppose evil in the name of his God and for his love of the family.

Somehow Sir John had taken away the Sikh's holy *kirpan* and had used the heavy knife to kill this good and faithful man and then perversely mount him on the wall as if he was just another trophy.

In Lawrence's heart, sickness gave way to grief, and grief crumbled in the face of rage. It was more than the beast that howled within his chest. Those things that made Lawrence Talbot the man he was screamed now with bestial wrath as terrible as that of the wolf.

And then the strengthening moonlight coaxed a gleam from something small that hung from the dead Sikh's throat.

The key!

Lawrence steeled himself and took a step toward Singh's body. He curled his fingers through the silver chain and with great delicacy slid it over Singh's head and turban.

"I'm so sorry," he said to his old friend.

The chest had been knocked on its side, but Lawrence righted it and bent over it, wasting several precious seconds trying with trembling fingers to fit the key into place. He dropped it twice and once had to fish for it after it bounced and rolled under a shattered dresser. Then he managed to slide the key in the right way and turn it. The lock clicked and Lawrence tore the drawer out.

There they were, standing in neat rows. At least fifty silver bullets for the four-gauge hunting rifle.

Lawrence sobbed with relief as he scooped out a handful of them and shoved them into his pocket. He took two more, broke open the gun and shoved the shells solidly into place. When he closed the rifle, he felt the very first shred of hope take root in the black soil of his heart. At very worst he could at least take his own life and save his own soul from further damnation.

Setting his mind for the grim work ahead, Lawrence headed for the door.

He tightened his grip on the gun and screwed up his own resolve.

"For you, Ben," he said through gritted teeth. "For you, Singh. God help me . . . for all of us . . ."

Then a sound intruded into the shadows of the room. Soft, light, musical, as if the silvery moonlight itself had found a voice and was whispering to him.

Lawrence stood stock still, straining to hear.

It was music.

The quiet, haunting notes of a strange melody. Played on the strings of a piano.

Lawrence left the room and in the hallway he could hear it more clearly. Someone was at the grand piano in the Great Hall, playing a sad song to the ghosts of all the Talbots.

Sir John?

It had to be . . . but it was so strange, so bizarre a thing. And the music was so delicate, so skillfully played that it spoke of a degree of control totally at odds with the carnage Lawrence had found.

As he crept to the head of the stairs, he heard the music more clearly.

He *knew* that music. It was there in his earliest memories. A sweet song from some exotic land that his mother sometimes hummed to him as he lay with his head on her lap. And for a fractured, hopeful moment Lawrence held the irrational hope that it was Solana down there in the Great Hall, seated at the piano, playing sweet music to soothe the beast within her son's chest . . . and within her husband's.

Lawrence began descending the steps, holding on to that fantasy, willing it to be true. Even if it was her ghost, then perhaps this night could end differently. With understanding. Without more blood.

"Mother," he murmured, "please . . ."

Even as he said it, he raised the gun and aimed it over the bannister.

The music continued. Unbroken, flowing like scented water through the landscape of that old house.

At the bottom of the stairs, Lawrence took a steadying breath, unsure now whether he walked through Talbot Hall or through drug-induced nightmares back at the asylum or through a dream. But when he entered the Great Hall and saw who it was that sat at the grand piano, he knew that he was not in dreams or his own home. He was in Hell.

Without looking up, Sir John murmured, "Father, I have sinned against heaven and before thee."

Lawrence stopped, hope dying in his heart.

Sir John said, "I am no more worthy to be called your son."

Lawrence's heart was hammering in his chest, and the world felt twisted and unreal.

Finally Sir John looked up. His white hair was unruly, his eyes dark and wild. "And lo and behold, here he stands, the Prodigal Son returned. . . . Shall I have my own robe brought to be placed upon your shoulders? Rings for your fingers and shoes for your feet?"

Lawrence raised the rifle. "I'd say you should pray now, you son of a bitch. But we both know it wouldn't do any good."

"I take it you have one of Singh's silver bullets in my gun."

"Yes," Lawrence hissed in fierce triumph.

"It seems you have me at an advantage. But . . . it makes me happy, you know."

Lawrence frowned. "What does?"

"Seeing you here like this. It truly *is* glorious, isn't it?"

"No! It's hell."

"Hell?" Sir John said softly, amused. "The beast isn't evil."

"Damn you!" growled Lawrence. "It's the essence of evil."

"No. It's just a beast. Beating it into submission is the mistake."

Lawrence shook his head. He did not want to hear this. He had sworn to himself that he would not allow his father to weave his sorcery, but Sir John pressed on and Lawrence didn't pull the trigger.

"Locking it up . . . that was a mistake. It enraged the beast." He chuckled and played another few notes, but now they were random and disjointed. "Here's my advice: let the dog have its day."

Lawrence adjusted his grip on the rifle, steeling himself to take the shot.

Sir John nodded approval. "Still remember how to use that? Not that you need one anymore. Perhaps we should take a hunting trip together? A grand tour? The Continent . . . Africa. America. So many places . . . so much fresh meat."

It was too much. Lawrence could feel the change screaming within him; he could feel the beast howl in agreement with what his father was saying. And he could not bear it.

"Father," he said thickly, "God damn you to hell . . ."

Lawrence pulled both triggers.

And absolutely nothing happened.

CHAPTER FIFTY-FOUR

L awrence stared at his father down the length of the useless rifle. He pulled the triggers again . . . and again.

Nothing. Just the dull click of the firing pin on the brass casing.

"That's it, boy! Excellent," said Sir John, looking immensely pleased. "Didn't think you had it in you."

Lawrence backed away and hastily cracked open the rifle, flung the shells away, fished two replacements from his pocket and jammed them into place. He slammed the rifle shut and jammed the stock hard against his shoulder.

Sir John waited patiently throughout, his face beaming with approval.

Lawrence squeezed one trigger and then the other.

Nothing.

Lawrence retreated, backing all the way across the Great Hall, as Sir John, chuckling quietly to himself, rose to his feet and followed. Just inside the doorway Sir John stopped by the grand piano. There, laying atop the polished black wood, was the wolf-headed sword cane. Sir John picked it up and considered the weight, then nodded toward the hunting rifle Lawrence held. "I emptied the powder from those shells years ago. Singh never knew. I doubt he ever suspected. But . . . God, if I'm not pleased with your nerve."

Sir John thumped the silver head of the cane into his palm. Lawrence began backing away and his father kept pace with him, whacking the cane against his palm in time to their steps.

"Finally you're the man I always wanted you to be," he said. "What do you say then, boy? Will you run with me?"

" 'Run with—'?"

"Or am I going to have to beat some sense into you?"

Lawrence reversed the rifle in his hands, holding it by the barrel.

"You can try," he said with more steel in his voice than he felt in his arms. Then he lunged at Sir John, moving as fast as he could, swinging the heavy rifle in a deadly arc, aiming for the grizzled white hair, aiming to kill. The rifle stock whistled through the air.

But Sir John was not there.

He moved with incredible speed. Not just fast for an old man, but fast for any man. He moved so fast that for a moment it seemed to Lawrence as if the rifle stock passed through his body. The power of Lawrence's swing spun him in a half-circle and he staggered sideways off balance. As Lawrence wheeled around he saw a flash of silver and then the head of the cane crunched against his jaw. Blood flew from his mouth and he twisted around and fell to one knee.

Sir John used the cane to hook the rifle stock and with a grunt of effort he tore it from Lawrence's hands and sent it flying across the hall. It smashed into the Ming vase and exploded it into a thousand jagged fragments.

Lawrence crabbed backward and then scrambled to

his feet. His jaw was a mass of pain but his rage was building now and he let loose with a fierce bellow and waded toward his father to swing a vicious hook punch. But Sir John stepped inside the punch, blocking the fist on his left elbow and chopping a short uppercut into Lawrence's floating ribs. Lawrence gasped as if all of the air had been suddenly sucked out of the room and he stumbled backward.

Sir John stepped toward him but as he did so his face *changed*. His eyes flashed with yellow fire and his skin darkened as the wolf inside screamed to be let out. The old man growled sharply—not at Lawrence but at the force of his own transformation, and the wolf suddenly receded. His eyes turned cold blue again and Sir John maintained dominance over his own form. At least for the moment.

Outside the moon continued to rise.

Lawrence fought for breath, and as he was finally able to drag in a chestful he stepped back toward his father, wanting to grapple with him before they were both lost to the inevitable transformation. Sir John was no longer smiling. His face was set into a vicious snarl as he tossed aside the cane and moved to meet Lawrence in the center of the hall. He checked Lawrence's punch and hammered him with a short left and then an overhand right that knocked Lawrence to his knees, but he didn't stop there. Sir John rained down another overhand and another, splitting the skin over Lawrence's eyebrows, bursting his lips against his teeth, pulping his right ear, breaking his nose. Lawrence had no chance at all. Not against a man who had studied bare-knuckle fighting in dives and thieves' dens in seaports all over the world. Lawrence was outclassed as a fighter and overmastered as a predator.

Sir John grabbed Lawrence by the front of his shirt and hauled him to his feet and then turned and flung him onto a small table and held him down with one hand while he continued his assault. Punch followed punch. Lawrence could feel the bones in his face crack and break.

Then Sir John stepped back and let Lawrence roll off the table onto the leaf-strewn floor. Lawrence landed hard and lay there gasping, watching with bulging eyes as Sir John walked slowly over to where the cane had fallen.

Sir John bent and picked it up by the shaft, and then turned chopping at the air with the head of the cane. As he walked toward Lawrence, Sir John's dark smile blossomed once more. Cruel, impassioned, in love with his own violent skills. He raised the cane high overhead, his whole body trembling with power as he prepared for the killing stroke. Then with a cry of awful delight he brought the cane down with savage force.

And Lawrence caught it.

It was a reflex action powered by fear and desperation and it shocked both of them into a moment of stillness. Lawrence's hand closed on the shaft just under the silver collar and the shock of the impact drove splinters of pain into his wrist. He immediately darted out with his other hand and grasped the wolf's head. Lawrence turned his wrist and heard the *click!* as the hidden lock was released.

Sir John struggled to free the cane, not yet realizing his threat . . . and Lawrence twisted and whipped his arm away so that the handle parted from the shaft and the glittering length of the rapier swept through the air like silver fire.

Sir John staggered back a step, holding the wooden

shaft of the cane, blinking in shock and surprise—he saw the blade and understood on some primal level that the weapon was not just polished steel, but steel coated with silver. Sir John knew that his death was in his son's hands, and he paused.

And in that one second of hesitation Lawrence pivoted from the floor and drove the entire length of the silver rapier through Sir John's upper chest. The thin blade tore through muscle and bone . . . but it missed his father's black heart. Sir John clamped his hands around the carved hilt of the sword and held fast as Lawrence climbed to his feet. They strained against each other, locked in a contest of strength that drew on resources both human and unnatural.

Then Sir John chopped at Lawrence's ankles with a vicious foot-sweep that sent his son crashing to the floor again so hard that his head struck with a meaty crunch. Lawrence lost his grip on the rapier and rolled away, dazed beyond thought or action.

Standing wide-legged, chest heaving, Sir John stared down at Lawrence for a long moment, teeth bared in pain and fury. With an inhuman scream he ripped the blade out of the wound. Blood sprayed Lawrence's face and the floor.

Sir John looked at the sword for a moment and then threw it the length of the hall where it struck and rolled out of sight. He drew a deep breath, expanding his chest muscles against the damage as if daring the wound to bleed. The flow of blood slowed and stopped, though because of the silver coating on the blade the wound did not close and vanish. Even so, Sir John smiled in dark satisfaction.

Lawrence, his mind still numb, was trying to crawl along the floor. He made it as far as the entrance to the

Great Hall, but Sir John stalked over, grabbed him by the collar and belt and lifted him off the ground and threw him all the way across the Hall. Lawrence hit the settee and tumbled over it to land in the coals of the dying fire. Sir John came to examine his handiwork, pleased at the pool of blood that was spreading under Lawrence's head.

Chest heaving—more from passion than effort, Sir John stood still for half a minute as he fought the animal beneath his skin. He wanted his human side to experience this. Then he bent and knotted his fingers in Lawrence's hair and dragged him from the fireplace, hauled him across the room toward the great window that looked out onto the patio. Beyond the gleaming brass of the telescope the landscape fell away to offer an unrestricted view of the moon.

It was vast and white and now only a sliver of it remained below the horizon.

The Goddess of the Hunt ruled the sky . . . and the hour of the wolf had come.

Chapter Fifty-five

"Oh my God!"

The cry was torn from Gwen Conliffe as she reined her horse to a whinnying stop halfway along the road to Talbot Hall. She stared at the high walls and tall towers, but all she could see were the flames. Tongues of fire licked upward from every window, thick columns of smoke spiraled upward into the sky like the pillars of heaven.

ONCE MORE LAWRENCE opened his eyes to pain and destruction. His life seemed to be composed of nothing else. He rolled over and spat blood onto the tiled floor. The room was far too bright and as his senses returned to him he realized with horror that the house around him was on fire. He gasped and smoke filled his lungs, sending him into a paroxysm of coughing.

"She's almost here," said Sir John behind a pall of smoke, his voice loud and rough.

Lawrence raised his head and saw his father standing above him, his back to the window. Flames clawed at the timbers overhead and they cried out as the house died.

Sir John nodded past him, and Lawrence turned to see the fully risen moon hanging ripe and lush over the moors. "Can you feel her?"

"No . . ." said Lawrence weakly, putting the lie to what he knew to be true.

"You were the heir to my kingdom."

"Why are you doing this?" Lawrence asked wretchedly as he climbed to his knees.

Sir John pressed his palm to his chest where the silver rapier had stabbed him. He held out his palm to show that it was red with blood. There were splatters of it on the floor. "The wound won't stay closed as long as the beast is caged."

"I should have aimed better!"

That made his father laugh. "Do you know what wolves do to their unfit young?"

Another coughing fit tore through Lawrence.

"It's purity, really." Sir John's eyes were no longer human. The irises had taken on an unnatural yellow tint. As Lawrence watched, his father's ears grew into points, and when Sir John smiled his fangs gleamed in the moonlight. "Untroubled by conscience. Oh God . . . to be free of it."

"Father . . ."

Sir John opened his eyes. "Sweet animal oblivion."

"Lawrence!"

The cry came from outside the house, drifting through the thick smoke. Sir John and Lawrence both turned toward the sound. Sir John smiled; Lawrence's mind tottered on the edge of the abyss. *No! She could not be here. Not here.*

"Gwen? . . ." He murmured.

Sir John laughed aloud, and his voice was like thunder. "This is perfect, boy! Now everything will be as it should be. A true pack. An alpha, his pup . . . and now the alpha will have his *bitch*."

Lawrence knew that his father meant it. Sir John's

covetous lust for Gwen had led to Ben's death and to the damnation that now faced Lawrence this night. Now that he had decided to let the beast have total murderous freedom, Sir John would take whatever he wanted. He had the will, the coldness of mind, and the power to do it. Nothing human could stop him.

Nothing.

Something suddenly snapped in Lawrence's mind. The fear and despair that were wrapped like barbed wire around his soul *broke.* Weariness dropped away like a discarded garment and all that remained was a towering rage that gave him the power to get off his knees and climb to his feet.

Sir John was not impressed and mocked him with laughter that shook the heavens.

Gwen. It was the only thing in Lawrence's mind. Everything else had been burned down to a screaming howl of bloodlust.

Sir John's smile faltered as he saw his son's eyes change from brown to a yellow that was hotter and brighter than the flames that rose all around them.

Then Lawrence threw himself at Sir John, slamming into his chest with hands that had already begun to shift and change. The impact was far more savage and powerful than Sir John expected and it drove them backward a dozen steps, sliding and slipping in the blood. Lawrence grabbed his father's throat and pressed forward with his thumbs, trying to crush Sir John's windpipe—but his father's throat thickened beneath his fingers, the tendons expanding to force Lawrence's hands apart. With a grunt of effort Sir John shoved Lawrence back, and as he did so his own eyes flared from ice blue to hot gold. He snarled with black lips as sharp teeth began tearing through his gums.

"Lawrence!" Again Gwen's voice cut through the smoke and the roar of the blaze.

"The bitch is *mine*, boy!" Sir John bellowed in a voice that had lost all traces of humanity.

"Be damned!" Lawrence shouted back and slashed at his father with the claws that had sprouted from each finger. He opened up rents in his father's clothes and droplets of blood seeded the air. For the first time, Lawrence wanted the change to happen; he willed the monster to emerge so he could tear this man . . . this true *monster* . . . apart before he could bring harm to Gwen Conliffe.

But the beast had lived in Sir John far longer than it had in Lawrence.

Even as Lawrence tore at him, Sir John transformed. Sir John's chest and shoulders suddenly swelled with enormous muscles, silver-gray hair erupted from his skin, and the gaping mouth elongated as wicked fangs grew to needle points. One moment Sir John stood there and in the next it was the Werewolf.

Monstrous, huge, and with the fires raging behind it, the creature looked like the Beast of Hell itself. The Werewolf roared its challenge and lashed out with a backhand swipe that was so shockingly hard and fast that Lawrence never saw it. The impact broke a huge bell in his head and suddenly he was flying through the air, smashing furniture to kindling, rolling and tumbling until he crashed into the blazing stone fireplace. Smoke billowed up around him and the flames glowed like hellfire.

THE WEREWOLF STOOD there in the center of the burning Great Hall: powerful, invincible. But then it winced as pain flared in its chest. The wound from the silver rapier had not closed. It had not vanished as all of the other injuries had over the years. The Werewolf felt a tiny flicker of doubt.

It heard a sound and turned toward the fireplace. A shadow moved weakly behind the smoke, and the Werewolf bellowed its fury. It stalked forward, swatting furniture out of the way, aching for the kill, *needing* it with a passion hotter than the flames that chewed the walls.

It reached the fireplace and saw only a broken chair sagging into the flames.

There was a guttural sound behind him and the Werewolf turned to see something huge and dark leap through the fiery smoke on the far side of the room. It crashed down ten feet away, snarling, its eyes ablaze.

The Wolfman.

Chapter Fifty-six

The Wolfman stalked the Werewolf across the burning room, its claws rending the heated floor tiles. The furnace heat made steam hiss from the clothing that still hung in tatters from its powerful frame. It snarled at the creature that stood twenty feet away. The Wolfman could see the glow of blood seeping from a wound in its shoulder. It sniffed again, expecting the stink of fear to accompany the wound, but there was nothing but challenge. This was not wounded prey—this was a wounded predator. The Wolfman narrowed its eyes, its instincts igniting both caution and hatred.

The same intensity of vigilant bloodlust was mirrored on the Werewolf's evil face.

The Werewolf abruptly moved sideways and began circling; the Wolfman turned to match both pace and distance. They were both massive and built for destruction; armed with fangs and claws that could tear through anything and driven by a blood hunger beyond all control. Above the Hall the Goddess of the Hunt watched as her two most powerful children began a battle unlike anything ever fought.

Time after time the Werewolf faked lunges at the Wolfman, trying to coax its enemy into a foolish and ill-timed attack, but each time the Wolfman only slashed at the other monster. The fire grew bigger and hotter around them. All through the house windows exploded outward.

The monsters attacked.

They both moved at the same time, each of them becoming a blur of lethal speed. They collided chest to chest in the middle of the room, inches from the glass dome, and the light from the dome painted their bodies with fire as they slammed together. The impact was so intense that shockwaves tore tiles from the floor and the last of the windows splintered to glittering dust.

The monsters fell to the floor, locked together in a slashing tangle of fangs and claws. They tore at each other, cutting through muscle and tendon and bone, but the wounds closed almost at once. The pain only made each of them more furious, pumping more murderous energy into their attacks. Each of them tried over and over again to go for the one injury they knew on the deepest of instinctive levels that the other could not withstand: a savaged throat. But just as they knew the best attack their instincts gave them the preternatural reflexes to avoid the fatal bite over and over again.

GWEN LEAPED DOWN from her horse and ran toward the house, heedless of the tongues of flame that licked from the black mouths of the shattered windows. Heat buffeted her in waves as she flew up the stone steps to the front door. The doors stood ajar and she whipped them open and rushed inside.

And then froze as she beheld a scene beyond anything nightmare could produce. There, surrounded by roaring sheets of flame, two great creatures fought. They were more dreadful, more terrifying than anything she had imagined, far more powerful than the monsters described in the books she had read. Here were her worse fears multiplied tenfold, made all the more terrifying because of the implacable reality of it.

The Werewolf slewed around on all fours and darted in low and fast, and it clamped its jaws on the Wolfman's arm. Instantly it began thrashing back and forth, trying to use its mass to tear the arm from the socket. That would not kill its enemy, but it would leave it crippled and helpless for the killing attack.

The Wolfman howled in agony as the jaws locked on its arm and snapped bones and ruptured tissue. They toppled backward and rolled, and the Wolfman bit and slashed to try and dislodge the Werewolf. But the Werewolf held on, and a gleam of malicious triumph began to blossom in its eyes.

With a shriek of pain and anger, the Wolfman got its legs under it and rose to its feet, dragging the Werewolf with it. Nothing alive should have been able to rise up with that amount of injury and bearing such ponderous weight, but the Wolfman was drawing on energy that tapped an unbelievable reservoir of darkness. Once upright, the Wolfman began driving its enemy backward toward the fireplace. The Werewolf buried its claws in the Wolfman's shoulders and dug its toes into the floor, and though it slowed the push it did not stop it.

The Wolfman grabbed the wounded and still bleeding shoulder of the Werewolf and gouged deep into the rapier wound with its claws. With a snarl it tore at the puncture, rending it, widening it, tearing away chunks of meat.

The Werewolf could not bear the pain and it opened its jaws and threw back its head to howl out its agony.

And in that instant the Wolfman struck!

It lunged forward and buried its powerful teeth in the

Werewolf's throat and bit down with every ounce of fury and power it possessed. Then it picked the Werewolf up and threw it against the stone edge of the fireplace. The creature was instantly wreathed in flame, tearing a howl of pain from its damaged chest.

The Wolfman bent low into a crouch and roared at its fallen enemy. Then it grabbed the burning monster with its mighty hands and pivoted, turning with all of the power of its hips and shoulders and hurled the Werewolf away. It vanished into the smoke and crashed down out of sight.

UNSEEN DURING THE battle, Gwen Conliffe stood in the doorway, unable to move, unable to even blink at the horrific spectacle playing out before her.

THE WOLFMAN WAITED for the death cry . . . but the moment stretched.

Then out of the smoke, blazing like the sun, the Werewolf came stalking forward. It was entirely engulfed in flame. With each step it burned a print into the tiles. Its clothing and hair turned to ash and still it came. With a titanic bellow of hatred, it threw itself through the air, and the Wolfman bared its fangs and stretched its claws out to meet this impossible attack.

And the Werewolf crashed down onto the floor a yard short.

The Wolfman took a step forward, expecting a trick.

The burning creature got shakily to its feet and came forward, tried to leap once more at its enemy, and once more fell short. Sparks flew around it as it collapsed.

The Wolfman held its ground, still wary of a trick.

The Werewolf struggled to stand but could only rise to its knees. It was being consumed by the fire. It *was* the fire. Layers of flesh ran like tallow down its body. Muscle fibers peeled away. Heat contracted its lips, making the creature's grin more hideous and frightening.

It reached out a hand that was now no more than a tangle of burning sticks. The nails were charred and cracked, the tendons of the wrist contracted from the evaporation of all moisture, leaving the hand curled into a futile parody of its own killing claw.

The Werewolf dropped to all fours. It was diminished now, its mass boiling away in steam and hot ash. It managed one more single step forward, and then it collapsed to the floor.

DEEP, DEEP INSIDE the mind of the beast, almost completely submerged in red shadows and primitive instincts that existed without conscious thought, Lawrence Talbot somehow looked out through the eyes of the Wolfman. He saw the beast that had been his father. He watched as the withered limbs twitched and twisted in the flames and the Werewolf became the husk of Sir John. The process took seconds, and those were the last seconds of Sir John Talbot's life.

When the transformation was complete, Lawrence could see the wreck of his father lying bloody and dead not fifty paces from the spot where his mother died— where his mother had been *murdered*—all those years ago. The same spot where he, himself, had perished; where the innocent boy he had been was torn out of a normal life, driven into insanity, reclusiveness, bitterness and cynicism. That spot was where the world had completely changed for Lawrence Talbot. It was there

that he had *ended* . . . and now, just removed from that
sacred and yet unholy place, was where his father ended.

As he watched he could feel a dark joy boil up in his
heart, but almost at once it was overwhelmed and then
wholly consumed by the beast. As the Wolfman threw
back its head to utter its victorious howl, Lawrence felt
himself disintegrate into nothingness.

Chapter Fifty-seven

Gwen Conliffe stood twenty feet from the monsters—dead and alive—staring in horror at what had just happened. The thing that had been Sir John was gone now and she instinctively knew that it was gone for good. She looked at the creature who had been Lawrence. Was any of him still in there, or had the beast consumed him just as the flames had consumed Sir John? She raised her hand toward it, knowing the gesture was futile, and her lips were parting to call his name once more when the air behind her seemed to explode and she saw the Wolfman spin away from the burning corpse in a spray of blood.

As she spun to her left, Gwen saw Inspector Aberline come striding out of the entrance foyer, his pistol barrel smoking. He raised the weapon for another shot.

"No!" Gwen cried and she flew into him, trying to push the gun up and away, but she was a split second too late. Her attack spoiled his aim so that the bullet struck the Wolfman in the hip, knocking it back.

Instantly the monster attacked, knocking Gwen aside and driving Aberline back and down. The inspector's gun went skittering across the floor, and a second later Aberline screamed as the Wolfman clamped its jaws around his shoulders. Blood exploded from around the monster's muzzle.

Gwen bent and hastily snatched up the gun.

"Shoot him!" cried Aberline, and Gwen turned to see the Wolfman shaking the inspector in its mouth like a terrier with a rat. *"Shoot him!"*

Gwen raised the heavy pistol in both hands, but the monster was worrying Aberline back and forth with insane speed. It was impossible to get a clear shot.

The Wolfman saw the pistol and understood what it was. He dropped Aberline to the floor and turned toward Gwen. Blood and spit dripped from its mouth to sizzle on the hot floor tiles. Aberline's face was white with shock and twisted in agony.

"Run!" cried the inspector.

Gwen ran.

She whirled and flew toward the front door, and the creature followed, but its feet were so slick with blood that it lost a moment finding purchase. By then Gwen was out of the house and running as fast as she could. The Wolfman was torn between pursuit of one prey and a meal close to hand, and it hesitated at the doorway.

Hesitation came with a cost.

Something struck him in the back with great force and his chest blossomed with pain. The monster looked down to see the wickedly sharp blade of a Masai spear sprouting from its chest.

It spun toward the Hall. Its meal was far from dead. Wounded, bleeding, Aberline stood with a second Masai spear, ready to hurl.

The Wolfman curled its long, crooked fingers around the spearhead and yanked, pulling the shaft of the weapon through his chest. It pulled again and again and then tore it completely free and flung the weapon away against a blazing wall.

It peeled back its lips, bared its teeth and hissed at Aberline.

A cracking sound made both of them look up. The ceiling was hidden behind roiling black smoke, but pieces of flaming plaster and timber were beginning to fall. The house could not stand much longer.

Aberline used the distraction. He hurled the second spear, knowing that it would do as little good as the first, and then lunged for the wall of weapons. He snatched down a heavy claymore. The sword was four and a half feet long and weighed almost seven pounds. Even without the terrible wound in his shoulder it would be a cumbersome weapon; now it was merely something to hurl as the monster began hunting him through the smoke. He flung it and saw it rebound from the massive chest. A chest that no longer showed any trace of the spear that had passed entirely through it.

Aberline shifted away, his vision dimming from the thickening smoke and the loss of blood. His foot hit something that screeched along the tiles like metal and he glanced down to see a slender rapier with a blade that gleamed with silver purity. The weapon had a snarling wolf's head pommel.

He bent and swept the sword off the ground as the Wolfman came closer.

The creature saw the rapier and froze, eyes fixed on the silver blade.

"Yes," wheezed Aberline, "that's silver, you son of a bitch. Come and get a taste."

The Wolfman crouched, its muscles bulging for a leap; Aberline raised the point of the sword.

And then the roof of Talbot Hall collapsed inward with an earsplitting crack of dying timbers and a dragon's roar of flames. Tons of burning rubble plunged down through the house as if Lucifer Himself stood above the Hall and drove His fiery fist through the old house's heart.

The shock hurled both combatants away.

THE WOLFMAN SLAMMED into the wall, gagging on dense smoke, snapping at the burning embers that nipped at his flesh. His prey was gone. Even his scent was erased by the smell of burning debris.

Outside movement caught him, even in the midst of the conflagration, and he turned to see the other prey running across the lawn toward the woods.

Instantly the Wolfman smashed through the remains of the window and gave chase.

GWEN CONLIFFE RAN faster than she had ever run, the heavy pistol clutched to her breast. She kicked off her shoes and ran barefoot across the cold autumn grass, straight into the forest, her speed fueled by terror and hopelessness. Trees and shrubs plucked at her dress, tearing away ribbons and bits of cloth. Gwen ran and ran as the scream behind her died away into a dreadful silence. She ran until she could no longer hear the hungry, wet sounds of the monster as it savaged the man who had died trying to save her.

The ground began sloping upward and she raced along it, hearing the roar of running water to her left. She followed the rising cliff wall up into the moonlight. Even with hysteria chewing at the fabric of her mind she was able to think. She had no illusions as to whether the creature could track her through the night, but she had to try. If she reached the waterfall maybe she could cross it and somehow confuse the thing, but first she had to reach the gorge and after that follow a winding path through a forest so dense that not even moonlight as bright as this could help her find a path. She ran . . . but she knew that running was only delaying something that now seemed terrible and certain.

The ancient trees rose around her as she fled into the forest, splashing through streamlets that led to the waterfall. She heard the sound of something fast and heavy crashing through the woods. She stopped for a moment with her back pressed hard against the trunk of a giant yew, listening to the jumbled sounds of the forest. Was the thing up here on the ridge or down by the moors? She couldn't tell and she did not dare risk looking for fear that if she saw it then it would immediately see her.

The sound died away and Gwen left the shelter of the old tree and circled back toward the cliff. If the monster was out here now, then maybe she could sneak back to the Hall and find her horse. Not even this creature could outrun a horse. Could it?

Doubt was a gnawing thing that tore at her as she ran.

The ground before her was spread with shadows and she almost ran through them until she realized that there was no ground at all: a deep gorge had been cut into the path by ten thousand years of rain and she almost stepped into it. Gwen edged around it and then turned to run toward the sound of the waterfall. She heard a rustle. A small, furtive sound.

Was it here?

Gwen raised the pistol.

"Lawrence," she said in a voice that shook as badly as her hands. "It's me. It's Gwen."

Another sound. Closer. Much closer. But she could not tell if it was to one side or in the shadows ahead of her. Was she walking right toward the creature?

"You know who I am," she said, fighting to keep her voice calm. To sound ordinary, unthreatening . . . and at the same time trying to reach Lawrence. If Lawrence still existed.

She could not hold the pistol steady.

"Lawrence? . . ."

In the darkness, not ten feet from her, were two yellow eyes. Fierce, unblinking, unnatural. Gwen froze to the spot, knowing that her luck and her life had run out.

The Wolfman came slowly out of the shadows of the woods, its eyes fixed on her. Gwen backed slowly away, feeling the marshy ground give way to the packed clay and rock that formed the edge of the cliff. The Wolfman came closer. She had not seen it this close before. It was enormous. Eight feet tall, packed with muscle, and twisted into a parody of life that was not animal and not man. Its claws twitched as if aching to rend and tear.

She stepped onto a loose rock that slid out from under her and she went down—and the Wolfman leaped at her, following her down to the hard rock, straddling her, looming over her, filling her entire consciousness with all of its dark promise.

"There must be some part of you left. Please . . ."

The creature's only reply was a bloody leer of naked hunger. Its clothes were torn, stained with gore, smudged with soot. There was nothing human about this *thing*.

Gwen started to cry. A sob broke in her chest and tears filled her eyes. She raised a hand toward the monster.

"Please. . . . Remember the things you said to me?"

Her fingers were inches from the monster's face. Gwen knew that she was going to die, but she could not accept that there was nothing of the good man she knew left within this fearsome form.

"Remember how you kissed me?"

The Wolfman's yellow eyes narrowed to predatory slits. Gwen was weeping, calling his name, her fingers touching the very tips of the creature's stiff black hair. The Wolfman's face changed for just a moment. It did not transform, but the snarl of hate eased for a second, the lips lowered to cover those awful fangs, and hope flared in Gwen's breast.

"Lawrence? . . ."

HALF A MILE away a line of torches moved through the darkness. The men of the Special Police squad had arrived. Aberline was with them, his face tight with pain, leaning on Adams as they moved away from the pyre of Talbot Hall. A dozen men from the town were with the officers, and they'd brought shotguns loaded with silver and a pack of hounds that bayed and howled at the scent of blood on the air.

Aberline's knees buckled and Adams lowered him to the grass.

"Leave me," the inspector gasped. "Find her." He waved the bloody rapier blade toward the forest. "Go!" he croaked.

The hunting party set off at a run toward the woods, following the hounds who had the scent.

Aberline looked down at the ruin of his shoulder. The fangs of the monster had torn muscle, cracked bone. The wounds burned and itched. It felt as if ants were crawling under his skin.

The moonlight struck silver fire from the sword's razor-sharp edge, and for a long time Aberline stared at the weapon.

"God," he breathed, amazed that he had survived the creature's attack when so many others had fallen. "Thank God. . ."

Gripping the silver sword, Aberline staggered forward into the murk, following the men, following Gwen Conliffe. Following the monster.

Chapter Fifty-eight

T he moment seemed eternal. Gwen lay upon the cold stone, one hand curled around the pistol butt, one finger laying alongside the trigger guard; the other hand lifted to touch the matted fur of the monster who crouched over her.

"Lawrence . . ." she whispered.

The Wolfman looked at her and for a moment all traces of hate and hunger were gone from its face. Gwen's heart lifted. She knew that *he* was still in there. Beneath the surface of this impossible thing, Lawrence Talbot still existed.

She raised her hand to touch his face.

And then they heard the dogs.

The Wolfman whipped his head around toward the house. Dogs brayed and barked. Men yelled and called to one another.

Gwen knew with a sinking heart that Fate, cruel and malicious, had stolen the moment away from her. From them. She could see the tension crawl beneath the monster's skin, tightening his muscles, putting back all of the animal fury that her words and her touch had taken from him.

The Wolfman turned its head slowly back toward her, and when Gwen looked into its eyes there was not the slightest trace of Lawrence Talbot. What remained, what she saw, was only the beast.

"No . . ." she said softly, but the monster peeled its lips back to show her the teeth that would be the last thing on earth she felt. It began a deep-chested growl, a promise of the howl that Gwen knew would mark the moment of her death.

Then the Wolfman reared back, throwing a howl toward the moon that was filled with all of the infinite pain and misery and torment that has ever troubled the world. The howl tore at the fabric of the night, slashing at sanity, clawing the face of the Goddess of the Hunt until the sky itself shuddered at the sound.

"I love you," Gwen said.

And then she pressed the barrel of the gun against his chest and fired.

The heavy gun bucked in her hand, the explosion was louder than all the sound in the world, and the silver slug tore through flesh and muscle and bone, destroying everything in its path.

The Wolfman howled in surprise and terrible pain and fell over onto its side. Screaming, Gwen shimmied and clawed and kicked her way out from under, bringing the gun back up. Sobs broke in her chest as she watched the monster's blood well out of wounds that would not close, that could not close.

The creature lay still on the ground beside her. The hunting party were yelling now, the dogs insane with bloodlust as they all ran toward the gorge.

But the creature did not move.

Suddenly it snaked a hand out and grabbed her hand. Gwen screamed. She struggled to break free . . . but the hand did not claw her, the talons did not tear at her skin. The Wolfman did nothing more than hold her. She froze, watching.

And as she watched, the hand *changed*.

The dark hairs seemed to writhe like grass in a breeze, but as she looked she saw that the hairs were retreating into the skin. The hooked nails thinned and retracted into the pads of each finger. The body changed, too. Even in death the process of transformation could not be stopped. Hands that had become twisted mockeries resumed their human shape. Bones straightened. The thick pelt of the werewolf vanished and the unmarked flesh of the man emerged into the moonlight until the Wolfman was entirely gone and only Lawrence Talbot remained.

With a cry, Gwen bent forward and pulled Lawrence to her, pressing his head to her breasts, kissing his tangled hair. Cradling him to her, she rocked back and forth as tears fell like rain from her blue eyes.

"Lawrence! Oh God . . . Lawrence. Forgive me. Please . . . forgive me. I'm so sorry. Forgive me . . ." Her words spilled out in a tumble as the sound of the dogs and the shouts of the men grew closer.

LAWRENCE COULD NOT find the strength to speak. He raised one hand and looked at it in wonder. Seeing his own skin, seeing his humanity. He felt no pain. All of his awareness was drawn by the purity of the goddess who held him. Not the fierce Goddess of the Hunt, whose face had become a twisted mask of disapproval and disappointment, but the smaller, more beautiful face of the goddess who clutched him to her breast and kissed him and wept. The goddess whose eyes were filled with tears and pain and loss. And with love.

The goddess who had saved him.

He wanted to say something to her. To tell her that he loved her. To say thank you, but there was not enough of him left. Lawrence used the last of what was left to touch her hand, to stroke the smooth skin. Would she understand? Would she know that there was no need for him to forgive her? Salvation does not require forgiveness.

His fingers trailed along the back of her hand.

It was all he could do.

He was safe now.

He could sleep.

GWEN CONLIFFE FELT him die. His body settled against hers and when she looked at his face, so clear in the moonlight, there was no trace of pain. His eyes were closed, and all of the pain and fear was gone. She bowed over him and wept as the hunting party swarmed into the clearing.

The men stopped and stood at the edge of the grassy slope, staring at the weeping woman and the man she held. The sound of her desperate, broken sobs struck them all to silence, and even the dogs stopped baying.

A moment later Aberline himself came out of the shadows. His wounded arm hung at his side, but the bleeding had stopped and he no longer staggered. The men held their ground as the inspector walked out onto the rocky lip of the gorge and stood over the sobbing woman.

Aberline looked at Lawrence Talbot's face and knew that this hunt was over. The poor man was at peace. He felt a strange twist of grief for Talbot, and more for the woman. Moonlight glittered on the blade of the sword cane he still carried. Aberline raised the rapier and looked at the reflection of his own eyes in the slender mirror-bright blade. Then he raised his eyes and stared at the laughing face of the Goddess of the Hunt.

ABOUT THE AUTHOR

Jonathan Maberry is a multiple Bram Stoker Award–winning author, magazine feature writer, playwright, content creator, and writing teacher/lecturer. His novels include *Ghost Road Blues*, *Dead Man's Song*, *Bad Moon Rising*, and *Patient Zero*. Visit him online at www.jonathanmaberry.com.